SOME OF US HAVE TO GET UP IN THE MORNING

SOME OF US
HAVE TO GET UP
IN THE MORNING

stories by
DANIEL SCOTT

TURTLE POINT PRESS
NEW YORK

ISBN 1-885586-21-3

LCCN 00-136363

Design and composition by Melissa Ehn at
Wilsted & Taylor Publishing Services

For my father, Walter A. Scott

Contents

SOME OF US HAVE TO GET UP IN THE MORNING

BYPASS

Afternoons Tina opens the back door and walks across the gravel in her open-toed slippers to the edge of the wild grass that separates the house from the highway. There are no people out here—the nearest house is a half-mile off—there's just the road, a bypass that skirts the heart of the town. But by this time of the day she's had her fill of housework and television shows and especially the muffled thumps that come from behind the refrigerator every once in a while. Tina is afraid they're rats. She keeps intending to mention them to Richard, but the noises never seem to happen after he comes home.

Tina had thought there was a chain-link fence between the house and the highway when she first arrived here, but she realizes now the fence is on the other side of the road, guarding the large ditch that runs between the highway and a dense cluster of trees. She'll refuse to have a baby here, she thinks. Not that they've talked about kids yet. But when they do, she'll tell Richard it's too dangerous. Semis on their way to the interstate a hundred miles east roll by so close, and at all times of the day and night. Three of them speed by in succession as she's standing there. The first two drivers lean forward a little to get a better look at her as they pass. The third one actually slows down and stops. The side of the truck reads Arcata, Nevada. The driver leans over and rolls down his passenger-side window. He's an older man, maybe fifty, with a day's growth speckling his chin and cheeks.

"Hi there," he says with a broad smile.

Tina smiles back, but only briefly.

"You look like you need a lift," the trucker says.

"No, thank you."

"Heading toward Omaha?"

"No," says Tina. "I'm not going anywhere."

"It's not safe, a pretty girl out here all by herself."

When it's clear the truck driver won't be discouraged, Tina turns and begins walking back to the house.

"Could be fun," he calls behind her, and then lets out a laugh. She hears the truck rumble to life and go on its way. When she reaches the door, she looks back and spots it just as it takes the bend and disappears into the trees.

She returns to the kitchen. The chicken will burn if she doesn't watch it. She lifts it from the oven pan with two forks and drops it on the waiting platter. It's burnt across the top and Tina swears. She doesn't think she'll ever get the hang of cooking. She strains the peas and divides them up between the two plates set on the table. She opens the jellied cranberry sauce and scoops out two helpings. She had to go to three stores to find it. "People don't eat it here," Richard told her.

She stops suddenly, hearing an approaching semi. She goes to the kitchen window. The truck stretches across her view and is gone in an instant. When she turns around again, she gasps and grabs her chest. Richard is there, on the threshold between the kitchen and the living room.

"Didn't you hear the car?" he says. He's in his driving examiner's uniform, a light blue short-sleeved shirt all officially patched and badged by the state of Nebraska, and dark blue pants that Tina thinks make his ass look fat, unlike his navy uniform, which made him look slender.

"God," he says. He shakes his head and drapes his jacket across the back of the kitchen chair. He grabs a beer from the refrigerator and sits down at the table. "Today was like . . . *really*. I'm almost too tired to eat."

"There's a ton of food here, Richard."

He nods. "I'll have a little." He twists the cap from his bottle of beer.

Tina slices the chicken. It takes her a few minutes, and when she's done the bird is hacked terribly. She looks at Richard. He's reading the label on his beer bottle. He's a label-reader, Tina has noticed. She goes to the refrigerator, takes out the margarine and a beer for herself, and sits down.

"This guy comes in today," Richard says after forking some peas into his mouth. "Big biker-type fella with a Harley Davidson T-shirt and this big droopy moustache. Worst driver I've ever seen. He kept punching the gas pedal and lurching the car ahead. Then he would slam the brakes on when he came to a stop sign. I told him, you're being tested on how smooth you operate the vehicle too, you know. Chicken's burnt."

"I know."

"So finally he turns into the wrong lane on a one-way street. That's a violation. I explain that to him when we get back. Then he says, you mean you're flunking me? And I said, no, you flunked yourself. Then all of a sudden he bursts out in tears. This big biker-type guy. I couldn't believe it. His learner's permit said he was 37 years old, for chrissake." He stops to peel the burnt skin from his chicken.

Tina looks up from her food. "I wonder why a 37-year-old man would be getting his license now," she says. "I mean, how'd he get by before?"

Richard waves her off. "I've seen 60-year-old ladies come in and get their license."

"I know, but I'm not talking about that. I'm talking about something completely different."

"I've seen a few women get teary-eyed when they failed the test. But you should of seen this guy crying. And not just crying, but really, you know, *crying*."

"All I was saying is that it's pretty hard to get by in life without a driver's license if you're a 37-year-old man. Especially out here. I mean, you've got a job. A family."

Richard shrugs. "I don't know, honey. I don't get into the personal stuff." He picks up the drumstick with his fingers and gnaws at it.

Tina scrapes lines in her cranberry sauce with her fork. After a minute, she says, "So then what happened?"

Richard pauses, still holding the drumstick in front of his mouth.

"I got out of the car," he says. He puts the chicken down and picks up the beer. His greasy fingerprints stain the bottle. "Some old guy was with him. Probably his dad. He stopped me and asked what happened. I told him, he turned into the wrong lane on a one-way street. That's a violation."

"Maybe you could have let that slide," Tina says.

"I don't write the laws, honey."

Tina thinks the license must have been pretty important to the man, but she drops it. Richard fills his mouth with beer, letting it down his throat little by little. Tina's never known anyone who drank that way. All of a sudden she hears two very distinct thumps from behind the refrigerator. This is the first time the noises have happened while Richard is home. She looks to him. He's straining forward, reading the cranberry sauce can.

"Didn't you hear that?" Tina says.

Richard looks up with questioning eyes.

"The noises," she says. "From behind the refrigerator. I'm afraid we might have rats, Richard. My mother said they have rats as big as dogs out here."

Richard laughs once through his nostrils. "This isn't Staten Island, Tina. There are no rats here." He shakes his head. "Your mother," he says, and he's right, Tina knows. She had long ago ceased to believe her mother "only meant well," as she always claimed, by the things she said, especially where Richard was involved. She knew Tina was frightened of rats ever since she was a little girl and found one in her hamper. But when that failed to dissuade her from Richard, her mother said, "You're marrying him too fast, Bettina. He's a hick. What's he gonna do when he gets outta the navy?" And then, when Tina announced she was moving with her newly discharged husband back to his tiny hometown of Bradenton, Nebraska, where his brother could get him a good job, she said, "Do you really think you can be happy out there?" To which Tina silently replied, "At least it would get me away from you."

"Then what are the noises?" Tina presses.

"I didn't hear anything," says Richard.

"That's because you don't listen!"

Richard leans forward and puts his hand on the side of her face. "Don't get upset, honey. I'll take a look behind there if you want."

"You will?"

"Sure."

"Okay." Tina looks down at her plate. She hasn't eaten at all.

"But not tonight." He leans back in his chair and yawns. "I'm too tired," he says. "I just wanna go to bed."

"It's not even eight o'clock yet."

"So what?"

"I don't understand how being a driving examiner can tire you out so much!"

"It takes a lot of concentration!" With that he gets up from the table. He goes to the sink to wash the chicken grease off his hands. When he returns, he puts his hands on her shoulders and they smell like dish detergent. "I'm sorry, honey. Maybe after I lay down for a while, we'll go out for a drive or something." He kisses her on the top of her head and shuffles off to the bedroom.

Tina stays at the table a minute, her arms folded across her chest. Then she gets up and clears the dishes. She tosses them into the sink recklessly, but none of them break. She turns on the garbage disposal and leaves it on long after all the plates are scraped. She supposes she's hoping Richard won't be able to sleep from all of the noise. But in no time, even over the garbage disposal, she hears him snoring. She knows they won't go anywhere tonight. Once Richard falls asleep, nothing can wake him up.

She snaps off the disposal and fills the sink with water to soak the chicken pan. She hears the thumps again, three this time. She spins around and glowers at the refrigerator. She looks down at the space between it and the stove and expects to see the snout of a rat poking out. But she doesn't want to see it, and she hurries to the back door and throws it open. A semi has just passed. She sees its round red taillights disappear—first one, then the other—behind the distant foliage. It's getting darker by the minute now. She looks up. Already there are more stars in the sky than she's seen on the darkest night in Staten Island. The light from the kitchen illuminates the gravel path. She walks it and stands with her toes on the edge of the wild grass. She can still make out the grasshoppers as they leap away from her.

She hears an approaching engine and looks down the highway. She can tell from the loudness that it's not a truck but a regular car, a four-door sedan as it comes into view, blue or possibly a deep purplish red in the fading light. The car doesn't have its lights on and takes the turn tightly, then instead of straightening out it keeps going, into the chain-link fence on the other side of the highway, knocking it down, and disappearing into the large ditch directly across from where Tina is standing.

Tina doesn't know what to do. It happened so quickly, and with practically no noise, that for a moment she's not sure it really happened at all. But she gathers herself, thinking first that she should run across the highway, which is empty at the moment, to see if anyone is hurt. Then she decides she should run in and wake up Richard. He'll know what to do.

But before she can move she spots arms, and then a head, clambering up from the ditch. When the man makes it to the road, he stands up. He's the man Richard had denied his license earlier that day—Tina is sure of it. He fits the description exactly: a large droopy moustache and a big barrel chest that sags a little in a black Harley Davidson T-shirt. He in fact appears just as Tina imagined him when Richard told her the story. The man peers up and down the highway, then brushes himself off. He looks up suddenly and spots Tina standing across from him. She thinks she should ask him if he's okay, but from the look on his face he does not seem glad to see her.

They stare at each other a minute, each not quite believing the other's presence. Tina is ready to be afraid, ready to turn and run back to the house screaming for Richard. But the man makes no move toward her. He looks up and down the highway again, then back at her.

Tina opens her mouth, then shuts it and then opens it again and calls, "Are you hurt?"

The man doesn't respond. Tina thinks he must be dazed from the crash.

"Is there anyone else in the car?" she calls. The man looks at her for a moment, then shakes his head no. In the glare of the streetlight she thinks she sees something shiny running down the side of his face. "Your head," she says.

The man touches his forehead. She hears him say, "Oh God."

"You need help," says Tina. "I'll call 911."

"No!" the man says. "Don't call anyone!" He suddenly seems frantic and starts across the highway, toward her. Tina backs away, almost tripping as she turns. She hurries toward the open kitchen door. But behind her, the urgency dies. She looks back. The man is on his knees, on the double yellow line in the middle of the highway. He is looking down, his hand against his head, the five fingers splayed out; it looks as though a big starfish is stuck to the side of his face.

Tina watches him a moment. And then, inevitably, she hears the distant sound of an engine. She knows it's a tractor-trailer. The man makes no attempt to move.

"Hey!" she yells. "Get out of the road!"

But the man does not seem to hear her, and still doesn't move.

Tina darts from the door, across the gravel, across the wild grass and onto the smooth asphalt. The man does not notice as she approaches. She grabs him by the arm and tries to pull him to his feet.

"Let's go!" she says. "There's a truck coming!"

"No," says the man. "Leave me here. I'll be alright." He looks up at her, still holding his head, and again is sad that she's there.

She is without words, she does not know how to speak, but she's just pulling, grunting with the strain, not even breathing, the engine getting louder and the headlights slowly exploding in the corner of her vision. She thinks that she should run away, save herself, be scared. But she is only pulling and pulling like the man is bolted to the ground.

A hot hiss is let into the air. Tina finally looks toward the rig. It is slowing down, and comes to a stop, well ahead of the two people in the road.

The man looks into the headlights, then down again.

The truck blows its horn.

"Come on," Tina says. The man gets up with a struggle, one leg first, then the other, Tina helping. She holds him with two hands as he begins to walk, holding him by the bicep, thinking that it's thick and bulky and a little soft, like someone who lifted weights for a long time and then stopped. It is only when they get through the grass and onto the gravel that the truck begins to move. It creeps by, curious, until the woman and the man disappear inside the house.

"Sit down," Tina says. "Please sit down." The man falls into a kitchen chair without ever looking for it. She examines the cut on his head. In the light she can see it is not bleeding, only a little bloody. "You should go to the hospital," she says. "I'll call an ambulance."

But when she picks up the phone on the kitchen wall, the man jumps up, grabs it from her and hangs it up. "Don't do that," he says.

Tina steps back. She thinks she should run in and wake Richard, or at least scream for him. But the man, expended from his outburst, falls back into the chair and groans.

"You're hurt," she says.

"It doesn't matter. I'm not hurt bad enough to die." He seems to regret this.

"I could take you to the hospital myself. Or my husband could." She gestures vaguely in the direction of the bedroom.

"No."

"We should at least call the police."

"Why?"

"Well, your car is out there in the ditch."

"That's not my car."

"Is it your father's?"

The man looks up at her. "How'd you know that?"

"I didn't. It just looked like an old man's car. Maybe we should call him."

"No." He makes like he's going to get up again, but can't seem to bring himself to it. "Please don't."

Tina can see his eyes filling with wetness. "Okay," she says. "We don't have to call anyone."

Suddenly the refrigerator thumps three times. They both look over. The thumps have never sounded so deliberate to Tina, so evenly spaced.

"I don't know why it does that," says Tina, thinking it will take the man's mind off his troubles. "Do you?"

"No."

Tina looks at the refrigerator again, then back at the man.

"My dad would know," he says.

"Does he know about refrigerators?"

"No. But he would know what's wrong. Some people can just figure out things." The man grabs his head again, as if a sudden sharp pain had entered it. "I don't know how they do it," he says. "They're just born knowing things. While the rest of us don't know nothing."

Tina is surprised not so much by what the man is saying as by the fact that he's talked so much all at once, and by his soft, almost lisping voice. He is on the verge of tears again and Tina tries hard to think of something else to say.

"Where were you headed?"

The man wipes his eyes. "East," he says. "I was gonna drive as far as Omaha, then hop a bus from there. Someone told me that people back East care less if you were an inmate or not. Here, when people look at you, it's all they can think of."

Tina feels her body stiffen. The refrigerator thumps again.

"Do you think that could be rats?" she says.

The man thinks a minute, then shakes his head. "Rats make more of a scraping sound. I know the sound of rats."

"You do?" She says this with hope.

The man nods.

"I think you're probably right." It just makes sense to her. She thinks she should not feel as relieved as she does. "Do you want something to eat? I've got a ton of food. I'd hate for it to go to waste."

The man doesn't want any food. "I just wanna get out of here, out of this town, before the cops come after me. I don't wanna go back to prison."

Stealing a car, crashing it, driving with no license—Tina knows he's right. The refrigerator makes its sounds again but that doesn't bother her now. She goes to the back door. She opens it and looks out at the spot across the highway where the fence is knocked down. "Maybe the car is okay. Maybe we can call a tow truck to pull it out of the ditch." But as soon as she says that, she realizes that won't be possible. Even if she could get a tow truck to come out here in the middle of the night, that would undoubtedly attract the police.

"No," the man says. "We ain't calling no one."

"Maybe we could get the car out ourselves," she says. "I have some rope around here somewhere. We could use my husband's car to pull it out."

"Your husband's car?"

"We could try. Let's at least go look at your car." Tina grabs a flashlight from the kitchen drawer and helps the man up. They walk together to the end of the gravel path, where the man stops. Tina can see he is looking at Richard's car, parked on the adjacent side of the house. "Come on," she says, and the man allows her to take him across the grass, then across the highway. Tina is wondering what the man will do if his car can't be retrieved. They arrive at the ditch and Tina shines the light onto the wreck. It is instantly apparent the car cannot be driven again. The passenger side is completely caved in, the windshield is gone except for the top corner of the driver's side, which clings like a cobweb. She thinks it's a miracle the man is not hurt more than he is.

She wonders what he will do now. She does not know what to do but follow him back across the highway. He is looking at Richard's car. Once they reach the grass, she hears an engine approaching. She knows from the sound that it's a semi. She waves the flashlight at it. The man, who has already reached the gravel path, turns to look at her as the rig comes to a stop. The driver rolls down his window. "Hi there," he says to Tina. "Need a ride?"

"Are you going to Omaha?" she says.

"Sure am." He pops open the door on the passenger side.

Tina turns to the man and signals for him to come. "I don't need a ride, but my brother does."

The driver makes an expression like he does not understand.

"His car broke down while he was visiting, and he really needs to get back home," says Tina, not knowing where the words are coming from. "I'd be really grateful to you. On the return trip, you can stop by here on your way back and I'll give you a home-cooked meal."

The driver seems charmed. "Well," he says. "Are you a good cook?" But the smile disappears from his face quickly as the man appears out of nowhere.

"All I ask is that you get me to Omaha," the man says to the driver, his back to Tina. She thinks he's somehow threatening the driver, who's staring down at the man's pants. She remembers seeing something hidden by the hang of his T-shirt.

"Just get me to Omaha and I'll take it from there." The driver nods. The man climbs up into the rig. He turns to Tina. "Thanks," he says.

"Sure," says Tina.

"You know," he says, "it could be a rat that's trapped. Sometimes when they're trapped, they'll flop around like that."

"Oh."

The driver is staring at Tina with pleading eyes, but before she can say anything the man pulls the door shut and Tina watches as the truck rolls away, slowly at first, and disappears around the bend.

She returns to the house and puts the flashlight back in the drawer. She washes the last of the dishes, dries them and puts them away. As she walks by the refrigerator, it thumps several times. Tina decides to put an end to it once and for all.

She stands perfectly still and waits for the noise again. When it happens, she grabs the refrigerator. Using all her strength, she succeeds in pulling it back a few inches. She grabs the flashlight from the drawer again, along with the hammer. She shines the light behind the refrigerator. There is nothing there but a thick gray layer of grime. In the morning she will pull it out all the way and clean behind there.

She shuts off all the lights and goes to the bedroom. She climbs under the covers and is surprised to find Richard's eyes are open. "What's going on out there, Tina?" he says.

It takes Tina a moment to think what she should say. "We might have a guest for supper sometime this week," she decides.

"What?" He is already falling back to sleep.

"If we do, I'll make chicken again. I'll try not to burn it."

COOKOUT

For it being Everett's last weekend before he went in the Marines, Mamma and Daddy had to decide if they should have a big cookout or instead take the family to Squanto Park for a day. It was weird because they had called everyone to the front porch to talk about it. And since when did we have cookouts *for* someone? But Mamma and Daddy—especially Mamma—were making such a big deal out of this thing, asking each of us what we thought and everything. So when she got around to me I told her what I thought: "The amusement park. We can have a cookout any damn weekend." Mamma shot me one sidelong. She didn't like the garbage mouth.

So next was Lily, who, big surprise, said the cookout. The long drive to Squanto Park always made her throw up.

"It doesn't matter what we do because Everett won't show up anyway," said Katy, the boss of the world.

"I'm sure that if Everett knows we're doing it specially for him then he'll show up," Mamma said.

"I bet he won't," Katy said. I *knew* he wouldn't.

"He will," Mamma said.

Daddy said that maybe we should have the cookout because Everett might be getting too old for Squanto Park. I had to laugh at that because Everett loved that place more than any of us, more than me even. He especially liked the Monster Lift. That's this metal compartment thing that you sit in and it shoots you high up in the air and then brings you back down again really fast like you're going to crash, but you don't. Cool. Everett went on it seven times in a row once and never threw up.

Then Mamma started saying that if we had the cookout we could invite all the relatives and friends and they could all see Everett before he left. Like the relatives cared about Everett all of a sudden.

"You can invite everyone but Carrie Battisti," Katy said, all smart-alecky. "I wouldn't invite her," she said. Mamma was bringing her highball up for a sip but she stopped and said, "Just keep your mouth shut, Katy."

"I'm just saying the truth," Katy said.

"And I'm saying keep your mouth shut." She took her sip.

Then Katy got mad and said something about how stupid it was to have a cookout for someone who didn't even want to go away. Mamma was set to jump up after her, but Katy stormed off into the house. Katy's very touchy. She's always ticked off about something and her latest thing was Carrie Battisti. Carrie and her used to be friends until Carrie started going out with Everett. Then Katy didn't want anything to do with her. Then Carrie and Everett stopped going out. Then Carrie never came around the house again. This just happened like a few weeks before.

"And a cookout would be less expensive," Daddy said. Mamma agreed and then I knew the idea of Squanto Park was dead and buried. Denny and Eddie and me were bummed, but Lily laughed. It got me mad and I asked why she didn't go off somewhere and puke. Then Mamma gave me a whack and said that I had a mouth worse than a boy's. I said I didn't know why they even bothered asking me what I thought about the whole thing, since no one ever listens to me anyway.

The whole week leading up to the cookout, Mamma must have reminded Everett about it ten times a day and every time Everett'd just grunt or not say anything at all, always when he was on his way out the door too. She kept reminding us about it, too. It was like she was possessed with the idea. She kept talking about "Everett's cookout" and "the cookout we're having for Everett." It was weird because Mamma never really made a fuss over anything. She even bought these gold cardboard letters that spelled out Everett's name to string up on the side of the house. It was like ever since Everett signed up to go in the Marines, Mamma thought he was the greatest. Before he signed up, there was no end to her complaining about how wild he was, and she was always either screaming at him about it or defending him to somebody. But now that he was going in the Marines, she was so happy about it. It's hard to say if she was more relieved, like finally he was someone else's problem, or more proud about it. Of course, she wasn't proud the time Everett was tough enough to punch his principal in the stomach, or the time he was tough enough to break into that ski shop and beat up that security guard. But she was definitely proud that he was tough enough to cut it as a Marine. People looked up to her for it, too, and congratulated her for it.

Like take Aunt Kit, Mamma's sister. She arrived at the cookout a little early to see if Mamma needed any help setting up—like she doesn't have eight of us kids to do all the helping she needs. Kit said that she thought it was a great thing that Everett was going to be a Marine. Not one of her boys would last a day on Parris Island, she said, and she called them scrawny little crybabies. Mamma just smiled, peeling apart the paper plates. I think she was a little surprised that Kit was even there, since she was not invited. Kit must have heard about the cookout from all the other relatives and just assumed that she could come, too. Mamma didn't want her there because, she said, she didn't want Willie, Kit's oldest, to start another fistfight with Everett. And, she said, she didn't want Sammy, Kit's husband, pitching any more horseshoes into the side of the house, which he always did when he had too much to drink, which was practically all the time, she said. But those weren't really the reasons she didn't want Kit there. I think the real reason was that at the last cookout Kit came to she brought fresh hamburger patties, the homemade kind, and put them on the grill next to Mamma's frozen ones. We all sort of looked at them and Lily even had the stupidity to ask what Kit's were. "What do you think they are?" Mamma said, and walked away mad. This time Kit brought beer.

Uncle Sammy said, "I don't remember anyone giving me a send-off when I went in the military," and he banged his horseshoes together. He was waiting for his turn in the game he was playing with Daddy. We called Sammy "the hick" when he wasn't around because he was originally from the South and he talked with kind of a Southern accent.

"That's because you went in the Army, not the Marines," Kit said. "Besides, you got drafted."

"What difference does that make? Drafted or volunteer, Army or Navy or Marines—a man serves just the same."

"Everyone knows the Marines are the toughest," Kit said. She was packing the beer into an ice cooler while she talked.

"Everett's so tough! Tell me how tough it is to join the Marines during peacetime! I was drafted into a war, I remind you."

Kit looked up at me and Lily and Mamma. "The Korean War ended two weeks after he got his draft notice," she said.

Then I heard Mamma say "Stupid hick" under her breath. She was trying to light the charcoal briquettes.

"Like that was my fault," Sammy said, and he was about to bang his horseshoes together again—a habit that drove Mamma up the wall—when suddenly he looked out into the street. This car, a long blue one, was slowing down as it passed our house. Mamma looked up at it like maybe she was expecting Everett to hop out. I thought it was just more relatives. But the car just picked up speed again and drove off without ever stopping. Sammy looked back at us and before walking off to take his turn he said, "You can bet though that if someone *had* given me a send-off, at least I would have showed up."

Mamma looked straight at him and said, like she could barely keep from screaming it, "He'll show up."

"I bet he won't," I said.

Then Mamma got mad and said I was sounding more and more like Katy all the time. Right then the funniest thing I ever saw in my life happened. This horseshoe whizzed right behind the back of Mamma's head. It nearly decked her. "Good Lord!" she said.

"Whoa there!" Daddy yelled.

"Sorry about that, Peg," Sammy said. I was *laughing*.

Then that same car, the long blue one, passed by the house again, only this time it was coming from the other direction. We all stopped to look at it. This time it slowed down almost to a stop. Then it raced off again.

When Mamma looked back she caught that pig Lily eating relish right out of the jar again. She pulled it away from her and asked if she was determined to get sick. When I looked back at Mamma, I thought about that horseshoe almost ringing her neck and I had to laugh again. She looked at me and said, "Don't you think that's enough?" but I couldn't stop. So then she told me to go in and tell Katy to come outside because people were starting to arrive.

When I went in Katy was watching TV. She had this mad expression on her face. She always does.

"Mamma says shut that off and come out and help set up," I said. But she was in one of her moods where she wasn't going to talk to you. I always take these moods as a challenge to make her talk. I said again, "Mamma says come out, Katy, because everyone's starting to arrive."

Still Katy said nothing.

"You sure are ugly, Katy."

Still nothing.

"Katy, you got lice in your hair."

"Why don't you shut your damn face for once!" she said. I knew I could do it.

"Should I run out and tell Mamma you said that?" I said.

"You can run out and tell her I'm not coming out. There's no way I'm putting myself on public display with this family. Horseshoe spikes in the middle of the front lawn! And with Daddy in that bathing suit? Forget it." Then she turned her eyes from the TV to me and said, "Can't any of you see that all the neighbors are looking at us?" Mamma always said Katy thought too much about what everybody else thought.

Then I said, "You better come out, Katy, because everyone's arriving and you have to help set up."

"I bet Carrie Battisti hasn't arrived," she said, going off on her latest thing again. But it made me wonder. The Battistis usually did come to our cookouts, but they weren't at this one. So I asked, "Why, Katy? Why didn't Mamma invite the Battistis this time?"

Katy turned and looked straight ahead at the television. A commercial for Mace came on. It showed a woman using it on a guy sneaking up behind her.

"Why, Katy?" I said again. She looked for a minute like she

might say. Then she said, "Why don't you just go back out there with all the other freaks."

So I said I was going to tell Mamma what she said and I went back outside. I found Mamma by the barbecue grill and I told her. She made a face and was about to yell for Katy when she just all of a sudden stopped. She was looking out into the street. Then I looked, too. It was that blue car again, this time coming from the same direction as when we first saw it. It slowed down again as it came by us and this time it stopped across the street, in front of the Wheelers' house. The sun reflected off the windows so you couldn't see who was inside. Pretty soon everyone was looking at it. A couple of times the brake lights lit up and went off again. Then the door opened and a lady got out. It was Mrs. Battisti, Carrie's mother.

At first I thought, Mamma *did* invite the Battistis, but Mrs. Battisti was by herself and didn't have anything with her, no food or beer. She just had her pocketbook hanging off her shoulder and her arms folded in front of her. She walked up on the lawn that way. Everyone was looking at her. Then suddenly I knew she wasn't there for the cookout but for something else, something more serious. She walked straight toward me and Mamma.

Mamma was standing like she was frozen. Mrs. Battisti stopped and looked at her and then at me. She had these huge sunglasses on that made her look like a fly. She looked back at Mamma, then Mamma looked down at me, then she looked back at Mrs. Battisti. But no one was saying anything. Then the two of them turned and walked away from me and stopped and started talking. Everyone was watching. Mrs. Battisti pulled her sunglasses down a little and looked over them while she talked. I could pick up some of what they were saying. Mrs. Battisti started by saying something about not wanting to say anymore about it, but when she drove by and saw us having a cookout she just had to. There was a bunch of whispering and mumbling and then Mamma stepped back a little, put her hand on her chest and said, "I don't know what more you want from us, Judy." Then Mrs. Battisti said something like Carrie won't even leave the house now and that she didn't know what to do with her anymore and that maybe he should be in jail for what he did to her. Then Mamma stepped back again and said, pretty loud, "I don't know what more to tell you, Judy. He's going away in to the Marines. That was what was decided."

I saw Mrs. Battisti's eyes get really mad before she covered them up with her sunglasses again. Then she was about to leave when she looked over at the gold letters on the side of the house that spelled out Everett's name. "It's a sin to be having a cookout for him!" she said, way out loud for everyone to hear. "Just a sin!" Then she hurried off the lawn and got in her car and drove off.

Everyone at the cookout went back to what they were doing, but in a more quiet way. Nobody even laughed when Sammy threw a horseshoe clear off the lawn and it landed with a big noise in the street, right where Mrs. Battisti's car was.

"We should've gone to Squanto Park," I said to Mamma.

She just gave me her face and walked to the far end of the lawn and made like she was checking to see how many charcoal briquettes were left in the bag.

I heard this gagging sound and I turned around to see Lily throwing up that relish in the bushes by the side of the house. Mamma would kill her when she found out.

Everett never did show up. I said all along he wouldn't, but no one ever listens to me.

FLUENCY

Jared Webb had received more acclaim than most in his profession. Spread out across the dressing table in his bedroom was the latest write-up, a darling piece in the weekly arts paper. Now that Jared was in the final performances of *Public Enema*, his triumphant one-man show, the press was going gaga. The article said that the show's surprisingly profitable three-year run at the Mother Stage in the East Village had broken him out of cult status and left him "if not swimming in the mainstream, then at least sunning himself on its banks." The writer, a fan from Jared's old days on the circuit, gushed on: "Webb won't divulge his future plans—he'll say only that he has several projects under consideration—but for now, he has made himself the most accomplished and best-known gender illusionist in New York—or anywhere—today."

Jared flipped the switch and the clear round bulbs that semi-circled the desk mirror made a soft glow around his face. He smiled at himself magnanimously. He tried to be amused at how the papers described him. "Gender illusionist" made him sound like some kind of cheap magic act, stirring his old fear that his place in the theater world was not very far removed—maybe one step up— from that of people who pulled white pigeons from behind the ears of gullible audience members. At least it was better than "female impersonator" (*The New York Times*' term), which he hated because when he was performing Jared did not feel he was impersonating anyone; in fact, at no other time did he feel more himself. His personal preference was "actress," for that was what he always dreamed of being and that was how he thought of himself now, though he hadn't publicly said that in a long time because it implied he took himself and his craft seriously. And if he'd learned one thing after years in this business it's that people won't stand for a self-important drag queen.

The picture they used pleased him, snapped onstage during the "sweeping divan" bit, in which Jared lays on a couch in a diaphanous nightgown while speaking on a French telephone to his family, who are together celebrating his nephew's bar mitzvah and are upset over Jared's mailed gift to the boy of a string of pearls. The camera flashed just after he delivered the last line ("So," Jared says to the nephew, "today you are a man. (beat) Of course, darling. I'll send the matching earrings, too.") and the expression on his face was priceless. At least, that's how Jared remembered the picture before it was ruined. Jared had left the article out for Enrique to see, laying it open on the small round table in the kitchen where his lover ritually consumed his fried eggs and guava juice before heading out to his midnight shift. When Jared came home from that night's show, he was hoping his lover might have something nice to say about it. Even if Enrique didn't speak English incredibly well, he seemed, if given the time, to be able to read it.

"My picture! Enrique—!"

"Wha'?"

"Oh, how could you do that?" Jared gingerly separated the bottom of the juice glass from the paper. The stain cut right through his face. "How could you do that!"

"O," Enrique said. "I diddun see."

"Oh, for Godsakes!"

"Was a ahcciden', Jare'."

"Aren't you even going to say you're sorry?"

"I sorry, Jare'." With that, Enrique ran his finger across the plate to get the last of the yolk. Then he stuck the finger in his mouth and sucked it clean.

"For Godsakes, you're not living in a hut in some Puerto Rican village, you know," Jared said. "In America, we use utensils." It was a dreadful thing to say, and Enrique would have been right not to talk to him for a week because of it, just like he did the last time Jared's tongue got the best of him.

But Enrique just got up and slipped on his jacket. "I lif in a house in Puerto Rico," he said quietly.

"I know that."

Jared wasn't sure where these horrid comments came from, only that they never used to come at all. He'd known Enrique almost a year and had been living with him for nearly that long. It was only recently that he'd grown short with him, and begun to say things that left him feeling ashamed of himself. Even in his act, Jared strove to keep things elevated. Of course people expected drag queens to be outrageous, but that didn't mean Jared had to pander to their worst instincts—or to his. Sometimes, though, when he was angry or when he was ad-libbing hotly, the nastiest things would just pop out.

Jared thought he should tell Enrique how sorry he was for his callous remark. But something stopped him; maybe it was his years on the every-bitch-for-herself drag circuit that made him so averse to apologizing. "Are you leaving now?"

Enrique nodded. "Ahnthony no wans me late."

Enrique had just started this job, the overnight janitor shift at NYU. Anthony was his supervisor, and had gotten him the job in the first place. Jared never quite understood how they met—Anthony was somehow an acquaintance of Enrique's cousin Consuelo in the Bronx. Anthony was from Puerto Rico, too, though he'd been in New York for years. They began to hang out together and Jared was jealous yet he could never seem to bring that up to Enrique. But his fears subsided after he actually met Anthony. Almost twenty years Enrique's senior, he was also stout, almost portly, with Brillo-pad hair that had little curls of gray throughout. When Enrique introduced him, Anthony grinned and shook Jared's hand as if his life depended on it and told him, in impeccable English, that he had a son back in San Juan who was nearly Enrique's age. He had such an earnest manner about him, in the disarming way the Puerto Ricans seemed to have, that Jared felt embarrassed at having suspected him of even being capable of ulterior motives.

"You know, Enrique, you don't have to work," Jared said, moving closer. Jared's success had allowed him to accrue a hefty little nest egg, and he was more than willing to share it with the man he loved.

"I wan' to," Enrique said. And indeed, the whole time Jared had known him, Enrique always had some kind of job, often more than one. The janitor position was his first that wasn't part-time and low-paying. It gave him his own money, and his pride too, which Jared believed was very important to Latin men.

"I miss you at night," Jared said, stepping closer still.

"Bu' the job iss . . ."—he struggled for the words—"I ge' insurans. An' I ge' to the yunion ahfter six mons."

"I know. It's just that I miss sleeping with you."

Enrique fixed on his head the Yankees cap he was so fond of wearing. "By," he said, and the word to Jared was like a piece of candy, a little bonbon wrapped in a simple square of gold foil and tossed toward him in a glinting arc. Jared grabbed it.

"Rico," he said. He put his hand on the door before Enrique could open it. He kissed him on the lips. "I love you," he said.

"Me too," said Enrique.

Jared whispered, "In Spanish . . ."

Enrique obliged.

They kissed again. Jared slipped his hand into Enrique's pants. He was a little surprised to find him not even slightly aroused.

"No wen you dress lige tha'," Enrique said.

Jared took a taxi home from his show every night in full costume and makeup; he liked taking everything off in his bedroom, in front of his mirror, going over that night's performance in his mind. But Enrique preferred making love to a man who looked like a man, and actually Jared preferred being made love to as a man as well. But Jared was only trying to be spontaneous.

"I haf to go."

Jared backed off. He watched his lover shut the door behind him and listened to him lock the two locks. He was left standing in the kitchen in the glittering gold gown from the "grand ball" bit that closed the show. He looked down at his ruined picture and thought how this would be an ideal time to cry. He stood perfectly still, waiting for the tears. But they never came, no matter how bad he felt. He was bone-dry. It stymied him. At his darkest moments he believed that this was the difference between drag queens and real actresses. Actresses cried. They knew how to feel things. The whole mindset of the drag queen was a defense against being hurt. Most of the ones Jared knew were very cold people.

Jared retired to the bedroom. He removed his makeup more quickly than usual, knowing he needed to get to sleep at a decent time this night. He wanted to be rested for his big lunch the next day. His "several projects under consideration" was actually just one—but he just couldn't resist saying that to the press. It was more than a month ago now that he was backstage after his show when a note was handed him by a messenger. The note, scrawled on the back of an unfilled prescription for eye drops, was from Morton George. At first the name didn't mean anything to Jared, but slowly it sank in: the guy who directed *Loved Ones* a few years back—and didn't he win an Obie for that?—of course!—Morton George!—one of the more famous off-Broadway directors. "Impressed by your show," the note read. "May have part for you in upcoming prod. Call if interested," and the phone number.

Jared felt that he shouldn't have been as swept away by the note as he was. After all, he fully expected something like this to happen at some time. It was all part of his master plan. Yet he went home in a reverie that night, even treated Enrique to a late night on the town that turned out to be their last time out together, just before Enrique got the job at NYU. He was like a giggly schoolgirl when he told Enrique about the note, even showed it to him, but the significance of it seemed to pass Enrique by. When Jared first fell in love with Enrique, he promised himself that he would become fluent in Spanish so they could really communicate. This was one of those times when he wished he had followed through on that promise.

The next day he made the call to Morton George, who sounded older on the phone than Jared expected. It seems he was slated to direct a play by a promising young writer, and he believed Jared had just what one of the characters was crying out for. Jared pressed him for information about the role, about the play, but Morton George said they should meet in person to discuss it. He had to be out of the country for the next several weeks, but they set a lunch date for his return.

It was actually before the talk with Morton George that Jared had begun to tire of *Public Enema* and its grueling eight-shows-a-week schedule (including the Saturday and Wednesday matinees; Mondays he got off). But the talk definitely accelerated the feeling. For the first year of *Public Enema*, Jared was actually still writing the show, or at least refining it. He would add a line here, subtract some stage business there. Every night was a challenge. But in the last couple of years, having gotten the show down pat, he was slowly but surely giving in to the temptation to walk through the thing every night. As the show continued to pack them in most nights, Jared began to have nightmarish visions of becoming the gay equivalent of that guy who's been doing *Fiddler on the Roof* for the last hundred years.

So Jared made the decision to end the show, even before he knew anything about the part that Morton George had in mind for him, even before he was sure he had a deal. The theater owner told him it was a reckless decision, and Jared realized that was probably true. But then, it was a reckless decision for him as a kid of fifteen to go to the Ganlin, Ohio, Community Auditions dressed as Barbra Streisand and lip-sync to a scratched 45 of "The Way We Were." Now as then, he just had a feeling that he was doing the right thing. As an artist, he told himself, he hungered for a new challenge.

And maybe even more than that, he needed to show the world what he was truly capable of, what a real actress he was. He needed to show everyone who ever said he was crazy or sick, or that he would amount to nothing: his parents, who practically disowned him after the Streisand incident; Mr. Hofstedt, who ran him out of the audition hall that day; the handsome and cruel boys at school who never let him live it down. And those tawdry girls he rose up through the ranks with—and then surpassed. He wanted to show them, too.

Jared remembered how it was when he first showed up on the New York drag scene. The others were as pleasant as one could expect from their ilk. But once it became clear who the real star was, who got the biggest laughs and the loudest applause, they became the ragingest of cunts toward him. They spat at him. They made snide little comments. Katrinka Blue and Laverne DeFlowers actually conspired to trip him on his way out to the stage one night. And then there was the time backstage when Sistina Chapel announced, right in front of everyone, that his calves looked like full vacuum cleaner bags. (Sistina, like all in Jared's trade, had the talent for spotting weaknesses; Jared was more sensitive about his cliff-dweller calves than any other part of his body.) But Jared kept his dignity. He was different. He knew it, and so did they. Any one of them could zing effectively, but only he jotted down his remarks, sharpening the wording and delivery until they glinted with truth.

What's more, Jared made a point of keeping up his appearance. The others—the ones who were still around, that is; the ones who hadn't given it up or been carried off by the plague—had let themselves go after only a few years. The last time Jared saw Sistina Chapel, a couple of years ago at an AIDS fundraising event, he was deeply impressed by her deterioration. She needed a close shave, and her makeup looked like it been applied on the IRT, for Godsakes. And her act! It was never anything special, but now she had sunken to pimping her ever-expanding waistline. Jared long ago vowed that would never happen to him. He went to the gym—light workouts only because he didn't want to muscle up too much (especially in the calves). He avoided smoking and sweets and even drugs, for the most part. He shaved and plucked and waxed until his skin hardly felt human. And he positively refused to buy off the rack. He wouldn't be seen in rags.

Jared settled into the big empty bed, missing Enrique more this night than any other so far. He tried to sleep but kept wondering about tomorrow, what kind of character Morton George had in mind for him, what the part was that he was just right for. Something saucy, perhaps. Maybe a prostitute. He did a good prostitute. It was all in the shoulders. Or maybe a grande old dame type. Glasses at the tip of her nose as she reads her financial statement. Anyway, it hardly mattered. If Morton George wanted him to play the bathmat, he'd do it. Jared was seasoned enough to know that chances like this didn't come along every day, or even every year.

7:30 in the morning was not a time that theater people considered at all propitious. Yet there Jared was, awake, rested even. The way the light streamed into the bedroom made it look unfamiliar, and he was a little bit frightened when he first opened his eyes.

He made some tea and sat down at his dressing table to figure out what he would wear to his big lunch with Morton George. Jared wanted to look stunning for the great director and spent the better part of the next four hours making himself up to look just short of that, not wishing to seem too eager. The ideal appearance was one

of effortless glamour, one that said attractiveness was second na-
ture. After much fussing he settled on a classic white blouse with a
floral-pattern scarf dashed across one shoulder. He wore a very pale
lipstick and a whitish-blonde wig that made him look too much
like Dusty Springfield. So he switched it for a medium-length
brown number that accentuated the dimple on his chin.

After that, he practiced his how-nice-to-see-you expression a few
times, holding his hand out palm down the way his mother's Avon
lady used to do when she came to the house on Thursday afternoons. He thought of Mrs. Hollander fondly as he slipped on his
long purple coat. She was the first real lady to enthrall him. And the
treasure trove she carried in that small black box of hers! His heart
raced when she opened it, and later, when no one was around, he
would experiment for hours with the different creams and colors
she had left behind as samples.

On his way out, Jared glanced in the full-length mirror one last
time; he was pleased with the results. Just as he reached to unlock
the locks, they unlocked themselves. It was Enrique on the other
side. Jared glanced at the clock—11:40—and only then realized
that Enrique should have been home hours ago. His shift ended at
eight.

Enrique almost appeared not to recognize Jared when he opened
the door. Maybe it was the wig, Jared thought. Maybe it was something else.

"Hello," said Jared, adopting a smile.

"Hello."

Jared stood in front of him a moment, his arms a perfect V meeting at the hands, which gripped a small white purse. It was rather
an expectant pose, like that of a grade-school teacher awaiting an
explanation for bad behavior.

Enrique just yawned. Jared stepped aside. Enrique shuffled past
him and into the apartment.

"How was work?" said Jared. He knew it was not the question of
the moment. He didn't understand himself sometimes. Onstage he
could be so direct. He could be that way when he was angry, too, but
right now he was just perplexed.

"Alrigh'," Enrique said. He took off his jacket and a small something fell from his pocket. He bent down to pick it up.

"What's that?"

"Iss a book."

"Oh. What kind of book?"

"Jus' a book. Ahnthony gif to me."

Jared moved closer. "Can I see it?"

Enrique shrugged and handed it over. It was a small paperback with a faded red cover, thin and cheaply printed. It looked like something that had been baking in the display window of that old Communist bookstore on Bank Street, and indeed, it might have been, as the title was *Das Kapital*.

"Anthony gave you this?"

"Yess."

"Why?"

"To read."

"Oh."

Jared thumbed the book. He remembered reading it in college, at the small private university in Pennsylvania his parents shipped him off to. Even for him, who fared well in school, it had been a particularly abstruse assignment. And in this copy, the print was especially tiny and hard to read.

"Well, that was nice of Anthony to let you borrow this," Jared said. "But it may be difficult for you to understand. You can probably get it in Spanish at the public library."

Enrique snatched back the book, rather abruptly, Jared thought. "I no borro'," he said. "Iss a gif."

Jared could not bring himself to say, "Oh," yet again. He really didn't give a damn about the book. He wanted to know where Enrique had been all morning. His heart demanded to know. He took one step closer. His mind sorted the possibilities, and he found himself striving toward the most innocent of them.

"Did you work overtime today?"

"No."

To Jared, the cruelty of that terse remark seemed boundless. But then Enrique went on. "Ahnthony an' me, we go to bregfas' ahfter."

"For three-and-a-half hours?" The question was not asked accusingly. Indeed, Jared had managed to toss it off with an almost disinterested air.

"We talk a lot." And that seemed to be the end of it. Enrique yawned again and announced that he was tired. He took off his shirt as he headed for the bathroom. Desire welled inside Jared at the sight of his brown, muscular back; it seemed a long time since they'd made love. He wished he wasn't dressed the way he was. He had a little time before his meeting. He heard the shower begin to run, then simply turned and left.

When Jared got back late in the afternoon, Enrique was not asleep, as he expected. He wasn't even watching television, which wouldn't have surprised Jared either. He was sitting on the couch, munching dry cereal from the box, reading (or attempting to read) the book Anthony gave him.

Without saying a word, Jared untied the scarf and slipped it from his neck as he headed for the bedroom. He shut the door behind him. Twenty minutes later he reemerged in his favorite pink satin robe. His hair was mussed in spots, tangled in others, flat against his head near the ears; wigs wreaked havoc on naturally fine hair such as his. His face was raw and tingly from having just been scrubbed.

Enrique had hidden the book and the cereal box under the couch and was now watching television in his customary position: slouched, arms crossed against his chest like a pouty little boy, the ankle of one leg resting on the knee of the other. His expression was not very different from when he was reading: intensely focused, yet angry, like he was dead set on figuring out something he knew he could not.

"Enrique?"

No response. There was no way he couldn't have heard him.

"Enrique!"

"Wha'?"

"Aren't you even going ask me how my lunch with Morton George went?"

"O. How di' it wen'?"

"It's *go*, darling. 'How did it *go*.' " Jared did not like the sound of himself correcting Enrique's English. Only dreadful people with persnickety little minds did that sort of thing. It was just that the accent that so often tickled him—and which he still found so intoxicating in bed—sometimes came off like so much put-on baby talk. "Lunch was . . . interesting," he said.

He approached his lover. But it was clear that Enrique had already become reabsorbed in the television show. Jared went to shut the damn thing off but stopped short, bent down, and yanked the plug instead. He stood up with the cord, twirling it in his fingers like a freshly murdered daisy.

"Wha' are you doeen'!?"

"For Godsakes, Enrique, you watch too much television!"

"I am praticin' my Eenglish!"

"You are not. You're sitting there, zombified!"

"Wha' is tha'?—som-bi-fi—"

"Oh, forget it. Listen, sweetheart. Morton George asked me to be in the new play he's directing."

Enrique looked him up and down. He said, "O."

"Isn't that wonderful?"

"I suposs'."

"You suppose?"

"You don' seem hahppy."

"I'm happy." He fell back a little. Enrique knew things. Jared just couldn't decipher how he knew them. "I do have reservations, I guess."

Enrique let out a sigh. Jared sat next to him on the couch. He pulled his legs up underneath him. His fingers played with the fraying hem of the robe. He thought how he would have to get a new one; he hated going around in tatters.

"The part," Jared said. "It wasn't what I thought. It's the part of a man."

Enrique appeared to consider this information. "He no wans you in drahg?"

"No. He wants me to play a straight part. It's a big part, though. A good part."

The role was that of the dishonorably discharged brother-in-law of the main character whose cowardice and impotence are regularly trotted out by his hateful new wife and her family. It was hard for Jared to believe, at first, that this was the character Morton George thought was perfect for him. He refrained from giving Enrique the details about the role precisely because he was afraid of how absurd it might sound.

Nevertheless, Enrique, after thinking a minute, said, "Why does he want you?"

It was one of those rare times when Enrique spoke a line of flawless English, unadulterated by even an accent. He was, very occasionally, capable of transcending his limitations.

Jared bucked up. He tried to remember exactly the way Morton George had worded it, how he made it begin to make sense to him. "He says there's a quality about me when I'm onstage, something that goes beyond the clothes and the makeup. He says it's a kind of underlying dignity. It's exactly what this character needs, he says. When he saw me performing, he just got a feeling that I could play it."

"O."

"He said there must be a reason why I never took a silly stage name like other drag queens." And when Morton George said that, Jared felt vindicated. His decision to always use his real name was laughed at initially by the others, and frowned upon by the club managers. But he insisted (to himself only, initially) that it was him they were coming to see and not the dirty jokes and the wigs and the fabulous outfits. At first, of course, it was all those things that they came for—they didn't even know who he was. But that changed soon enough.

"He says he knows it's a stretch for me. But he thinks I can do it, Rico. He believes I can."

Enrique looked at him. "You are gonto be a mahn?" There seemed to be a flicker in his eyes.

"That's right, sweetheart." Jared reached out and touched his lover's face. "I'm going to do it."

"En spi' of wha' hahppen lahs' time?"

Jared pulled back his hand. "What last time?"

"You know . . ."

"That was totally different! That has nothing to do with this!"

"O."

"For Godsakes, Enrique!" Jared sprung from the couch and stalked his way around it. Then he stormed into the bedroom and slammed the door. He was hoping Enrique would come after him, but a minute later he heard the TV going again.

Jared sat at the dressing table. It was scattered with varieties of lipstick and rouge, eyeliner, nail polish. He put his hand on his chin and rested his elbow on the desk, looking away from the mirror. *The last time.* Jared had managed not to think of that at all in connection with the Morton George project. Why did Enrique have to bring it up?

It was not quite a year ago, during the peak of *Public Enema*'s popularity, and not long after Enrique moved in following a courtship of exactly eighteen days. Jared had a friend on the board of the Theatre Arts Society who got him invited to speak at a symposium on "The Interchangeability of Gender Roles in Certain Plays by Shakespeare." Jared jumped at the chance. It was a little-known fact about him that he had minored in Shakespeare. This seemed like a prime opportunity to show the world he had a mind. He remembered laughing out loud at the thought of any of those other drag queens giving a talk on Shakespeare; Katrinka Blue had trouble reading the instructions on a Woolite bottle, for Godsakes, Laverne DeFlowers was an ignoramus, too, and Sistina Chapel must have been named by someone else because she appeared utterly unaware of the high-culture reference she was making. (Privately Jared admitted that whoever thought up the name had done a pretty good job; it gave the dress-wearing Catholics a nice knock and invoked that fruitcake Michelangelo.)

So Jared set about writing his speech. He wanted it to be a serious, scholarly talk. It had to do with the practice during Shakespeare's time of using young boys in the roles of women. It was quite a speech: well-reasoned, eloquently executed, and deadly dull. But that's not what really killed the evening. It was his decision to go dressed not as Jared Webb the noted entertainer but as Jared Webb the unknown man, complete in a double-breasted suit bought just for the occasion, cuff links, tie, even a musky aftershave. He was there to showcase his intelligence, not his wardrobe, he told Enrique, who accompanied him as his date.

The moment they walked in, however, Jared knew he had made a momentous mistake. Clearly it was the drag queen everyone expected to see. His friend was polite and introduced him to people, and most of them knew the name after failing the face. Only the most comfortably artificial among them didn't register their disappointment in some way. And then, once they got over the shock of his appearance, people started pressing into him to say something witty or at least outrageous. But Jared, to no one's greater astonishment than his own, was an utter bore. His off-the-cuff remarks were tepid at best, prompting polite laughter, which, as everyone in the theater knows, is not quite as bad as no laughter at all. By the time he gave his talk, which for some reason sounded rather stiff and halting, the crowd had dismissed him altogether. They would have settled for one good joke, one trenchant ad-lib, but anything Jared thought up was stillborn by the time it reached his tongue. Up there in his suit, he just couldn't find it in himself.

That night ranked as one of the worst of Jared's life. It revealed just how much of him was the wigs and the outfits and the jokes. Those things transformed not only the way he looked, but the way he talked, the way he comported himself, the things that came into his head. When he was in drag, the tiniest lift of his eyebrow spoke volumes, and resulted in howls of laughter.

"I died," Jared told Enrique after they got home. Enrique held him in his arms, the way he used to. Jared remembered thinking at the time how it was a good chance to cry. "All they wanted was the clown show."

"Don' woary, Jare'."

"They weren't interested in anything I had to say."

All they wanted was to show each other how buddy-buddy they were with him, how hip to him they were. It occurred to Jared that his success was based merely on his coming along at the right time, that the New York elite were primed to embrace a drag queen exactly as *Public Enema* received a rave from *The Village Voice* and, a few weeks later, *The New York Times*. He had become the "safe" drag queen: no silly name, no overly garish ensembles, no off-color remarks that would hurt anyone's feelings.

But the next day, after he'd had time to recover, Jared reflected that he had simply gone about it all wrong. He could have been the hit of the evening, if only he'd gone better prepared. The men's clothes were not a mistake; the men's clothes without any self-knowledge, without self-consciousness, without any acknowledgment of it in any way—*that* was the mistake. Now his mind brimmed with amusing things he could have said: "I'm dressed this way as a tribute to one of America's greatest drag queens—We love you, Gore Vidal!" When Jared realized his mistake, he was even able to laugh about it. He tried to explain it to Enrique and got a nonplussed look for his trouble. Again he wished he had learned Spanish like he said he would. Nevertheless, Jared knew he would never let anything like that night happen again. He would not go into the Morton George project with blinders on, thinking he'd be a natural success. He'd work at it. He'd work at it harder than he'd ever worked at anything.

The scheduling for the play, called *Fatalities*, was tight. There were to be three weeks of rehearsal followed by thirteen nights of previews before it opened. This was due to another project that Morton George had signed on to do right after *Fatalities*. As it happened, the first rehearsal came just four days after the last *Public Enema*. Jared had hoped to have more time than that to rest up and spend with Enrique. After all he'd been working for three years straight without any real break. But long ago he accepted that being in show business meant working harder and longer than regular people, and he didn't really mind.

That first morning, he tried not to fuss too much over what he should wear. Even so, he changed three times before deciding on the jeans, light blue shirt and dark blue blazer that he'd picked out initially. He looked in the mirror. He didn't understand how he could have such commanding shoulders in a dress, yet in men's clothes look like some undernourished adolescent. But he tried to block such thoughts out of his mind.

He looked in on his lover before he left. Enrique slept soundlessly, his naked brown body all curled up. He had come in more than two hours after his shift ended that morning. Another breakfast with Anthony. Another book brought home. This one a ranting tract called *Slave State: The History of Puerto Rico*. Jared was beginning to think he didn't understand Anthony at all, but then Anthony could have been the reincarnation of Che Guevara and Jared wouldn't have really cared. He was too consumed with the jealousy that grew in him with every minute Enrique went missing. He was determined to find out just what was going on between them. But that feeling retreated when Enrique walked through the door. Then, all Jared wanted was to be held and reassured. But when Jared saw the book, the jealousy charged forward again.

"Enrique, I don't like it when another man is giving you gifts all the time," he said, saying the words quickly so he wouldn't stop himself.

"No is gif," replied sleepy-eyed Enrique. "I jus' borro'. I haf to gif bahck."

That deflated Jared, or maybe it was Enrique's seeming obliviousness to his anger. Enrique yawned and went off to bed.

Undeniably, Jared had begun to wonder about Anthony again. It was possible that Enrique just needed a friend, a fellow countryman, a father figure. He was only twenty-four, after all. And Anthony, from all Jared could glean, wasn't even gay. Yet Jared couldn't shake the sensation that Anthony was working some kind of change in Enrique. Enrique was less talkative than he'd always been, and when he talked he laughed less. He stopped wearing his Yankees cap, and one day Jared spotted it in the trash. He began to forgo TV in favor of poring through the books Anthony gave him. He read them with apparent great difficulty, hunched over at the small round table in the kitchen, fingers caressing his angry brow, lips silently mouthing the words. Once Jared ventured to ask him what he was reading about. Enrique came back with an odd, snappish, painstakingly enunciated reply, something about how Jared wouldn't understand because he was a "United Statesian."

Sex was different, too, and not just in that Enrique seemed less interested. They had actually made love over the weekend, twice. Normally Enrique talked up a storm during sex—in Spanish, the way Jared liked. But Jared never before had to prompt him to do it, and then Enrique used words that were unfamiliar, harsh-sounding, even hostile. And while Jared enjoyed the more-brutal-than-usual manner in which Enrique pumped away, that made him wonder, too. Afterward he did not dare ask Enrique what he was saying. It was enough to lie in bed and be held by him like he hadn't been in a long time.

Perhaps the worst thing about that morning was that it put Jared in a strange and conflicted mood. He would rather have appeared more confident as he walked into the theater for the first rehearsal.

The first person he saw was the actress who would be playing his wife.

"Hi," she said. "Who are you?"

The atmosphere was casual as the cast introduced themselves. They seemed to be a nimble, amiable bunch—the fact that Jared had never heard of any of them encouraged such kind thoughts. Morton George made a jovial, grandfatherly ringmaster. The only sour note came from the playwright, a small, anemic-looking Yale graduate named Barnett. Jared couldn't figure out if that was his first name or last; it was all anybody ever called him and it was all that appeared on the script. Barnett had dark-rimmed glasses and a black goatee so bristly you could probably cut your fingers on it. He seemed from the first to regard Jared with a mix of horror and revulsion, rather like he'd walked into his kitchen in the morning and found a cockroach in the coffee pot.

After introductions, everyone settled down for an initial read-through of the play. Jared had read through his part already, of course, and found his first attempts at saying his lines—in the privacy of his bedroom, in front of the mirror—to be rather wooden and lifeless. Now, as he read along with the others and heard how they brought the words to life, he thought his voice sounded almost entombed. And he tripped over his lines often enough for Morton George to say, "Just relax, Jared," with an encouraging smile.

After that they read through it again, and then again. It seemed to Jared that he did an even worse job with each reading, but no one said anything. At some point they stopped to eat. After that they worked late into the evening on blocking the first act. Jared stumbled there too—literally.

"Just relax," Morton George said to him again, right before they called it quits for the night. "You just need to loosen up."

Still, Jared went home with a vague, uneasy feeling. He was glad when Enrique failed to ask how his first day went. In fact, he hardly looked up from his book at all while he ate his eggs and juice before going to work. Jared was plagued by the desire to talk. He wished there was something he could say that would make Enrique simply stop what he was doing and look up at him with eyes that sought to ease his pain. But he did not know what those words were.

Jared's unease only grew as the days of rehearsals became weeks. His line-reading and stage movements improved somewhat, but they were still very tentative. There was none of the grace and flow that had always come naturally to him whenever he took a stage. Moreover, his character did not make any more sense to him now than it did at the beginning. The guy was such a terrible wimp! In one scene, his wife smacked him across the face. The first time they rehearsed it, the actress clocked him so hard that he actually hit her back, out of instinct. The poor girl was not seriously hurt, thankfully, and Jared apologized profusely. But the incident seemed to point up for everyone how little he had grasped the character.

Not that anyone ever said anything to him. In fact, from the beginning, everyone (except Barnett) was exceedingly polite toward him. At first, Jared assumed that was because he was the biggest star in the cast (although he did not have the starring role) and he responded with the appropriate noblesse oblige. But later it became apparent that something else was going on. Jared watched how the other actors worked together, exchanging suggestions, experimenting with different readings. And he saw how Morton George and Barnett would say things to better their performances. But no one ever said anything critical or even substantial to Jared about his performance. They'd talk to him—about the costumes, about what a great artist Morton George was, about the Triangle Shirtwaist fire for Godsakes (it came up somehow)—about anything but his acting. When Jared was performing, a pall seemed to descend from the rafters. Everyone went still and silent, helpless to prevent what they were seeing: unaccountably lifeless reading, stage movements that reminded Jared of an armadillo crossing a highway back in Ohio. And his hands! Jared just didn't seem to know what to do with them. In drag they floated and fluttered all over the place and Jared hardly even had to think about it. Now they either knocked over props or just hung in front of him like the paws of a begging puppy.

Not even Jared himself could broach the subject of his acting.

The extent to which putting on a play was a collaborative art threw him. He was simply not accustomed to working with other people, to sharing insights. On the drag circuit, sharing insights was tantamount to giving your act away. Most of what he had learned about performing had come through trial and error. He was used to keeping to himself, practicing in privacy with the bedroom mirror. But this was no one-man show.

There was one instance resembling an actual discussion between Jared and one of the other actors, a neophyte named Cliff Ellinger. Although he had only one line and was onstage for all of forty-five seconds, he was so thrilled to be in his first real production that he walked around with a big, stupid grin all the time. Jared was leaving one night when Cliff said, "Boy, you've got a great part." Jared smiled mildly in response, managing to construe the remark as a compliment.

The whole business began to weigh heavily on Jared. He was filled with dread when he woke up in the morning and dread when he dragged himself home at night because he knew he would fall asleep only to wake up to it all again. In his despair, his performance actually worsened; any improvements he had made erased themselves. Also, he was disheartened by a trip he'd made to the public library to look up some articles on Morton George in the hopes of getting a clue as to what he wanted from his actors. He found the glowing pieces from when the director was in his heyday, but the more recent ones had a different thread running through them. They spoke of his "great lapses in judgment" since he had started winning awards. They cited his all-lesbian reworking of *A Doll's House*. Then there was his musical version of *The Miracle Worker*, which he co-wrote. It was true that at one point he was convinced that *Fatalities* should be set on a Martian colony in the future "to bring in the element of the universe." Jared couldn't help but wonder if he wasn't Morton George's latest mistake.

The previews, not surprisingly, were even more disastrous than the rehearsals. The play was no longer just a private debacle between a small group of people who went home hushed and exhausted each night. Now it was out in the open. Half the audience disappeared during intermission. The dialogue was punctuated with coughs and squeaking chairs that were definitely not in the script. And at the curtain call, the applause, never more than just barely polite, diminished perceptibly when Jared took his bow. He rushed home at night, dreading the reviews.

As *Fatalities* careened toward opening night, an air of desperation gripped the production. The night before opening night, Morton George decided to hold one last full dress rehearsal. Jared was in the middle of a scene—the scene where his character finally gets up the courage to ask his wife why she married him—when all of a sudden the veil of politeness that had shielded him dropped away. Morton George just blew up.

"No no NO!!" he thundered. "Jared, you're reading the lines but you're not understanding them! You're not listening to what the character is really saying!"

Jared was mortified. Sistina Chapel could not have been more cruel. But, as with Sistina, there was truth in what he said and Jared knew that.

Jared went home wondering if there had ever been a worse time in his life. The four-floor walk up to his apartment had never seemed so daunting. He was finally on the verge of tears, and he wanted to wake up Enrique and cry in his arms. As he approached the apartment door, however, Jared could tell that Enrique was not asleep. The salsa station could be heard. Underneath that, there was talking. The voice sounded somewhat like Enrique's, but it appeared to be in conversation—but wait, there were two voices, very similar-sounding, speaking in very urgent and serious tones that belied the frivolity of the music. And these people—one of them? both of them—*Someone* was speaking English, clear unaccented English. He immediately thought of Anthony. Jared could feel the blood pulsing in his temples. He went in.

Enrique and Anthony were seated at the small round table in the kitchen, drinking beer from clear bottles. Enrique had his radio set up on the table. Anthony smiled broadly at the sight of Jared and jumped up from his chair, bumping the table as he did. He didn't seem so fat as Jared remembered. He was more thickset, and quite robust.

"I invi' Ahnthony ober."

"I see that."

Anthony extended his thick, callused hand. Jared was a little taken aback by his dark, smoldering eyes and shining skin.

On the table was a stack of yet more books. In the past weeks Enrique had brought so many home that they were forming stacks on the floor by his side of the bed. From the bindings Jared could tell that these latest had been checked out, or perhaps stolen, from the NYU library. *The Sugar Trade. Viva Zapata! Properties of Gasoline.* Next to them was an open map of Manhattan.

"We are planning a protest!" Anthony announced when he saw Jared's questioning face. He lifted the map and showed Jared a newspaper article that was underneath. It said the Governor of Puerto Rico was visiting New York tomorrow and was scheduled to meet the mayor at Gracie Mansion.

"What are you protesting?" Jared said.

"He is nothing but a puppet for United Statesian interests!" Anthony said.

"United Statesian?"

"We no say American," Enrique put in.

"That's right!" said Anthony. "Because we are all from the Americas. The United States has stolen that from us too."

Then Anthony showed Jared a flyer for the protest, which was to take place at ten the next morning. It called for the "Independence of Puerto Rico."

Jared couldn't help but say, "Independence from what?"

"From the United States!" said Anthony. "Puerto Rico is not a toy for you to play with!" He said this with such violence that Jared became a little intimidated.

"Puerto Rico's not part of the United States," Jared tried to reason.

"Iss a ter-ri-to-ry," said Enrique.

"It's all about economics," Anthony said assuredly.

"I thought the United States and Puerto Rico were friends."

"Hah! With friends like that ..." Anthony was confident enough to know he didn't have to finish the phrase.

"What are you doing tomorrow morning?" Anthony said to Jared. He seemed almost fevered.

Jared would be working tomorrow, of course. Morton George

had told everyone to get to the theater early, where they would work on "trouble spots" until the big opening at eight. The despair Jared had momentarily been delivered from returned, even worse than before.

"You're quite the revolutionary, aren't you?" Jared said, heading for the sofa, not really caring what Anthony would think.

"No, no," he said, eschewing the label. "I only do what's right!" His voice was deep and reckless somehow, dangerous even.

Jared plopped himself down, his back to the two conspirators. He listened as Enrique and Anthony talked, mostly in Spanish, which felt to Jared like a pure affront. Even though he couldn't understand them, it was obvious that they had a rapport, that they enjoyed talking, that they liked one another. He was also struck, again, by the similarity of their voices; they both had a sunburned sound to them, a dry cracking that ruptured their words and let their emotions come out.

Jared seethed with jealousy and desperately wanted Anthony to leave, not just for now, but forever. Once he was gone, Jared would tell Enrique that Anthony was no longer welcome in the apartment.

It wasn't long before Anthony realized that Jared wanted him to go. So he told Enrique—in English—that they'd continue their discussion at work, and then he left.

For several minutes Jared listened to Enrique knocking around in the kitchen, shutting off the music, clearing the beer bottles.

"So this is what's been going on?" Jared said at last. He immediately thought that Enrique wouldn't understand him, wouldn't get what he meant.

But Enrique said, "Oh, Ahnthony iss bery—how you say?—passionate."

Jared smirked at this latest instance of perfect English.

"He iss plahnning to ligh' on fiyer on Sahturday."

Jared wasn't sure he understood.

"What?"

Enrique seemed to think about his words, whether or not he had used the right ones.

"Did you say he's going to light himself on fire?" Jared said impatiently.

"Yess. Ahss a protess."

Jared turned around and looked Enrique in the face.

"You mean he's planning to kill himself?" Jared said.

"Yess."

Enrique turned his eyes to the floor. He seemed genuinely disturbed by this in a way that inflamed Jared.

Jared thought he should tell Enrique that he had to stop him, that he couldn't let Anthony go through with this. Instead he said, "Is he crazy or something?"

Enrique took obvious offense. "No. He jus' belifs bery strong. Strongly."

Enrique went off to take a shower. Ten minutes later he left for work. They never said another word.

Jared just sat there. He could try to stop Anthony himself. But it occurred to him that overly emotional crackpots like Anthony would find a way to follow their crazy lights no matter who tried to stop them. He even managed to make a joke to himself about what a great bit of theater it would all make.

He decided to go to bed. The weight of his own problems did not lift, but he felt strangely invigorated by what he had just learned. He'd rather Anthony not have to be horribly burned or worse, but at least he knew now that there was no affair going on, and that there would never be a chance for one to begin. He believed now that Enrique was infatuated with Anthony, and he knew his death would hit him hard. It would give Jared the perfect opportunity to console him, to show how much he cared.

The day of opening night, Jared woke up with a determination that reminded him of the old days. He would get this role down. He quickly showered and dressed and decided to get to the theater early. He would put on his costume and his makeup (such as it was) and he would say his lines and practice his blocking and he would do this thing the way it was supposed to be done. He would show them all.

But when he arrived at the theater, everyone else was already there. Obviously a meeting had been called that he was not invited to. Something—or rather, one very specific thing—was up. The cast was huddled around the coffee canteen, their backs to him.

Barnett and Morton George were talking to one another on the other side of the theater. Their arms were folded and they stood very close. They turned and looked at Jared. Morton George waved him over, not smiling. Jared approached just as Barnett abruptly broke away to join the other actors.

He agreed to be let out of his contract with surprising alacrity. He shocked himself because he was not one to let things go easily, especially not hard-won professional gains like this. But Jared heard himself say, "Yes. Alright. I understand," and found himself pleased to know the press would be told it was "creative differences" that led to the "mutual decision." Morton George said nothing like, "I still believe that with the right role, you can shine." Rather, he appeared to Jared right then like a confused old man with eyebags and gray whiskers and the yellowest teeth he'd ever seen.

Cliff Ellinger knew Jared's part by heart, and would be playing it on opening night. Barnett himself had agreed to take Cliff's walk-on role. Apparently Jared was never considered for it, and in a strange way he took that as a compliment. Morton George, though, did not seem to believe that the last minute changes would save the show. Indeed, the last thing he said to Jared was, "What happened—it wasn't all your fault."

Jared walked home feeling lighter than he had in a long time. When he entered the apartment, he found that someone was home. Enrique should have been with Anthony at the protest. But the TV was on, though no one was watching it. It took him a moment to hear the talking in the bedroom over the jabbering of the TV.

He stood still a moment, tracing the voice. He approached the bedroom door. It was closed. He stopped with his hand on the knob. He listened to the voice.

"No, it's alright."

Flawless English. He thought of Anthony. Anthony in his own bedroom. But how could that be? Anthony was scheduled to become a smoldering carcass right about now.

"It was a good protest anyway."

Oh yes. That warm, dry, cracking voice.

And yet there seemed to be no second person, no Enrique. No one was responding. Anthony must be talking on the phone. He imagined Enrique lying in bed next to him, listening to the voice of the man he really loved.

"Yes. It was good. It was better than good."

Jared couldn't listen anymore. He opened the door. He did so with the intention of surprising them, but he had done it so smoothly and silently and gracefully—exactly the opposite of how he'd been onstage—that Enrique, alone in the room, seated on the edge of the bed with his back to Jared, didn't even notice him.

"It doesn't mean that you've betrayed the cause, Anthony. It just means that you want to live. Please stop crying."

Jared fell back a little, but kept his bearing. Enrique's English was not flawless, he realized, but it was pretty damn good, far better than he'd ever heard Enrique speak, far better than he ever thought he was capable of.

"I don't think that at all. I still think you are a great man. I'm glad you didn't do it. I would have missed you."

From the slight angle Jared could see that Enrique never looked more handsome, with his dark brow ridge and full lips and day's heavy beard. He was maturing into serious manhood. It was time.

"No, he'll be at the theater all day and all night."

Jared felt his heart begin to tear open.

"Yes. Come on over."

Perhaps, he thought, this was the ideal time to cry.

"*Sí. Te amo tambien.*"

With that, Jared retreated. He knew enough Spanish to understand what that meant. He closed the door without a sound and floated back through the apartment. Out the door and he was gone.

He wandered awhile. He thought the Village had never looked so much like an ordinary neighborhood, full of people rushing around doing things they'd have to do anywhere. It had turned cold and rainy and he was not dressed for it. He passed the revival house on 8th Street and, realizing that he hadn't been to a movie in ages, decided to go in. It was a "Classics of Drama" festival from the '30s and '40s, Jared's favorite period. He took a seat and let himself get caught up. Rita Hayworth had just been granted a reprieve, but unseen forces were busy contemplating her next great challenge.

THE WHEREABOUTS OF ME

"Hi," I said, leaning out the window of the rig, smiling the way you do at cops, like you're the most cheerful and innocent person ever to get behind a steering wheel. And the whole time the blood was pounding so hard in my head I thought it was gonna knock my sunglasses off.

He asked me if I was aware that the driver's-side brake light on my trailer was, as he put it, "not operational."

"Really?" I said.

Just then Matt, my advance driver and the only friend I had in the world, jumped out of his pickup and came over.

"We did know that, officer," Matt said, sounding sensible. "And we told our boss about it. Only he hasn't got around to fixing it yet."

"Duane Dolman," the cop said. Either he'd eyed the stenciling on the side of the rig or Duane had become too well-known to the cops around these parts. Ever since he blew into town not so long ago and set up Dolman Homes, the house farm just north of the bypass, there'd been violations and citations up the wazoo. And complaints too, since Duane's homes were nothing but terrible cheap little crackerboxes with no foundations that usually ended up sinking on one side or infested with spiders or flooded through with every good rain. Still, the prices were so low that young couples came from all over southeastern Kansas just to buy a Dolman Home. It was Matt and me's job to haul the homes to their plots of dirt and plop them down.

I thought we were gonna get off with just another write-up for

Duane and I even started to take the rig out of gear when without hardly even moving his lips the cop said, "License and registration, please."

Actually, for a second there, I thought about just letting it happen, just letting the cop discover how I didn't have a CDL—you're supposed to have one to operate a tractor-trailer legally—and after he ran a background check he'd find out about the warrant for my arrest and then at least I wouldn't have to go on living this shadow of a life that I hated so much. But I had Shayla to think about. I believed it would kill me if I never got to see my baby girl's face again, if the next time I saw her she was a walking talking stranger all snotty and resentful like her mother, her head filled with God only knows what lies about me.

So I gunned it. Now, gunning a tractor hitched to an entire two-bedroom house is not the same thing as tearing off in your big brother's GTO. At first the engine raved hysterically. Then, instead of taking off, the rig started to creep ahead real slow, almost like it was trying to sneak away from the scene unnoticed. "Stop the vehicle!" the cop barked. He ran alongside me aways, screaming at me to turn the engine off and step out of the truck. He even made a jump for the door handle, but I'd picked up speed by then. By the time he ran back to his cruiser and got in and came after me, I was a pretty good distance ahead.

The engine was spitting and hissing and crabbing underneath the roar. Duane of course had to buy the cheapest clunkers he could find. But I pushed it to the hilt. That's a two-bedroom house traveling down the highway at 75 miles an hour. Cars were driving into ditches to get out of my way. At least the drivers would have something to talk about at supper when they got home.

I straightened my sideview to check on the cop. He was swerving all over the road, trying to keep from getting hit by the shingles that were peeling off that cheap Dolman roof. Then I watched as a piece of gutter tore away, flew through the air and landed smack in the center of the cop's windshield, shattering it. The cruiser went into a crazy skid and then disappeared from my view.

I guess it was about then that I started to think I really could get away. The Oklahoma line was only twenty miles south. Once over, I could have ditched the rig and disappeared into the woods along the interstate. I was figuring to leave Kansas anyway, and soon. But the thing was, I was planning to take Shayla with me. She was the only reason I took this job in the first place, to save up enough so that her and me could start fresh somewhere where nobody couldn't find us. I hadn't got a chance to work it out whole yet. I just knew that if I left Kansas now, the odds of me being able to sneak back and grab Shayla were about as good as the odds of me becoming the next Loretta Lynn. So with the cops off my tail for the time being, I decided to try for her.

There was no sign of the law by the time I reached Route 306 and that's why I drove north instead of south. About thirty miles up was a turnoff that led to my baby.

I had no way of knowing if Christine would even be home, and I didn't know how exactly I was gonna take Shayla away from her. I wouldn't have minded just knocking Christine aside, but then she wasn't the type of girl who went down easy. She was a scrawny little thing, but she knew how and where to hit a man. But I'd find a way. I had to. I just couldn't let Shayla go. I'd already lost one kid. I couldn't stand to lose another.

It was that other kid I'd lost, my little Mikey who I hadn't seen in more than two years, that drove Christine and me apart, though not in the way you might think. I had been living with Mikey's mother, Bernadette, some three years when all of a sudden she decides to take up with some building contractor and the next thing I know my key doesn't fit the lock. I snuck in through the basement window that didn't lock and came up through the cellar. You would have thought I was the creature from the black lagoon, the way Bernadette looked at me. She cussed me out—right in front of little Mikey too—and she threw at me the laundry she'd just folded. Let me tell you, you wouldn't think a balled-up pair of sock could hurt that much. "What does it take for you to get the message?" she screamed.

"What message?" I said.

"That I want you out! That I'm tired of you leeching around here! That I don't love you anymore."

"Jeez, Bernadette," I said. "You could have just *told* me."

But after thinking about it I decided that I wouldn't go. Why should I have? I had a right to be there. That was my home and my son and up until a short time from then my woman. I wasn't going anywhere, and I let Bernadette know that.

That's when she slapped me with the big one. She'd seen a lawyer, she said, and together they figured up a number of 13,000 dollars that I supposedly owed her in child support. She claimed I hadn't worked an honest day since Mikey was born, which I suppose was true if you don't consider changing diapers and middle-of-the-night feedings to be work. Then she filed a complaint against me with the police and warned me if I didn't leave she'd call and tell them where they could find me. Deadbeat dads were getting ten, fifteen years these days, the lawyer told her. I sat there at the kitchen table that I myself had shellacked and I thought how it had to be the building contractor. There was no way Bernadette would have come up with that on her own.

That same day I packed up. I didn't even get a chance to say goodbye to Mikey. I drove clear across the state, to Lily Springs. It was the only place I could think to go because I knew Matt Bailey, a friend of mine from high school, had moved there a few years before.

Matt let me lay low at his place while I figured out my game plan. It was a predicament. I couldn't do anything to alert the state to my whereabouts. I couldn't fill out a job application or a tax form or renew my license when it expired. I was afraid to leave the house for fear of running into the cops somewhere. But Matt was real good to me for a good long while. He brought home groceries, played cards with me, gave up watching baseball when I wanted to watch wrestling. The only time I ever noticed him bothered was on laundry day.

Finally he said, "I think you can take your own dirty stuff to the laundromat, Paul."

"I don't know, Matt," I said. "What about the cops?"

"It's two blocks, Paul. Here's some quarters. I don't think the cops in Lily Springs are looking for you too hard anymore, if they ever were."

It was the first time I'd been outside in weeks. The sun and the wind against my face felt good. And Matt was right—there was no sign of the cops. I began to think that maybe the worst was behind me.

It was at the laundromat that I met Christine. She stood at the counter and made change for people. She had her blonde hair pinned up and didn't care that everyone could see her dark roots. There was this round sticker on her sweater that said KISS ME IT'S MY BIRTHDAY. I wanted to, but instead I asked her how old she was.

"36," she said, and I remembered liking her right off because she didn't lie or ask me how old I thought she was or play any of the games a lot of women do when it comes to their age.

I asked her out. Within a couple of weeks I moved in with her. Matt seemed concerned, but more relieved. He was downright perturbed though when, about a month later, I told him Christine was pregnant.

"Damn, Paul," Matt said. "Aren't you two moving awful fast?"

I said, "Yup. We're movin' at the speed of love." Love will make you say things like that.

"You sure about that?"

"Sure as I'm standing here."

"You're not standing, Paul."

"Well you know what I mean."

"Boots off the couch, please."

We were watching the Buzzsaw Brothers annihilate Willie the Fort Sumter and Captain Ahab.

"You gonna marry her?" Matt said.

"Jeez Matt, you know I can't do that." I might as well have just walked into the police station and given myself up.

"Isn't she wondering why you haven't asked her?"

"Nope. She hasn't mentioned it at all. I told you, Matt, she's not like other women."

Matt seemed to have more to say, but he washed it back with some beer. It occurred to me then that Matt had known Christine for longer than I had, at least from the laundromat.

During the commercial I said, "You ever hear anything about Christine before I met her, Matt?"

"Like what?"

"I don't know. Just anything."

He thought for a minute and then he said "No" and then he seemed to chase it back down his throat with a big swig of Budweiser.

"You plan to ever tell her about Bernadette?" he said. "And your boy? And the reason you came here to Lily Springs?"

"Yeah. Soon. It's kind of a hard thing to explain.—Whoa! Did you see that? The Buzzsaws had Ahab pinned, then he bucked them both right into the ropes!"

Matt rolled his eyes. "Wrestling's not real, Paul. You shouldn't get so excited about it."

"Jeez, Matt. That's just what Bernadette always told me."

Matt went to the kitchen to get another couple of beers. He tossed mine at me when he came back. "You know," he said, "I guess I maybe did hear something about Christine before you met her."

"Yeah? What?"

"Just that she was married once. And that they had a kid together. And that the kid got killed by a hit-and-run driver."

That's the kind of news that'll make you sit up a little. I cracked the beer and it foamed all over my hands. Matt threw me the roll of paper towels. "How come you didn't tell me that before?" I said.

"I guess it never came up. How come *she* never told you?" I decided to go home and find out.

Well, she just burst into tears the instant I brought it up. I'd never seen Christine cry before or since. She said she wanted to tell me but that it hurt her to talk about.

"Still, honey," I said, "that's kind of thing I really should know."

Then came a new round of sobs. About all I could get out of her was that the little girl was two when she died and that the marriage fell apart after that. The rest of the time she just cried. It was kind of nice because she let me hold her—ever since she'd gotten pregnant, she didn't want to be touched much. In the end she said she was sorry and I told her it was alright, that me and her were making it alright by being in love and having this child together.

I suppose that would have been a good time to tell her what she really should know, about Bernadette and the arrest warrant and how I lost a child too. But I didn't. I was happy just to have her sobbing in my arms.

The next morning, Christine acted like everything was back to normal. She yelled at me for using the rest of the mouthwash. I told her I'd buy her some more. "With what?" she said. "Your looks?"

I knew pregnancy could make a woman irritable. But more and more it got so I couldn't be in the same room with Christine without feeling I was doing something wrong. I kept hoping that she'd go back to loving me after the baby was born. But something told me that wasn't gonna happen. The day Christine went into labor with Shayla was when she broke the news that she wanted to break up. We argued about it in the car on the way to the hospital. She said the worst things to me, in between contractions. "You're a bum!" she said. "You lay on the couch and watch wrestling! You won't work! You won't even apply for welfare!" It was the first time she'd ever complained about any of those things. "You'll never provide a future for me or the baby—Oh, shit!"

"Breathe, Christine!" I said. "Short little breaths!"

"Hooh hooh hooh I don't want my daughter raised around a person like you—Jesus Christ!"

"Breathe! We're almost there!"

"Hooh hooh hooh . . ."

"And it could be a boy, you know."

"No!—hooh hooh hooh—it's gonna be a girl!"

"How do you know? Did you have one of those tests without telling me?"

"No—hooh hooh—it just has to be a girl"—from the get-go she said she didn't want a boy—"hooh hooh hooh—I swear—hooh—if a boy comes out I'm giving it up for adoption!"

I stayed in the hospital with her for eleven hours. It was hard to tell, but she seemed glad to have me there. She ranted and raved so much they finally had to knock her out.

Afterward, when they brought in little Shayla, the three of us were all together. It was nice. We felt like a family. I sat on the edge of the bed. I thought about Christine asking me to leave.

"Marry me," I said, all of a sudden.

I thought that maybe it would be alright, that maybe enough

time had gone by that the state had forgot about me. But Christine looked at me like I just laid a fart or something.

"I love you, Christine. I want you to marry me."

She rolled her head back on the pillow and said, "God, Paul."

"You don't have to answer me now," I said.

But Christine wouldn't even give me that. "No, Paul," she said flat out. "I already told you. It's over between us. I want you out."

I slipped back and fell into the chair that was beside the bed. The nurse came in with a clipboard to take down the information for the birth certificate. When she got to the father's name, Christine said, "Unknown." I realized I couldn't say anything. And I got the feeling that Christine knew that, too.

Before she left the nurse told her that her parents had called and were on the way.

"You better go," said Christine. "You know how much they hate you."

I didn't exactly prefer their company either. I leaned over and kissed the baby and then Christine, on the forehead. She didn't try to squirm away or make a face or anything.

"I'll pick you up in the morning," I said.

"Don't," she said. "My parents will do it."

"I can take you home just as good as they can, Christine."

"I'm not going home, Paul. I'm moving in with them." She wouldn't even look me in the face.

"When was that decided?"

"It doesn't matter."

"But you hate your parents."

"I do not! Besides, I can't afford day care for Shayla when I go back to work."

"Day care? Christine, that's what I'm here for!"

"Are you deaf, Paul? I told you already. I want you out of my life forever!"

"No, Christine. That's my daughter too. You can't just take her away from me . . ."

"Paul. Just go home, pack a bag, and don't be there when I come to get my stuff tomorrow."

"I won't go along with this, Christine."

"Oh yes you will." She reached over Shayla to pick up the phone that was next to the hospital bed. She looked straight at me, and I knew for sure that she knew.

I showed up at Matt's again. I told him what happened. I couldn't figure how she ever found out.

Matt sat me down and looked me square in the face. "It was me, Paul. She got it from me. That's the only thing I can figure. It was when you first moved here, before she ever even met you. I was at the laundromat and she said it looked like I had more clothes than usual. I told you were living with me. I told her everything, Paul. I'm sorry."

I looked at him and I could tell he was real broken up about it.

"I guess I should have told you earlier, Paul. But I wasn't sure she'd put two and two together until now. Hell, I didn't know you were gonna fall in love with her and get her pregnant."

Matt put me up again. This time he took really good care of me. He got me the job with Duane Dolman that paid under the table and didn't require me to show a CDL. He cooked real good meals. He put on wrestling without my asking. Finally I told him to stop fussing so much and that I forgave him. He hadn't done anything on purpose to hurt me, not like Christine, who'd used me from the start. I decided I didn't want my daughter raised by *that* kind of person. That's when I started making my plan to steal Shayla away.

I didn't tell Matt about it. That was no reflection on him. I'm sure he would have kept the secret for me. But I kind of liked having it all to myself, something that I knew that nobody else did. And I was still the only one who knew it as I flew up 306 in that speeding house-hauler, getting closer and closer to the only other living soul I would tell—my Shayla.

I could see in the distance that the black Buick Christine's dad drove was gone from the driveway. I took that as a sign that maybe things were starting to go my way.

The brakes howled when I brought the rig a stop in front of the house. The engine rumbled in an uneven way, like it was asking me a question—maybe Are you sure you want to do this? I ducked my head under the sun visor. The house was totally still.

Then the front door swung open and there was Christine. It was funny but even at that distance, with her behind the dirty haze of the screen door, I knew the expression on her face exactly—squinty and suspicious but not too angry, which surprised me. I thought the mere sight of me would have set her right off.

She kicked open the screen door and stepped out on the porch. Now I could see she was carrying Shayla. I couldn't believe how much she'd grown in a few months. And she had a full head of hair, sandy brown like my own. I got out of the truck, but I kept the engine running.

Christine walked down the steps and across the lawn. It didn't take long to realize that she wasn't looking at me. It was the house hitched to the truck that was drawing her attention. As she walked toward it she reminded me of how the new homeowners looked when Matt and me first drove up. They were always excited but a little anxious too, like even more than the house itself they wanted the reasons they were buying the house to hold up. They wanted the person they were gonna live with in it to always love them, the kids they were gonna raise there not to disappoint them. And I remembered then the newlyweds over in Shreve who were waiting for this very house, how they were looking up and down the road, thinking it'll be dark soon, standing in the dirt where their living room was supposed to go.

"Like it?" I said.

Christine finally turned my way. She didn't seem to know it was me, so I took my sunglasses off.

"Paul?" Her expression turned angry in a snap. "What the fuck do you think you're doing here?"

"Jeez, Christine. Is that any way to talk to someone that just brung you a present?" I'm not sure how I came to say that. The whole time Christine and me were together, I could never get away with lying to her. She'd squint her eyes and my mouth would start twitching or one eye would sort of half-blink and she'd just know. But not this time. Lying was easy this time, I realized, because I didn't love her anymore.

"It's got two bedrooms," I said. "It's got two bathrooms." I didn't know if it really had two bathrooms. But the important thing was, Christine's eyes were getting wider and her grip on Shayla was starting to slip. Her mouth was moving with wanting to say something, but words that weren't nasty and hateful were sort of like a foreign language to her.

All of a sudden Shayla turned and looked at me with her big watery eyes. I knew there was no way she could have recognized me, but I was still hoping somehow that she would. I went to touch her, but Christine pulled her back.

"I'm serious, Christine," I said. "You always said I could never give you and Shayla a real home. Well, here it is."

Let me tell you, it had been a long time since I'd seen Christine that unsure of what to think. She turned to the house again, sort of gaping. The blown-away shingles and the missing piece of gutter were plain in front of her, but she didn't know enough to notice them. Shayla let out a shriek.

Christine said, "I don't understand this. I don't understand this at all."

"Understand what?" I took a few cautious steps toward my Shayla. "I bought a house is all."

"*You* bought a house?"

"I put a down payment on one."

"Where'd you get the money?" She squinted at me like she used to, but I didn't even flinch. "Did you do something illegal?"

"Christine!" I managed to sound good and offended. "I've been working a lot the past few months. I even put a down payment on a plot of land for the house to go on."

I almost had her. And I knew I was running out of time.

I walked over to the passenger side of the truck and opened the door. "Hop in and I'll show it to you. It's only about twenty miles from here."

Christine didn't make a move. She pulled Shayla up the side of her hip. "No, Paul," she said. "I can't."

I knew what she couldn't accept was any notion of me and her getting back together.

"Look," I said, "I didn't buy this house for the three of us. I bought it for you and Shayla. To live in. Without me."

Christine truly did not know what to think.

"Why would you just give me a house, Paul?"

"Because Shayla's my kid too." I told her that when she threw me out the way she did, it got me to thinking. She was right, I said. Everything she said about me was true. So I decided to make amends. I got myself a job and socked away the money. "I know there's no chance of us getting back together. But that doesn't mean I can't give my little girl a home of her own to grow up in."

Christine's face went all soft, then her body, like her anger, was streaming out the bottoms of her feet. She let Shayla slide down a little more.

"Of course," I said, "you can go on living with your folks, if you want." I gestured toward the truck. "Come on," I said. "It can't hurt to at least look at the land. Let's the three of us go. Right now."

She walked over, but stopped just short of getting in the truck. It was the closest I'd got to Shayla so far. I could have grabbed her then and pushed Christine aside, but for some reason I didn't.

She looked down at Shayla and said, "You wanna go for a ride?"

Christine climbed in, Shayla clutched tight to her chest, and I shut the door behind her. All I cared about was getting Shayla in the truck. If that meant Christine had to come along too, then I'd have to deal with that later.

I rounded the front of the truck and got in and took off in the direction heading away from 306, where the cops would be heading in from. A few miles ahead was a remote tree-lined road, 143, that would take us south and into Oklahoma.

"This is such a surprise," Christine said. "God, Paul, why are you driving so fast?"

"It's not that fast." I had to keep her occupied until I could figure out how to get rid of her. "So you're surprised, huh?"

"Of course! It's not every day someone drives a house up to your front door and tells you it's yours!" She looked out the window, at the trees rushing by in a blur. "It really is sweet of you, Paul."

"Yeah, well. I guess I have my good points too."

Christine looked down at Shayla, who was playing with her mother's necklace. "You know, Paul, I never meant for things to end up as bad they did.

"Yeah. Well, I guess sometimes people don't mean the things they do." I didn't know what I meant by that. I only knew I had to keep my anger under wraps for the time being.

"I didn't know what else to do to get you to leave."

"It's alright," I said, trying to hard not get riled. I was glad she wasn't looking me in the face right then because I could feel my lip starting to curl up. I was on the verge of blowing the whole thing with the anger screaming under my skin.

"Has it been . . . hard for you?" she said.

"It's been rough." I cocked my head away from her and forced out a little laugh. It was almost despite myself that I then said, "I have to check my back all the time. I have to constantly be afraid of going to prison." I was afraid that sounded resentful so I laughed again.

"But really, Paul, it was that way for you before you ever met me."

"Yeah, you're right. My mistake."

"But it's worked out okay for you. You've got this job. You're on the right track now. The Paul I knew would never have done something as sweet as this."

Some kind of small explosion came from under the hood then, almost like a piece of the engine fell off, although there was no sign of that. All I knew was that the rig was slowing down despite my efforts to keep it going. We rolled another couple hundred feet or so. I pulled the rig as far over to the right as I could.

"What are you doing?" Christine said.

"Damn that Duane." I'd been running the truck hard ever since I got away from the cop. It just didn't have anymore to give. "I'm sorry, Christine . . ."

"What are you saying?—Fix it!"

"I can't. I don't know what's wrong with it."

"Jesus Christ!"

"Now don't upset the baby."

"What are we gonna do, Paul? We're out in the middle of nowhere and it'll be dark soon!"

I looked at the sky. It was inky in spots. I was amazed at how something could be so wide open and so right there and still not be any way to escape. I checked the road. 143 never got much traffic, but I wondered how long we could go before someone came along. I slipped my sunglasses back on.

"I'd like to know how we're gonna get out of here, Paul."

"Well." I was thinking that I could tell her I'd walk to get help. I wondered if there was any way to convince her to let me take Shayla with me. "We'll flag somebody down," I said.

"Who? There's no one coming."

"Then we'll wait until someone does. Jeez, Christine. You could be a little nicer, considering everything I'm doing for you."

"I never asked you to do anything for me. I certainly never asked to be stranded out in the middle of nowhere."

That was Christine all the way. She could only be grateful in small spurts. I know she didn't really have anything to be grateful to me about, but Jesus, she didn't know that.

"I am sorry, Paul," she said. She rubbed her forehead. "I don't know why I act the way I do sometimes."

"It's alright." I felt like an idiot not running. I could have told her I'd be back in an hour. I could have told her that there was a garage a couple miles up. But I couldn't leave Shayla, not like this, not when she was so close to me, right next to me.

But I didn't like just sitting out in the open, waiting to get caught.

I reached over and banged on the glove compartment. It fell open. I took out a heavy duty flashlight. I held it between us for a minute. Christine had never been scared of me and she didn't know enough to be scared now.

"Maybe you wanna take a look inside the house while we're waiting," I said. I pulled from my shirt pocket the key I was supposed to give to the young couple in Shreve. It was shiny silver and dangled from a white plastic ring. Shayla made a grab for it.

"I think we should just wait," Christine said. She folded her arms against her chest and let out a big sigh.

"Aren't you a little bit curious to see it?" I said.

A smile started to spread across her face. "I guess I am."

We got out and went to the side of the house where the front door was. I put the flashlight in my back pocket and climbed up the side of the trailer to unlock the door. The door swung open with the incline of the road. I jumped back down.

"Okay," I said to Christine. "I'll boost you up first, then I'll hand up Shayla." She looked at me, suspiciously I thought.

"You can boost her and me up at the same time," she said.

"Okey-dokey."

I made a step of my two hands and Christine lifted her leg, holding Shayla with one arm, balancing herself on my back with the other. Up they went. Then I pulled myself up. I shut the door behind me, and locked it.

The inside was just walls and floors and ceilings. The windows were boarded over like they always were for transport. It was the first time I'd ever actually been inside one of Duane's houses. It wasn't much, but I could see how a person could want one for their own, a place to be that was theirs.

"It's dark in here," Christine said.

I pulled the flashlight out of my pocket and held it out to her. She looked at me a moment, then handed Shayla over in exchange. I had never before held my little daughter. She seemed to take to me right away.

Christine wandered off into the next room. I could see the projection from the flashlight whipping around the walls. I thought, finally, my chance had come. I walked over to the front door and unlocked it.

"Paul?" Christine called.

"Yeah?"

"I can only find one bathroom here."

"Keep looking."

"Okay."

I turned the knob and pushed opened the door. Night had come fast. I looked out as darkness was filling in the gaps between the trees that lined the side of the road. I didn't want to take Shayla into it. It seemed too many bad things could happen to her out there.

"No, Paul." I heard Christine coming back. "There's just one bath—" She saw me with Shayla at the open door. "What are you doing?"

"I was just looking out here, imagining, I don't know, a driveway. With maybe a mailbox at the end."

Christine walked over and looked out with me.

"Does this land you bought have a driveway?"

"It will."

"Does it have a lawn?"

"It can."

I could see her imagining it herself, thinking she had a future standing at this front door. Suddenly I felt her kiss my cheek.

"Thank you, Paul," she said. "I mean it."

I sat down with Shayla at the door, letting my legs dangle out. Christine sat down next to me and did the same. We were silent. I wondered why things never turned out the way you wanted them.

"Christine?"

"Yeah?"

"Did you ever love me? I mean, at the beginning, even a little?"

"Yes," she said.

We went quiet again. Then I handed Shayla to Christine and said, "I'm going for help."

"Don't, Paul. There's no lights on this road. Just wait."

"There's a gas station a couple miles up. I'll be alright. You two stay inside the house."

"At least take this." She held out the flashlight.

"I don't wanna leave you two in the dark," I said.

"We'll be okay until you get back."

I kissed Shayla and jumped to the ground. I walked in the direction the truck had been heading. I waited until the house was out of sight, then I ducked into the woods. I shined the flashlight in front of me, but I couldn't see much of anything. It was only when I walked smack into a tree that I realized I still had the sunglasses on.

INFECTION

At night, the baby bangs himself against the side of the crib.

All the way downstairs, over the television, the mother and father can hear it. The glance they exchange is simple but dark, both knowing and unbelieving. The mother removes from her lap the pile of little girls' socks she's been folding and gets up from the couch. She goes upstairs to make the baby stop.

The banging gets louder at the top of the stairs, louder still—a regular racket, she thinks—just outside the baby's door. Then it stops. The mother halts. The baby must hear her outside. Then she pushes the door open and flips the light switch. The baby boy, who has banged the crib clear across the room, looks up and around to see where the darkness went. The mother walks toward him, shaking her head, wondering. She stands above the crib, arms akimbo. The baby returns her questioning stare.

She drags the crib back to where it's supposed to be. The four wooden legs scar the floor as they move; the wheels had been taken off by the father some time before in the hope that a more stable crib would discourage the baby's banging. (When it didn't, when the baby simply banged harder, the father said that he had never seen such a strong little boy and he tried to see some good in that.) Shoving the crib back into its corner, the mother leans down, gives the baby a small whack on the bottom and says, "Now I want you to lay down and go to sleep and stop this infernal banging." But the baby is unfazed by the scolding; nothing ever seems to make him cry. She picks him up and lays him down on his back. She says, softly now, "Do you understand me? Do you hear me?" But the baby does not hear her. He is listening to whatever it is that's inside him, whatever it is that makes him bang against the crib at night.

The mother flips off the light switch and shuts the door behind her. She does not know that, through the sole window in the baby's room, the moon is smoldering in the sky, casting the big-eyed grinning giraffes on the walls in a lurid light.

The mother goes back downstairs and reseats herself on the couch. The father is sitting in the adjacent chair, his feet soaking in a small basin of warm water. They say nothing, but continue to watch the hockey game until a commercial for spray starch comes on.

"I wonder why he does that," the father says, turning to the mother.

"It's just a phase," the mother says, lifting the pile of socks back to her lap.

"I don't know how the girls sleep through it," the father says.

"He'll grow out of it," the mother says.

"Maybe I should nail the crib to the floor," the father says. But the mother makes a contemptible face and turns it on him and says, "Who ever heard of anyone doing something like that?"

But who ever heard of a baby that bangs his crib across the room at night? The mother knows the father is thinking this. Then he says, "There must be something."

The mother, looking down, stops in mid-fold and says, "The floor up there is getting to be a real mess."

Right then, just as the game's fourth period is starting, the television screen becomes a white blank. They turn their eyes to it; something has gone wrong. The whiteness on the screen does not jump around or flicker, but is a solid block of light. It bathes the room in a glow of simulated daytime—it would never pass for a sunny day, but for an overcast one, maybe. They wait and watch, and listen too, for there is no sound coming from the TV either, not the *shhhhhhhhhhh* of white noise or even the low hum of transmission. This goes on for several minutes. Then the blank screen is abruptly replaced by a still photo of a small girl smiling and holding a daisy.

Next to her are the station's logo and the words WE ARE EX-PERIENCING TECHNICAL DIFFICULTIES. PLEASE STAY TUNED.

The father says, "Maybe if we buy a stuffed toy or something and put it in the crib with him. Maybe that would make him stop."

"We buy him that and the girls will want something too," says the mother. She begins folding the socks again, two by two, into small balls.

The father lifts his feet from the basin and looks them over. The water drips from his heels. Then he says, "Maybe we should take him somewhere, Meg."

"The baby?"

"To a doctor somewhere." He thinks about what he's going to say before he says, "Could be there's something wrong."

The mother stops folding the socks and looks up. She says sternly, "There's nothing wrong with him, Jack. It's only a phase. He'll be over it in a few months' time." She says this even though she remembers saying something similar some months ago.

The father nods.

The hockey game comes back on. Two goals have been scored in the last, lost minutes.

"There's no need for any doctors," the mother says, and they watch the television.

The next night, the baby bangs so hard against the crib that two of the wooden slats break and he falls through the space to the floor. The mother and father scramble upstairs at the crashing sound, the father's wet feet tracking the whole way. When they push open the door, they are able to see the baby in the fullness of the moonlight, apparently unharmed and trying to sit himself upright. Around him are the broken slats. The parent are relieved. But when the mother flips the light switch, she gasps audibly and the father falls to his knees in front of the baby; there a large scratch extending from the corner of the baby's right eye to the lower part of his cheek. The wound seeps blood like a river overflowing its banks. On the splintery edge of one of the broken slats are bits of blood and skin.

"Good Christ," the father says. "Call an ambulance—"

"No," the mother says. "We'll drive him to the hospital ourselves."

The baby is not crying at all.

They have to wake the girls up and take them along, since they are too young to be left to themselves and neither parent wants to stay behind while the other goes to the hospital. The girls are tired and sleep in the back seat all the way. The father drives and the mother has a sour expression on her face as she holds the baby in her lap and gently presses a wetted dishcloth against his wound. She glances down at the baby, who seems to be in no pain, then looks up again. She begins to feel the baby rocking in her lap, and quickly she clamps him to her breast. The baby squirms under her grip, still wanting to rock, and she tightens her arm around his body. Perhaps she is hurting the baby, but it is only in the name of protecting him, she thinks. No one in the car is talking. Outside, the night highway is deserted. The mother peers ahead; the pavement and the sky rushing past her seem equally black and she is glad she is not driving because she is sure she does not know where she is going. Above and behind them, out of their sight, the moon trails along.

In the distance, they see swirling lights and hear gurgling sirens. "Must be an accident," the father says, as they move closer. The accident in the middle of the highway seems to involve several cars. A police officer waves the father on even though he has not slowed down to take a look.

They arrive at the emergency room and take the baby to the nurse's desk to check him in, but the nurse tells them the wait will be long due to a bad accident on the highway. For hours they sit in a room crowded with anxious, sleepy people, all of them listening to the urgent sounds of the medical staff in unseen rooms and corridors. The girls are curled up asleep in two of the chairs. The mother, still holding the baby tightly, stares at the floor, but manages to take in the whole of the room: a few seats down from her sits a man with a bloody nose and a bored expression; opposite her is an elderly woman with moist eyes, wrapped in a shawl and muttering incantations; and across the room she notices a young woman not very unlike herself, tired-looking, with two small children in her charge, one bawling, the other, a girl, silent and pop-eyed and gripping a Phillips-head screwdriver. She is staring at it and slowly turning it, as if every aspect of the thing revealed some new fascination. When the girl's parent notices the mother is staring at her, she tries to take the screwdriver, saying "Will you put that damn thing away?" But the girl won't let go. She has both hands on it in a tug of war with her mother. Finally the mother lets go.

High in a corner of the room, a TV is running, but the snowy picture rolls over and over and no one seems to know it's there.

When the doctor finally calls them, the mother goes in with the baby and the father waits with the girls. The doctor is a smallish man with glasses and he appears exhausted. Blood specks the bottom of his white coat. His first question pertains to how it happened, and the mother tells him he fell out of his crib. He is skeptical of her answer, looking into her eyes, but she does not suspect this. The mother wonders a moment if she should tell him about the baby's incessant banging and how she was nearly at the end of her rope with it, but she doesn't know how to say it, how to phrase it, so that it doesn't sound horrible and strange.

The doctor says the wound looks nastier than it is, and that it is not something to be overly concerned about. He leaves the examination room and returns with a bottle of brown liquid and some bandages. When he applies the disinfectant, the baby wails furiously, kicking and swinging his arms about. Both doctor and mother are taken aback; the child had been so silent up to that point, it was almost as if he weren't in the room, as if he was only a possibility they had under discussion.

The mother holds the screaming baby by the shoulders while the doctor affixes the bandage. The mother is privately appalled at the sight of the baby's bandaged-over face—it makes him look disfigured. When he finishes, the doctor hands the mother some extra bandages and a large, half-filled bottle of the brown liquid. He opens a drawer and finds a sheet of paper and hands it to her. "These are instructions," he says, "on how to change the baby's dressing and apply the disinfectant—once a day for the next four days." He adds before leaving, "Try to watch him more carefully."

In the car, the father says, "I heard the baby screaming all the way out in the waiting room. It woke the girls up—"

"Remind me to call the insurance company tomorrow," the

mother says. But what she doesn't realize is tomorrow's already here. The sun is coming up as they pull into the driveway. It is Saturday morning. The girls are wide awake now. They chatter over the novelty of waking up where they did, and the bandaged baby elicits from them varieties of awing and cooing, which the mother puts a stop to.

The day is long and exhausting for the mother and father. The girls have to be told several times to keep away from the baby and his bandage. The baby himself is serene and takes a series of naps on a towel laid across the couch—he sleeps fine in the daytime. The father repairs the broken slats of the crib with some like-sized strips of wood he culls from the cellar. While he's at it, he tightens the crib's loosened joints.

By nightfall, the girls are sent to bed and the baby is dandled on the father's knee. There are dark rings under the baby's eyes. He yawns and part of the adhesive tape holding his bandage on unsticks. The father presses it back into place, careful not to hurt the baby.

"Maybe we should change the bandage now," he says.

"Tomorrow," the mother says. "I put the medicine and bandages on the changing table in his room so I can do it first thing in the morning." She does not take her eyes off the television. She is by now used to the baby's bandage, or she is too tired to care, but she does not want to look at it. The baby yawns loudly.

The father says, "Meg?" and the mother looks over at him. They realize that neither of them wants to put the baby to bed. The weary baby bobbles his head around the room, stopping momentarily to see the flitting images on the screen. The mother yawns. It is getting to be very late.

Finally the mother gets up from the couch. She lifts the baby up under its arms.

"It's much too late now for babies to be up," she says quietly, not really looking at him.

Both the mother and the father go upstairs to put him to bed. The father opens the door for the mother and turns the light on. He sees the disinfectant and the bandages arrayed on the changing table. The baby yawns.

"Maybe we should put pillows around the crib," the father says. "So he won't hurt himself again."

"We don't have that many pillows," the mother says, still holding the baby and looking down at the waiting crib. She wants to put him down, but doesn't. She shifts him from one arm to the other.

The father says, "Maybe he should sleep in our bed tonight, Meg."

"You'll have him spoiled," the mother says, and without lingering further she leans over and lays the baby in the crib. "You be a good boy now," she says. Almost as soon as she straightens up, the baby's purple eyelids drop and the parents share a profound relief.

They are very tired, the mother and father, having been awake now for some forty hours straight. But they stay up anyway and watch television for awhile. There is a peacefulness in the house now that they are reluctant to abandon, even for sleep. The eleven o'clock news is on and while the father is following the story of the stabbing at the mall, the mother is not. Through the window behind the television she sees the moon hanging low and full. Her eyes begin to close, her lids quivering a little, and she allows herself to nod off.

But she is awakened again, suddenly, by the sound of the baby banging.

The sound is loud and jarring and it scares her. She glances at the father; he is shamefaced and looks away. Then she drops her head and fights the need to weep by tightening her fist and pressing it against her forehead. The father makes motions to get up, but she tells him to stay put and goes upstairs herself. She pushes the baby's door open and stands framed in the dark doorway. She can see the baby clearly in the moonlight, banging. He has not gotten the crib very far and seems to have banged the bandage off, for it is laying on the floor outside the crib. She steps forth into the blue darkness and is bathed in the same light as the baby. Through the window she spots the moon, surrounded but not obscured by smoky, swift-moving clouds. She wishes suddenly that she could banish it from the sky. She walks toward the window to pull the curtains shut, but in her haste she kicks the changing table and hears the sound of a bottle falling to the floor and smashing. The baby still bangs. The mother looks down; she can see the bandages have fallen also. She picks them up but they are soaked with the disinfectant. Then, beneath the table, she spots the instruction sheet and picks it up. It too is soaked and she holds it up; in the moonlight she sees the ink lifting from the page and dissolving before her eyes. She catches the last of the words, at the bottom of the page, before they too blur into indistinctness: IF INFECTION PERSISTS, it reads, CONSULT A PHYSICIAN.

THE RIGHT OF WAY

She was born with a hole in her heart the size of the head of a pin. That's how Dr. Jankum described it. Only, in his passionless old voice, it sounded much more believable, much more like something that could actually happen. He sat us down in his office and in that same voice told us we had the option of putting her in some kind of special hospital where she'd get the attention she needed. "No way," said Penny, who hadn't stopped crying since she delivered. 'That's my kid."

So we took her home. We knew she'd take some explaining to the other kids. Dr. Jankum said the young ones wouldn't know the difference, but the older ones would probably have questions. He said to wait until they came to us, then sit them down all together and calmly explain that sometimes babies are born a certain way and there's nothing anyone can do about it. Turned out they never came to us. In fact, even though the baby was kind of strange-looking, with kinky red hair and stiff arms and legs that made her look like a ventriloquist's dummy, everyone accepted her without a problem. She was even cute. Everyone thought so. Except Penny. Penny didn't think anything was cute for a long time. She'd cry whenever we were alone and act like she was holding back from crying when the kids were around. "Quiet," I told her. "It's no-body's fault."

She was in and out of the hospital that whole first year, Tish was. That was what we named her. Tish had one problem after another, and they all took her to the verge of dying. "Go home now," the night nurse would say to us. "There's nothing you can do here." The top half of the waiting room walls were painted light gray and the bottoms were painted dark gray and the room was lit only by the one lamp in the corner where Penny sat. It gave you the feeling of being submerged in cold, dirty water, not like you were drowning, but just submerged, holding your breath until the tide went back out. I hated the place but each time Tish was in the hospital Penny refused to leave until she did. She'd stake out that little corner, picking apart the styrofoam cups I brought her coffee in, or saying the rosary. I'd remind her there were four other kids at home that needed taking care of. All she'd say was, "You go." But of course I stayed right with her.

Her first Fourth of July, when she was six months old, Tish caught an especially bad cold. We'd brought the kids to the Brackett Fairgrounds to see the fireworks when she started coughing and gasping for air. Turned out her little lungs were all stopped up and she was barely able to breathe. Penny and me were in that waiting room until early the next morning. The doctor had just left us. He wasn't very encouraging, though he tried to be. "God knows she's a fighter," he said.

Penny wouldn't let me comfort her. Every time I went to her she walked away. So I said, "What, Penny? Why won't you let me come?" And then she was out with it. "It's my fault!" she said. "I'm to blame!" "For what?" I said. "For Tish's being retarded! I'm to blame!" she said. "No," I said, "Dr. Jankum said it was no one's fault." "No!" she said. "The doctor didn't know! I was too ashamed to tell him!"

Turned out what the doctor didn't know—and what I never knew either—was that when Penny was five months along with Tish she paid a visit to Annie Beladonica. Annie lived next door to us in the old neighborhood in the city and was the godmother of our oldest. At the time Penny visited her, Annie's little ones were all down with the measles. Penny was convinced that was what made Tish retarded. "I shouldn't have stayed," she said, "but I wasn't sure and Annie didn't say anything about it. But I should have known Annie wouldn't know!" I told her to quiet down, that it didn't mean anything. I told her that sometimes babies are just born a certain way and there's nothing anyone can do about it. It was all I could think of. Penny just shook her head and said that she was being punished. Then, finally, she let me hold her. Tish lived through that cold, and after that Penny began to cry a lot less.

The second year was easier on us. Tish wasn't sick as much and Artie and Lois were getting to an age where they could start helping Penny out, changing diapers and whatnot. Meanwhile, we had another kid—a healthy one, thank God—and it got to be like Tish was just one of the brood. She didn't start walking or talking at the pace of the other kids, but it was like we almost stopped thinking of her as retarded.

In time we started to notice that her right foot turned out and the joints in her hands were large and bony, making her fingers curl in. The fingers could not be helped, but Dr. Jankum told us to encourage her to walk with her foot pointed ahead, which she could do if she made the effort. She tried, but like all our kids she was lazy at heart. "Walk right, Tish!" Penny would say. "It can't be that hard!" Later on, other bad habits cropped up that were equally impossible to break her of. She used to sit in front of the television—I mean, not an inch away from the screen. And she would eat sugar by the spoonful, if you didn't watch her.

Penny and me made a point of giving her whatever the other kids got and treating her equally in every way that was possible. When it came time to send her to school, though, we couldn't do that. Because she was so slow she didn't enter school until she was eight years old. We looked into schools for special kids, but they all wanted money. So we sent her into the program the public school had, which we supposed was as good as any. Penny was uncomfortable with the idea from the start, but I convinced her it was for the best. Tish would make friends with other kids like herself and, I thought, it would take some of the daily burden off Penny. But school turned out to be hard—more for Penny, I think, than for Tish. Normal kids are mean little son-of-a-guns, we all know that, throwing rocks at the special kids' bus, calling them names. They did that even though Tish's bus picked her up right at our house. Tish never complained about it, but it ate Penny right up. Maybe it wouldn't have gotten to her so much if even Tish's own brothers and sisters, who were more than old enough by then to know better, weren't mean to her too. They wouldn't join in the taunting, that's true, but they would run out of the house in the morning before Tish's bus arrived so they wouldn't have to witness anything.

One winter morning we woke up unexpectedly to a heavy snow. The kids were hoping to get the day off from school, but had no such luck. Penny bundled them up and sent them off, but they were running a little late because everyone had to find their boots. Somehow, despite the snow, Tish's bus showed up on time. It was more a big boxy van than a bus, painted a metallic tan color, with what looked like every retarded kid in Brackett jammed into the back, four and five to a seat. It would pull right into the driveway and honk twice. Penny sent Tish out the back door and kept an eye on her as she trudged down the driveway. Our three oldest ones, Artie, Lois and Rose, hurried past their sister with their heads down—so they wouldn't see her trying to wave to them, I suppose. Then, out of nowhere, snowballs were flying all around Tish. It was those McCue boys from up the street. They were little terrors, the whole neighborhood knew it. They were shouting names and making faces in between throws. Penny got livid and ran right out into the snow in just her bathrobe and slippers, screaming at the boys. She had just raised her arm at them when a snowball smacked her right in the side of the head. The boys split up and ran off. Tish made it to the bus unhurt. I ran out to help Penny back into the house. There was snow in her hair and her left cheek was stinging red. She was muttering, "Those damn kids. Those godforsaken kids."

"I'll call up Bill McCue if you want me to," I said. "But it never seems to do any good."

Penny looked straight at me then and said, "I was talking about our kids." She walked away, into the house, shaking the snow from her head.

Of course Tish had to die. We knew she would. We were told it would happen before her fifth birthday. So when she made it to six, I guess we sort of tricked ourselves into thinking she'd be all right. She was still in and out of the hospital a lot, but Penny and me had started to see that as par for the course, and each time we were less scared. But it's a terrible thing to do, to trick yourself. And like most terrible things, it's so easy. You think maybe you'd learn. You'd think that at some point you'd say to yourself, "Well, up to now, I have gotten exactly nothing the easy way." You'd realize that only disaster can come from not staying on top of a thing. And that's what happened. We got lazy about Tish's staying alive. So she died.

Her death came three winters after the one I just told you out. It was February. I was at home recovering from the heart attack I'd had just after New Year's. My printing shop was not going so good and I was working sixteen-hour days right through the holidays and still we were struggling. Laid up in the hospital, with Penny refusing to leave my side, I got to thinking about my bad heart and Tish's, and how maybe it was something that ran in the family.

I was watching TV. Penny had practically made the living room into our room because the flight of stairs to the bedroom, she said, was too strenuous for me to be climbing every day and night. Penny was taking her afternoon catnap on the couch, like she always did before the kids got home from school. But this time she overslept. It was 2:45 when she woke up. She got a little bit frantic. Tish's bus was supposed to drop her off at 2:30.

The bus had started dropping her off at the corner, four or five houses up from ours, because our neighbors across the street, the Guidas, had complained. Mr. Guida had come to our door one morning sort of embarrassed and apologetic. He said the horn from the special kids' bus woke him up in the morning, and then again when he was taking his afternoon nap. So we worked it out with the driver and he started leaving Tish up at the intersection, which cornered a big empty field and had no houses that were very close by. In winter, it was vast and white and looked like a desert. It was just the place, Penny said, where a retarded kid should be dropped off. Every day at 2:25 she would mutter something bad about the Guidas, put on the boots and the parka and walk to the corner. I said to her, "It's not that far. She can walk it by herself." But I think Penny wanted Mr. Guida to see her out there in the snow every day, even though that was supposedly the time he was taking his nap.

Anyway, on this day, a Friday I remember, Penny was panicked because Tish was late. She dressed in a big hurry and slipped and slid her way up the street until I couldn't see her anymore. About ten minutes later she came back. Tish was walking ahead of her while Penny was yelling, "Straighten that foot!" By the time they reached the driveway, I noticed Artie, Lois and Rose coming down the path Penny and Tish had made. Artie looked the same as he always did, but the girls had their heads hanging.

Penny and Tish came into the house. Penny untied the hood to her parka and pulled it off—boy, was she mad. She yelled at Tish to get out of the wet things and ended up having to help her as usual. She got down on her knees and pulled her boots off, the good foot first, then the bad one. Artie and Lois and Rose walked in then. They stamped their boots on the mat at the door. Penny ignored them totally. She even threw Tish's boots into the corner where they were, practically hitting them. Artie didn't seem to notice and went right up to his room. Rose and Lois kept looking from the floor to their mother to each other. Tish ran off to plant herself in front of the television.

Later in the afternoon, when it was time for my medicine, Penny brought tea, salt-free crackers and imitation Monterey Jack cheese. Penny had started buying all the foods that were supposed to be okay for heart patients to eat, even though they cost extra and tasted funny.

She made sure I swallowed my pills before she started talking. "Godforsaken kids," she said.

"What's happened, Pen?" I said. Turned out when she got to the corner she found that a bunch of kids from the neighborhood had gotten hold of Tish, who instead of coming home when she got off the bus had waited there for Penny to meet her. The normal kids' bus stopped at that same corner about ten minutes after the special kids were dropped off. There Tish was, a sitting duck for the little monsters. Some of the kids starting teasing Tish and throwing snow at her. Somehow, they grabbed her and wrapped her up in this loose chain fence that ran along the sidewalk and supposedly kept the people from going into the field. Once they had her wrapped up, they kicked and pushed snow at her until it covered up to about her knees. When Penny got there, Tish was not crying at all, she said, but yelling out, "Stop that right now! Stop that, you godforsaken kids!"

The little culprits scattered at the sight of Penny. She dug Tish out of the snow with her hands, since she didn't think to bring her gloves. She had just unwrapped the fence from around her when she noticed Artie, Lois and Rose standing across the street, watching. They rode on the normal kids' bus. They must have seen everything. Penny just glared at them and pushed Tish ahead.

When I heard that, I had to yell out for the three of them to get in here now. Penny said to mind about my heart. But I just had to ask them, "Why couldn't you do anything to help your sister?"

Immediately the girls burst into tears, which they hoped would pass for an answer. But I was too mad to let them off that easy.

"Answer me!" I hollered.

"Hank . . ." Penny warned me.

Rose was the first to speak: "It's . . . it's just . . ." and she trailed off into tears again.

"You have no idea how embarrassing it is," Lois blurted out. For his part, Artie said nothing. He just leaned in the doorway with arms crossed against his chest.

Penny started cutting more cheese. I thought she would turn around and hurl the knife at them. But she just sat up in her chair, very stiff and rigid, and got very quiet and wouldn't look at any of them.

I turned away from them too. "Go," I said. "Get out of here."

"We were gonna help," Rose blubbered, "once the kids left her alone . . ."

"Go," I said again.

"You have no idea," cried Lois, "what it's like for us!"

"Get out!" I hollered. Finally they went. Penny and me were quiet awhile. I put a slab of cheese on a cracker and bit into it. "That's not too bad," I said. Tish ran in with her boots in her two hands and asked Penny to put them on so she could go play in the snow. Penny told her no. Tish said that Mick and Helen and Paulene were playing in the backyard and that it wasn't fair. All she needed was someone to put her boots on for her. She turned to me, but Penny warded her off. "Never ask your father to do anything like that," she said in a low, smoldering voice—she was thinking about the strain on my heart. Tish began to cry and ran from the room. Penny put a slab of cheese on a cracker and bit into it. She chewed twice. Then she drank some tea and swallowed. "That's not too bad," she said.

Tish was fine all that weekend—she never complained even when she was sick, unlike the other kids. Monday morning,

THE RIGHT OF WAY   75

though, she was coughing her insides up. It was hard to say if being buried up to her knees in snow had anything to do with it or not. She caught colds pretty easy and pretty often.

Penny kept her home for the day but by next morning she was much worse. We had sensed it at the beginning, now we were sure: it was time for another emergency visit to the hospital in the city. Penny said she would take care of it, but I insisted on going with her. She was my kid too, and I knew how much these things took out of Penny. Turned out Tish had pneumonia. At the same time they found out she was a diabetic. We spent all Tuesday and Tuesday night at the hospital. I suggested that one of us call home to let the kids know we'd be there all night. But Penny just motioned for me to sit down and said, "Leave them." I couldn't really feel comfortable with that, but I didn't want to upset Penny any more than she already was. So I told her I was going to the bathroom when actually I went off and called Lois. "It's your responsibility to get everyone up and off to school in the morning," I said, using my firmest voice because it was the only way she listened. Then I went back to sit with Penny.

The doctor told us Tish might not make it through the night. Penny was crying, but like I said, I had heard it all before. "Penny," I said, "She'll be all right." And it looked like I was right, too. Around three in the morning a nurse came into the waiting room and told us Tish's condition had improved. She was still very weak, she said, but she was conscious again and asking for us. The doctor came in behind her, very tired but smiling, like he'd just won the Boston Marathon. He said, "Looks like she's gonna pull through."

She didn't, though. We stayed with each other there in that waiting room a few minutes, content just to feel relieved. Then we got up to go see her. But when we got to her room, men and women in white coats and green pants were running in and out, three machines with thick black cords were wheeled in. For a minute we were just struck dumb. Then the doctor came out to us. He was very young. It must have been his first death because I'll never forget the expression on his face. "Her heart just gave out," he said, like he was trying to understand it himself.

Penny and me took it hard. We went back to the waiting room. There was no one else there. We just cried in each other's arms.

Whenever I broke into a new sob Penny would sob back, "No!" and put her hand very gently on my chest.

Finally I felt like I would drown if I didn't get out of that waiting room. The dark gray paint on the walls seemed to be creeping higher and higher. I said, "Let's go home now, Pen." She didn't move. I said, "Penny," and she got up. She insisted on driving. She said she'd read how driving makes the blood pressure go up. There was no arguing with her. One thing about Penny: she was an excellent driver, very courteous, which was due to her having learned so late in life, I always said. She obeyed the speed limits, signaled at every turn. She expected the same respect from other drivers, and whenever someone cut her off or denied her the right of way, she'd get very offended. Even when another driver was doing something wrong that had no effect on her, she'd say, "You're not supposed to do that, blue car." Good a driver as she was, though, she got lost easy outside of Brackett.

I thought she was lost when she missed the exit that would have gotten us off the highway and taken us home. I told her she passed our offramp. She didn't say anything. She was looking up at the green-and-white signs as we passed under them. She didn't even seem to be noticing the small ice patches we were riding over. After a while, I had to say, "We have to go home, Pen." But she kept on driving. I didn't know what else to say.

The highway was completely empty. The street lamps only seemed to make the darkness more noticeable. Now and then a sanitation truck rumbled by in the opposite direction. I tried to explain to her about the houseful of kids back home that didn't know their sister was dead, about how they should be told. But she made no reply.

By this time I was starting to feel more miserable, like I wanted to cry again. I felt Penny was the only thing I had left and that now I was losing her too. "Penny," I said.

"The kids can look out for themselves, Jack," was all she said.

I was sitting very far away from her on the passenger side. I wanted to cry but was suddenly overcome by a great tiredness. We passed the huge neon Shell sign that was always flashing the time. It was 3:44 in the morning. I got to thinking about the kids. No doubt, they were all asleep. What good would it do to go home and wake them up now? I looked over at Penny. She was crying quietly but her tears looked very thick and they would not run down her cheeks. They seemed to cling to her eyes, making them glint under each passing street lamp. I didn't know how she could even see the street with her eyes that way.

"Honey," I said. "Stop the car."

"I won't go back there, Hank! I won't!"

"Stop the car if you're gonna cry."

"Maybe there's someplace else we can go for a while, Hank. Just for a while!"

"Stop the car!"

Yelling at her was probably not the smartest thing to do right then. She just collapsed onto the steering wheel, sobbing. The car hit an ice patch and slid about three feet to the left. I grabbed the wheel and slid over to put my foot on the brake. We skidded to a stop. I got out of the car and took the wheel and drove to the next exit.

I told Penny to please calm down, even though by this time I was bawling again, too, as I made a U-turn and parked under the ramp. I yanked the keys from ignition. I could hardly see what I was doing. But at least we were safe. Then we just held each other like we did in the hospital room, crying and crying. Penny would murmur "Your heart" every now and then, and whenever she did it made me feel better, like she was coming back to me. Slowly the heat seeped from the car, but we didn't care.

It was a long time—daybreak—before we calmed down. We stayed holding each other, not saying anything. That was when I heard the tapping at the window.

I sat up. Penny's head fell a little against my chest. I realized then she had fallen asleep. I could hear cars sweeping up the ramp over our heads.

Then Penny said, "There!" Her voice came out in a cloud and hung in front of us. Penny was pointing to a woman walking away from the car. From the back she looked young, maybe mid-twenties, thin with a short coat and one of those zip-up-the-side skirts you think of secretaries wearing. She must have been freezing. She had her blond hair all done up in a bun. She looked like what I imagined people driving into the city in the cars above us must have looked like. She was headed for work, her job, like she was just an ordinary girl. She was heading for this green compact, one of those foreign jobs, parked about a hundred feet away from us.

"I guess she was checking to see if we were all right," I said. "We must have looked like we were dead."

When I said that, Penny and me just looked at each other a minute, remembering. But that was all right. We would have to get used to remembering anyway.

Penny lifted my arm and looked at my watch. She made a big inhaling sound when she saw the time. "Your medication!" she said. "You should have taken it an hour ago!"

I had forgotten all about it and the pills were at home. Penny went for the ignition, but of course the keys weren't there. The last I remembered was pulling them out, but I had no recollection of where I put them. We checked everywhere—glove compartment, pockets, the car floor. But they were nowhere.

Suddenly Penny called out "Wait!" She got out of the car and flagged the young woman before she could get into hers. The young woman walked up to her. I watched as Penny described the situation to her. The young woman kept nodding her head the way you'd expect a secretary to. Then Penny came back to the car and said the young woman would give us a ride back to Brackett.

As she drove, Julie—that was her name—asked us friendly questions, trying not to sound too nosy. You could tell she had manners. She said she noticed our car as she was getting on the highway to go to work. She said she thought we'd been in an accident and was ready to call the police. She spoke mainly to Penny, who sat up front with her. She must have been thinking of my heart condition. It was the only thing she knew about me. I was looking out the tiny triangular window in her seat. The highway heading into the city was crowded. It seemed like there were lots of pretty young women in compact cars. Every one of them looked as nice as Julie, every one looked as though they would have stopped like Julie did. At one point, a car cut right in front of Julie; all she did was pull back and let the speeder go on his way. "It's not a race," Penny said approvingly.

Penny, in fact, did all the talking for us. She erupted like some-

one who wasn't able to talk for a long time. I'd never known Penny
to lie much, but she was pretty convincing when she told Julie we
were on the way home from visiting somebody the night before
when we got lost, then very tired, and we decided to get some sleep
until daylight.

Julie said, "That makes sense." She was really very pleasant. Afterward, when we talked about it, Penny would say to me, "With
that personality, she'll go far." Turned out Julie was in insurance.
She said she was an underwriter. When we hit our street and started
to approach the house, I noticed the metallic tan van pass us in the
opposite direction. Penny didn't, though. She was operating on
some unreachable level. She didn't seem to see anything other than
Julie. At the house, Penny invited her in for coffee. She said no, not
wanting to be late at the office, but Penny, whose eyes were wide
open and whose brain was thinking fast, said, "You must already be
late. Come in and use our phone." It didn't seem to me such a hot
idea, what with all the kids and the news we had to break to them.

Once inside the house, though, we discovered it was empty. I
looked at the clock on the kitchen wall. It was just after 7:35, the
time the kids left for their bus. Then I remembered I told Lois to get
everyone up and off to school. I looked at Penny. She did not seem
interested in the kids at all.

"Sit down, sit down!" Penny said to Julie. She went to make coffee. "Hadn't your husband better take his medicine?" she said, just
like that, in perfect-sounding English. Really, she was so thoughtful. She was still talking to Penny, like I was some kind of deaf-and-
dumb invalid, but that wasn't her fault. Penny was acting that way
toward me too, and Julie was just following her like any polite person would do. Julie was a little surprised when I said to Penny I'd go
up to the bedroom and get the medicine—that was where I kept it,
in the nightstand on my side of the bed, out of the little ones' reach.
I left to go upstairs, but I felt sort of uneasy about leaving Penny. I
figured she'd be all right a minute in the company of the nice young
underwriter, who I heard say, "What a big house! You must have
lots of kids!" She was being nice, pretending not to notice what a
mess the house was. You could tell she'd been brought up right.

On the stairs, I was thinking what we would do about the kids
once Julie left. Pull them out of school? Wait until they came home?

But when I got to the second floor I heard snoring. It was coming from Lois' room. I knocked at the door and the snoring stopped suddenly. Then I pushed the door open, and Lois was sitting up in bed with the sleep still in her eyes. She looked at the clock radio on her bureau and then at me and said, "Oh my God!" "Jesus," I said. That Lois could never be relied on. "I asked you to get everyone up and off to school. Was that too much you to handle?"

And then Lois started to cry. I could tell she was trying to come up with something to say, some excuse that would make it not her fault. And of course, when they can't come up with anything, they start to cry.

I wasn't mad at her too long, remembering they really shouldn't have gone to school anyway. I just said to her, "Come with me." She got up and put her bathrobe on. We went to Artie's room and woke him up, then the younger boys' room and woke them up. They were still small and when they saw Lois crying they started in too without even knowing why. In a couple more stops I gathered the rest of them: Rose, Helen and Paulene—the last two were already up, playing some kind of game with their fingers. They all started to cry too. I said, "Come downstairs, all of you." And one by one, single-file, I guided them down the stairs. The whole lot of them were bawling, except for Artie, who had looked out the window at the top of the stairs and was asking, "That car, Dad. Is it someone from school?"

Downstairs, Penny and Julie had moved from the kitchen to the living room. Penny was showing her the houseplants on a shelf high above the little ones' reach. And Julie, God love her, was actually acting interested. They did not notice me and the kids coming downstairs. But when I started leading them into the room, they both turned around. Penny looked so startled I thought she'd jump out the window. Julie, you could tell, was all set to be pleasantly surprised until she noticed everyone was in tears. Everyone but Artie, I mean.

Penny burst out crying then. She turned away from all of us and walked toward the window. For some reason, probably because Julie was there, she tried to look as though she was straightening the knickknacks on the window sill. "Kids," I said—and I couldn't really keep my own composure—"Tish died last night." There was silence, except for all the crying that had been there before. I heard Julie mutter, "Oh dear," although she couldn't have known who Tish was—I doubt, in the state she was in, that Penny would have told her. But otherwise, my announcement had no visible effect. It was like I threw a rock into a dark well and was still waiting for it to hit bottom. Nobody moved. Julie looked around like she was confused at first, then she went to each of the kids, one by one, and offered some quiet words and gave them a little bit of a hug. They all accepted Julie's consolations without question. Then she went to Penny, who had taken to cleaning the knickknacks with a cloth that was on the floor, rubbing them one at a time until all of them were clean.

UPSIDE-DOWN HEART

She threw her arms around my neck and said, "Let's dance, Vic." Her ass had been buffing the stool ever since we sat down. Her knees were rubbing the insides of my thighs.

I wagged my beer at her. "I just ordered this."

Cloey let go of me and folded her arms against her bright orange tube top. I never understood how women with big breasts could achieve that. "You're the one who wanted to come all the way into Boston," she said. "When it was already so late and we hardly have any time before we have to turn right around and catch the last train back."

"Poor Cloey," I said. "You don't do anything you don't want to do, when it comes right down to it." I smiled without showing any teeth and she smiled back the same way. We liked that assessment of her, even if we weren't quite sure it was true.

I expected that to be the end of it, but then she called past me, to Marty. "The two of *us* have never danced!" she said. There was a reason for that. Marty and I had an unspoken pact about never seeing each other dance. We both talked about dancing, about what great fun it was. Marty even told me of mornings—years ago, I guess, before I knew him—when he woke up feeling like he'd fallen down a flight of stairs because he danced so much the night before. But seeing a person dance reveals something very intimate about him. It shows how well he knows his own body, how comfortable he is with his own self. Marty and I weren't ready to reveal ourselves that fully to one another. I doubted we'd ever get to that point, actually.

The strange thing was, Marty didn't refuse Cloey outright. She extended her hand across the table and he took it. Right in front of me their fingers were intertwining. I looked at him.

"I'm not a very good dancer," he said, grinning in the same way he had been ever since he'd picked us up at the train station.

"That doesn't matter. Let's go. Watch my pocketbook, Vic?"

I hardly had time to register my shock when they were off, Cloey dancing her way to the floor, Marty trying to find a spot to rest his hand on those nonstop black-jeaned hips of hers.

I almost couldn't look. Marty was tall and thin, and his dancing was best likened to a tattered scarecrow in a buffeting wind; his body seemed on the verge of flying apart. What shocked me most of all was that it was better—or at least less absurd—than my dancing. I'd danced with Cloey a few times before, at bars in Brackett. I felt the music, but if I let myself get too carried away I started doing ridiculous things, kicking my legs up like a Rockette or pointing to Cloey every time the song lyric referred to "you." Maybe it was this cornball gracelessness of mine, this admission that I really didn't know what I was doing, that I was keeping from Marty.

I focused on Cloey, who was a pleasure to watch. She was smooth and subtle in her gyrations. She had this way of closing her eyes and holding her arms over her head while she spun around slowly. As I watched, I felt the familiar stirring between my legs; there seemed to be no ridding myself of the desire. I had already jerked off that day (in our mother's cellar) no less than six times. The last time, when my cock was sore and screaming red for me to stop and I had to go to the bottom of my soul to eke out that meager load, Cloey appeared. It wasn't the first time. She was naked, of course, voluptuously so, and on her back, getting fucked hard. She always had her head thrown back, and I could never decide if that was because she was enjoying it so much or because she really couldn't stand it. The fucker was any number of men: her jailbird boyfriend Don, a cop she'd run into trouble with, some hot number I'd seen on the subway. More and more, he was me.

"She certainly can dance." The voice, deep and lilting with insinuation, seemed to come from directly over my head. I looked up—nothing—then around: an old lech in a white blazer and an aquamarine turtleneck. I'd noticed him earlier, hovering at our periphery, watching Cloey in particular. He was in his fifties, I'd say. His body was pear-shaped, and the shock of silvering hair on top made him look like some kind of mutant fruit that had dropped from its tree before it had fully ripened. The dainty way he had of holding his highball—thumb and forefinger in a pincerlike grip on the rim of the glass, other fingers splayed out like a fan—made me wonder if it wasn't me he was eyeing.

"You should have danced with her when she asked you," he said. "It was you she really wanted."

I squinted my eyes. "Can I help you?" I said. I had meant to sound threatening, but probably came off more like an overworked stewardess. I turned back toward the dance floor.

"Now don't be hostile. I mean no harm. I think it's sweet when two people are in love. There's nothing I love more than two young people in love."

I thought he was gay for sure now.

"She *is* a lovely thing, isn't she?" he said.

I smiled. I figured he thought I was trade. There are few things a young gay man like myself likes more than to be taken for trade. In fact, now that I thought I was being lusted after, I didn't mind his presence at all. He leaned one elbow on the table. On closer inspection I could see he had an over-tanned face that made his unnaturally white teeth stand out even in the dim light of the bar.

I stepped up my observation of Cloey. "Yeah, she can move alright," I said.

He prattled on. But instead of coming on to me as I expected, he kept talking about Cloey, or Cloey and me as a couple.

"Have you known her long?" he said.

"Yes."

"Years?"

"Yes."

"That explains it, then."

"Explains what?"

"The resemblance between you two. It really is striking. You both have the same full lips and the tiny little nose. That's one thing

I've noticed after years of watching. When two people are in love—really in love, I mean, like you two—they begin to resemble one another. Though usually it takes quite a long time."

That stopped my beer in mid-swig. I looked at him, wondering if he knew something, or was just guessing, or was actually sincere. At any rate, I stopped feeling lusted after and started feeling interrogated.

"But, as you say, you've known each other for years, right?"

I nodded, slightly, like that might not have been true, though it was.

"High-school sweethearts, were you?"

I was growing tired of his questions and I would have turned to tell him so, but my attention was suddenly riveted to the dance floor. The lights were swirling and flickering and changing colors so at first I couldn't be sure of what I was seeing. I must have sat there for a full minute before the old lech, who had since followed my eyes to the dance floor and had clearly seen it too, said, "Don't you think you should do something?"

I bolted from the stool and muscled my way through the crowd. I don't know why, but once I made it to the dance floor I danced my way over to where Cloey and Marty were. I guess I thought it would draw less attention to them, Cloey in particular, who was spinning in her way, arms raised, eyes shut to the world, blissfully unaware that those enormous tits of hers had slipped out of the tube top and were bared for anyone who cared to look.

Apparently Marty couldn't believe his luck. He danced forward, trying to really take them in, his wide-open eyes crusting at the corners.

I stepped between them, my back to Marty, facing Cloey. She was just turning my way when slowly her eyes opened. She didn't seem surprised to see me there. She danced back a little, beckoning.

"Cloey," I said. The music was too loud. She smiled and held out her arms to me.

I shouted her name and she still couldn't hear me. It must have been the expression on my face that caused her to stop dancing. She stepped up and questioned me with her eyebrows. I glanced down at her breasts, then up again. She looked down, crisscrossed her arms against her chest and looked up again with a horrified expression. I put my arm around her shoulder and started to lead her off the floor. Somewhere during the trip back to the table she managed to refit herself into the tube top. When she took her stool, she had tears in her eyes. She kept saying, "Oh my God."

"Why didn't you do something?!" I shouted at Marty, who had followed us back.

"I didn't know! I swear!"

"You did too know. You were looking right at her!"

"I wasn't, Vic! I swear!"

"Oh my God," Cloey said.

I cradled her again. "It's alright, baby," I said. "I don't think anybody saw."

"You saw!" she said.

"I didn't. I wasn't looking. I just noticed something was wrong. I swear I didn't see."

Somehow she was convinced by that, even though it was obvious that I saw. How could I not have seen? They were hanging out right in front of me, two flesh balloons tipped with circles the size of silver dollars that were the palest pink and had little raised bumps on them.

"Marty saw," Cloey said.

"I didn't see!" he insisted. "I swear, I wasn't even paying attention. All of a sudden Vic showed up—I never saw a thing!"

His lie was as blatant as mine, but again Cloey seemed soothed. She wiped her wet face with a wad of bar napkins. Marty ordered a round and in the course of that beer she started to lighten up again. I ignored Marty and lavished all my attention on her. She announced that she had to go to bathroom, and that's when I noticed the old lech again, watching us from a safe distance. He smiled at me, then he turned, and I saw the crease where the back of his head folded into his neck. Then he disappeared into the crowd.

"When I come back," Cloey said to me, "we're dancing." I held out my hand to her and drew her close and kissed her moist cheek, very near the mouth.

Marty and I sat alone. I didn't know how to look at him. I thought of something brutal and cruel to say about his dancing. It wasn't even witty.

"I didn't know, Vic," he said.

I felt myself giving him the benefit of the doubt, though I didn't want to. After all, I hated Marty. We were only friends by default. He was actually the best friend of Gus O'Brien, who was my lover for almost four years. Gus didn't see it coming at all when I dumped him some months before. He even left Boston and moved back to his hometown in Wisconsin, where he had a standing offer to teach the history of American architecture at the public university. After that, Marty and I just sort of fell together. At first I couldn't figure out why he didn't hate me for running his best friend out of town. Months later, I still didn't know, but I didn't care either. I started bringing him along on our frequent nights out with my little sister Cloey, who I had gotten reacquainted with since having to move back to my mother's couch. Up until now, Marty had always shown a restraint admirable for a full-grown heterosexual male. Tonight, though, he'd been different: ogling her, dancing with her, brushing his arm too close when he shifted gears in the crowded cab of his truck.

"I would never have let her go on that way if I knew," he said.

"She seems to have recovered," I said. Still, I couldn't be sure.

"Has she heard from the boyfriend lately?" Marty said, tipping up his beer.

"No, I don't think so." The boyfriend was Don. Don Salvatelli. He was her ex-boyfriend, actually.

"Nothing since the letter saying he would kill any man she went out with?"

"He didn't say that."

"Oh. I thought that's what you said."

"No. He said he would fuck him up or something like that. He didn't say he'd kill anyone."

"Oh."

Don was doing seven years in Fullham State Penitentiary for the attempted murder of a man on Beacon Hill who had promised him some money and then stiffed him. Don had claimed the whole thing was a set-up, that the gun belonged to the man and it wasn't even loaded. But that didn't matter: when they hauled him in they found a mess of outstanding warrants on him—car theft the most serious among them. Cloey was in tears when she called me at the liquor store, where I had just started working two afternoons a week. I told her I'd be right there. My boss, old Ron, seemed unmoved by the family emergency. He just shook his head slightly and waved me off.

Don spent that night in a holding cell, and I spent it with Cloey, at the apartment they afforded together on the southwest side of Brackett, the small corner cut off by the interstate. I welcomed the change, since for the past month I'd been waking up with the embroidered designs of my mother's couch cushions impressed on one side of my face and the harsh downward glare of my mother's eyes on the other. Cloey spent much of the time crying or rolling joints—or crying and rolling joints at the same time. I sat next to her, my short-sleeve shirt untucked, holding her, and even when I wasn't our bodies were always touching, joined at the hip and thigh in the sagging center of her couch.

"You didn't know he stole cars?" I wondered. I brushed back the hair that clung to her damp cheeks.

"I knew he had priors. I thought it was all little shit."

"Why did this guy owe him money?"

She paused, shaking her head a little—not like she didn't know the answer to my question, but more like she knew the answer and it made no sense to her at all.

It was stupid of me to ask. I already knew the answer. Don was in construction but he also made real money selling his dick on the side. He was thirty-three—old for that sort of thing—but it still worked for him. He was lean, not an ounce of fat on him anywhere, with a craggy face that grew more handsome with age. And, oh yes, he had the cock of a farm animal. That was Cloey's testament, and I believed it. Don showed no basket at all, usually the case with a well-hung man, and besides, paying customers only laid out the kind of money he made for an authentic flopper.

("So, how big is it exactly?" I couldn't refrain from saying to Cloey, on some night in some bar.

"Exactly? I couldn't say." But the length she approximated between two fingers in the air was enough to confirm my suspicions, and maybe a little more.)

When Don was sentenced, Cloey cried for twenty-four hours straight. Again I stayed with her through the night.

At first Don's letters were constant, four or five a week. They were usually long, often wrenching, and occasionally illegible. Cloey read them out loud. He couldn't go very long, it seemed, without insinuating harm against anyone planning to replace him in her life. Cloey would look up and give me an embarrassed smile. It could have been that she was embarrassed about being loved that much, enough to kill for. Or it could have been that she knew Don was referring to me, probably among others.

It was true that Cloey and I touched and hugged and held hands —something, by the way, that we never discussed but just accepted, and something that was especially thrilling for me, who up to that point had never said "I love you" in a voice loud enough for anyone but my love to hear. But it wasn't even that which made Don suspect me. Cloey had told Don all about Conrad, our older brother, with whom Cloey had had sex from the time she was seven to the time she was fourteen. It was just that kind of family. So it was hard to blame Don for thinking along those lines.

The last time I talked to Don, it was obviously on his mind. He was awaiting trial on the attempted murder charge. The lawyer who had taken his case, a man named Larry Smalls, was someone Don had "known"—Cloey's word—before. (Later, in a moment of inebriated candor, she said he worked "pro boner.") Smalls did Don the favor of paying his bail, which was considerable. That allowed Don to spend his final three weeks of freedom with Cloey, a conviction and a long sentence being foregone conclusions. Given that, I would have thought Cloey would be grateful to Smalls. But she seethed whenever she talked about him.

Don was down to two days of freedom when I popped over to their apartment, expecting to find Cloey, of course.

"She got held up at work," Don said. "One of the old farts died." Cloey worked in a nursing home.

Don invited me in, or at least he didn't close the door when he walked away from it. The TV jabbered. He was edgy.

"I hope you two aren't planning on going out tonight," he said.

"No." I was actually there to pick up twenty dollars Cloey said she would loan me.

The television bridged a minute or two, then he came out with, "She admires the hell out of you, you know." He shook his head like he couldn't figure it out. "Because you lived in Boston for four years, I guess, and you been to New York and all that. And you did so good in college and got a degree. I told her: we could've gone to New York if she wanted."

"Cloey said those things about me?"

He pushed air noisily between his lips; some spittle shot out too. "Yes," he said. "She loves you more than anybody." He lit a smoke, holding the match longer than necessary so that the end of the cigarette turned black. "She'd kick the shins of anyone who said a bad word against you."

It was clear he was talking from experience. "So what did you say about me that got her mad, Don?"

He turned and looked at me. It was the only time in the conversation he took his eyes away from the television.

"You can tell me," I smiled. "I really want to know."

He turned away again. "Well, I didn't say I said anything," he said. He bit his lip with those crooked teeth of his. "It's not that I'm knockin' you, Vic," he assured me. "I'm just saying: your shit stinks as bad as everyone else's."

"That's true."

"But she doesn't wanna hear that." And then, after a pause, "You're supposed to be gay, I thought. Right?"

"Yes."

"Well, where do you get off acting the way you do?"

"What do you mean?"

"You don't act like a fag. I mean, a little you do. But not a lot."

I wasn't afraid of him, not then; Cloey was the amulet around my neck. Actually, I was getting a little peeved.

I said, "I am gay, but maybe it's not that simple. You're supposed to be straight and you have sex with men."

For a moment he sat there, hunched over, the cigarette smoldering between his fingers. Then all at once his body sank; obviously there was nothing he could tell Cloey that wouldn't make its way to me. He let out of big cache of air and never seemed to inhale again.

"I'm sorry, Don," I said. I actually liked the man.

"It's alright. You got brains. You know how to talk, to twist things around. Maybe you really do have some big plan like Cloey seems to think."

I asked him what Cloey thought that big plan might be.

Don sat back on the couch and played his fingers through the goatee he had grown since his arrest. I think he hoped it would make him look bigger and stronger than he was. "She says you always had a big plan," he said. "She thinks you just need time to get back on your feet after breaking up with your boyfriend there."

"Gus." Before Gus left he called me foolish and said I'd never find anyone like him again, and he demanded an explanation. All I could tell him was that I thought it was for the best. After he left I sat on the stoop of the South End townhouse where we lived and bawled like a child.

"Then she says you're gonna move to New York or something," Don went on, "then she's gonna visit you in your apartment there, go to the top of the Statue of Liberty. You should hear her go on about it. Somebody told her about this wicked bong shop there that sells all these different kinds of bongs. Ones that're shaped like turtles or, you know, they say things on them."

I nodded. I was the one who told Cloey about the place.

"She never says anything about taking me along," Don said.

"You can come."

"I mean, I've never been to the top of the freakinass Statue of Liberty."

"You should both come."

"Can we stay at your place?"

"Sure. I'll get one of those couches that folds out."

"Yeah, that'd be fine. Nothin' fancy." He smiled a little. I saw how it was with him. He could occasionally believe he was not going to be locked away in a matter of days. So I could believe I had a big plan that was going to get me a New York apartment with a fold-out couch. I even threw in their own set of keys so they could come and go as they pleased. "Yeah," he said, nodding, it seemed, with his entire upper body.

I was hoping he'd like me more now, and he seemed to. But as soon as Cloey arrived, and she hugged me and sat closer to me than to him at the kitchen table, the suspicion returned. I looked his way and everything about him was a threat, or a warning. And I couldn't exactly blame him for feeling the way he did.

*

"I think he was just letting off steam anyway," I said to Marty. "I mean, he's in prison. That would piss me off, I'd think."

"I guess so."

"There are probably times when he wants to kill everything and everybody."

"Probably." He started to peel the label off his bottle of beer, then said, "Aren't you afraid of when he gets out?"

"In seven years?" I shook my head. "You can spend seven years doing a lot of things, but not waiting for someone." Already Don's letters had dropped off. "Cloey has nothing to be scared of."

"Yeah," Marty said. "But I was asking if *you* were afraid of when he gets out."

I turned to Marty, then turned away just as quickly. "No," I said, as if I didn't comprehend what he really meant. And I repeated: "Cloey has nothing to be afraid of," turning around to look for her. She was nowhere in sight. I knew she had gone to the ladies room, but I had a feeling she was somewhere else.

Just as I turned, she was walking up. I was happy to see her, but she wore a somber expression. I stood up and took her hand.

"I'm ready to dance," I said. I knew Marty was watching and I wanted to show him I no longer cared.

But Cloey said, "No, Vic. I just wanna go. It's time to go. The last train's in fifteen minutes."

She had done a complete turnaround. Gone was the party girl that I and Marty had come to depend on.

"What's wrong, Clo? I told you, nobody saw what happened before."

"It's not that. I'm just tired. It hit me in the bathroom." She put her hands over her face and sighed into them. "Some of us have to get up in the morning, you know."

So we finished our beers and left. We crushed ourselves into the cab of Marty's truck—Cloey in the middle, flanked by us guys, as usual—and were silent as Marty drove us to Park Street Station.

"I'm sorry, guys," she said. She was feeling the burden of ruining the evening. "That's what happens when you live in the 'burbs." Marty laughed—big surprise. I did not. The last thing I wanted to do was go back and face my mother. Cloey had at least found a new apartment. We'd both had to find new places to live when our relationships ended. She was with a girlfriend of hers and her two small children. She didn't have to shield herself anymore from Mom's looks, those eyes lamenting her lingering motherhood. On the phone to her bowling partners, Mom had lately started talking very loudly: "No sooner do I get rid of one then another one shows up," like we were those warts she always gets on her eyelids.

Not that I could blame her, really. I knew when I got home that she'd be up late watching the all-gardening channel. Then she'd realize she'd have to go to bed so that I could crash in the place she was sitting. Christ, I thought. Let the old lady watch her show about tomatoes.

Marty pulled over on Tremont Street. I got out, followed by Cloey, who said goodbye to Marty and hustled her way to the doors of the station. She turned to look back, put her hands on those hips of hers, and called, "Let's go, Vic. It's almost 12:30."

I leaned on Marty's door. He was all I had left. "You wanna stay out?" I said.

Marty shrugged. "If you do. But Eve's expecting me home at two o'clock."

"That gives us time."

"I wish Cloey could stay though."

"Yeah," I said. We glanced across the way at her. She was searching that pocketbook of hers, probably for her token. She had one of those enormous pouchlike pocketbooks that carried everything. It was made of some brown hairy fabric and it must have been a burden to carry because she kept shifting the position she carried it in. She'd tote it on one shoulder, then the other, then she'd hold it under one arm, then sling it across her back. She looked like the weary mother of a restless baby orangutan.

"Especially since this is the last night I can see her," Marty said. I glanced up.

"Eve is getting fed up with it," he said.

"With what? I thought Eve liked it when you go out at night. I thought she liked the time to herself."

"She likes it when I go out with *you*. Gay men are fine. But she draws the line at twenty-four year-old blonde women. She wants it to stop. She only let tonight happen because you two were already on the train in."

It sort of made sense now, the way he'd been acting all night. Tonight was his last night of freedom, and he'd decided to enjoy Cloey all he could. As for Eve, Marty's live-in girlfriend, it never occurred to me that she would be jealous. She always acted so superior when it came to Cloey. They only met once, briefly, when Marty forgot his wallet and we had to stop back at his place. Nobody spoke because Eve, after coldly shaking Cloey's hand, never turned down the classical music she was listening to on the public radio station. But I'm sure she knew all the dirt on my little sister, since I'd told Marty everything. I shouldn't have, I suppose, but I did. It was hard for me to find things to talk about with Marty.

"Let's go, Victor!" Cloey called.

"You don't have to tell Eve if Cloey comes along," I said to Marty.

Marty shook his head. "I can't lie to her. I'd never get away with it."

"All I meant was, it's not as if there's anything to lie about. I mean, there's nothing going on between you two, right?"

"I know. It's just how Eve feels."

"Victor!"

"Let me just see that she gets on the train alright," I said.

"You still sure you wanna hang out?"

I nodded. Anything was preferable to my mother's.

"What are you gonna do after I go home?" he said. "Wander around all night again?"

"I suppose."

"You don't want to go back to Brackett and have sex with Cloey?" He added a laugh to that. And though I heard him clearly, just as I had heard him in the bar, I behaved as though his comment didn't register.

"I'll just be a minute." I left him with the engine idling.

So: Marty thought Cloey and I were having sex. He must have been awfully sure of himself to just come out and say it like that. Maybe though, as it was with Don, it was a natural thing for him to assume with a family like ours. Or, it could have had something to do with the way Cloey and I acted toward each other. It was hard to tell what was appropriate and what wasn't. I had no experience in loving a sibling, even less a woman. My entire heterosexual career ran the duration of a single slasher movie in high school. The girl's name was Joyce and I never touched her. I hardly even spoke to her. The most memorable part of the evening for me involved my trip —three trips, really—to the men's room. I remembered thinking: I'm gay. I see that, I understand. I was petrified, but I knew for sure.

Cloey was holding open the dirty plexiglass door when I reached her, and she was three steps down the stairwell before I could say, "I'm not going, Clo. I'm gonna stay in town with Marty. But I'll walk you down to the turnstiles."

"You're gonna crash at his place?"

"No. Marty never offers that. Even if he did, I wouldn't take him up on it."

"What are you gonna do then?"

I shrugged.

"You're gonna walk around the streets of Boston all night the way you always do," Cloey said. She shook her head. "How can you do that, Victor?"

I couldn't answer her. For the first time she seemed appalled with me and I didn't know what to say.

"I worry about you sometimes, Vic. You always had it so together, but the way you live now . . ." She shifted her pocketbook from one shoulder to the other. "It's like you're one step away from being a homeless person."

It had seemed like that to me too, from time to time.

"Why don't you just come back to Brackett and go to Mom's? You'll end up there in the morning anyway."

"I can't go. Not now. I can't stand the way she looks at me when I walk through the door. I feel like an intruder. When she comes down in the morning and sees me on the couch, she jumps."

"You don't have to sleep on the couch, Victor. She's got three empty bedrooms upstairs."

"I couldn't stand that, Clo. That's too permanent." And yet I couldn't tell myself that my mother's was a temporary situation until I got back on my feet again, since I had no interest in getting back on my feet.

Cloey let out a hot breath through her nose. I suddenly felt too heavy for standing, and sat down on the steps—fell down, was more like it. I wanted to cry, I felt it would be good for me, but there was nothing there. I had gone past the point of even pitying myself. I squandered my time and now each day dropped off without repercussion. It was different when I was with Gus—the discussions we had, the winding walks through the city to view the architecture, the sex, the rug-like fur on his chest that I used to lay against. At that time I was sure of the virtues he saw in me: my intelligence, my drive to do well in school, my willingness to love him.

I felt Cloey's hand on my shoulder. "Come home with me, Vic," she said.

"You have no room for me. And your roommate hates me there. I can tell."

"Don't worry about her."

"I can't, Clo. Marty is waiting . . ."

"Go up and tell him you're taking the train home with me."

"I don't know." I rested my head in my hands.

"I'll do it," Cloey said. I looked up and watched as she climbed the steps, her ass the shape of an upside-down heart. The pocketbook sagged off her shoulder, weighting her slightly to the left. Her low-heeled shoes clomped even after she disappeared. I thought that I shouldn't let her go alone, that she'd get mugged, or worse. But the heaviness held me in place.

I wondered what Marty would think of it, my going home with Cloey.

I turned and looked at the long stretch of steps before me. They descended to a low-ceilinged landing. Everything after that dissolved in a dirty green mist not unlike that of a bog, which, Gus had told me, was what much of Boston once was.

I don't think I even noticed the sound until the steps beneath me started vibrating, tickling my balls. A couple, a man and a woman, entered and tried not to look at me as they hurried into the mist. The vibrations ceased and the squeal of a brake escaped from the tunnel below. Then, after a moment, the rumbling began again, tickling me and leaving me aroused by the time it was gone, that last train back to Brackett.

The plexiglass door opened. Cloey wore a kind smile around the corners of her lips. She kneeled to me. "You look a little better."

"Yeah. I feel a little better."

"Good. Let's go before we miss the train."

"We missed it already."

She didn't move. She didn't even blink.

"It came while you were gone."

She shot to her feet. "You better be kidding me." She turned and clomped her way down the steps, no doubt to ask the token booth clerk if there wasn't just one train left. She rematerialized a moment later, wearily pulling herself up by the railing.

"Why didn't you come and get me?" she said.

"I couldn't have run out and gotten you and still made the train. It was here and gone so fast."

"Shit!" She smacked the railing. "Goddam motherfucking shit!"

"Calm down, Clo."

"How are we gonna get home?!" she demanded to know. "—Oh my God! Marty! Maybe he hasn't left yet." She charged up the stairs, taking them two at a time. She tripped once but recovered quickly. I trudged behind. When I stood up, my cock strained hard against my jeans. I stuck my hands in my pants and arranged it in such a way that it was less noticeable.

When I reached the top of the stairs, Cloey was coming back from the curb. Her jaw was set on edge. She looked at me with Mom's unforgiving eyes. I took off my jacket and casually held it in front of my crotch.

"What the hell are we gonna do, Victor!"

Two men walking on the other side of Tremont Street looked over. Lover's quarrel, they probably thought—no, wait, maybe the woman was a prostitute.

Cloey became aware of their presence and backed down. But she did not lose her sense of urgency. She walked to one of the benches that traced the periphery of the Commons and sat down. I joined her. The two men were safely away now. My erection hadn't eased. I laid my jacket over my lap.

"I want to know," she said in a calmer, more despairing tone, "how we're gonna get home."

"Now just relax a minute. Come here." I took her in my arms. She huddled against my chest. Her elbow came to rest, unknowingly I think, on my hard cock. She started to crush it and I shifted position.

"It's a beautiful night," I said.

She sighed heavily. "I'm tired. I just want to go to bed. I can't believe we missed the train!"

"It's not that bad," I assured her.

She broke away. She pressed the indent between her eyes with her middle finger in exactly the way of our mother when we did something she couldn't countenance.

"Can't we take a taxi?" she said.

"I have one dollar and change."

"I have three dollars."

"A taxi to Brackett will cost forty, fifty bucks. Plus tip."

"Dammit!"

"We could stay out all night . . ."

"No, Victor! I'm not like you! I can't do that."

"The first train to Brackett in the morning is 5:45. Right now it's 12:30. That's only five hours from now." I wanted to get her to see: the night doesn't go on nearly as long as we think. Compared to the day, it flies by. "It's beautiful tonight," I said. "This could be fun." I'd often wished during my wanderings that Cloey was along for companionship. If only she could get into the right frame of mind. She was spoiled, though. She was used to sleeping in her bed at night. She sat, angry and sullen, with lids half-closed like an over-tired child's. She didn't have nearly the stamina I did when it came to these things. I didn't know if I could win her over.

She looked up at me and it seemed that she was searching my face for the thing that made this alright with me. She turned away, unable to find it. She straightened up on the bench. "We'll call Marty. He's probably home by now, don't you think?"

Marty lived in the South End and probably had made it home by now. "What do you expect Marty to do?" I said.

"Maybe if we explain what happened, he'll give us a ride home."

I laughed out loud.

"At least he could let us crash at his place."

I was shaking my head back and forth. "That's not gonna happen."

"Why not? You two are friends, right? And he's my friend too, I think."

I just smirked. Marty and I had said goodbye already, in our way. I wasn't planning on seeing him again.

"What else can we do? We can't just be trapped out on the street all night."

"We're not trapped," I insisted. She was looking at it all wrong.

"I'm calling Marty. Where's a phone?"

I sat back on the bench and breathed out.

"Take me to a phone please, Victor."

I got up. I walked her ten feet to a bank of pay phones that lined the wall outside Park Street Station. I was thinking that I'd overestimated her. She had no will at all; she was just a lazy, coddled Brackett girl, and I understood that because there was a lazy, coddled Brackett girl in me too. I felt her, she stirred still from time to time, though she had long since been beaten senseless by the hoodlum of my insane will, which drove me to the untenable circumstances in which I thrived.

Cloey tried a phone, frigging its shiny chrome clit several times before slamming down the receiver. She tried another, then slipped it a quarter. "What's the number?"

I sighed.

"Number please, Victor!"

I gave it to her, making each of the seven digits sound like something she had failed to learn because of her laziness. My hard-on had died away, so I slipped my jacket back on and walked off a few steps as Cloey dialed.

Across the street were storefronts and doorways, buildings built with no regard for one another, thrown up in the haste of commerce. "The incongruity!" Gus would say whenever he walked down Tremont, shielding his eyes, cursing the succession of ungainly protrusions and darkened retreats along the sidewalk. It was in one of these hollows, an entranceway to a bank, that I noticed a man. He was gaunt and hollow-eyed, small-boned and a little old before his time. There was a familiarity to him, and he returned my gaze like he recognized me. I could make out a white cigarette sitting behind one ear. He seemed to be rocking back and forth a little where he stood, like he was keeping time to a rhythm from inside himself. He wore a long coat entirely inappropriate for the mild evening. We watched each other for twenty-five, maybe thirty seconds before I turned away and walked back toward Cloey. She had just slammed down the receiver.

"Do you know what he said to me?"

It occurred to me then that he could have said quite a lot.

"He said he was home now, and that's where he was staying. He didn't care at all that we missed the train!"

"What else did he say?"

"He said I could spend the night with you. He said you'd really like that."

"Well, I do think it could be fun."

"Yeah," she said. "Real fun." She shook her head. "And after he kissed me too."

I had been standing in a lackadaisical pose, with my hands in my back pockets and all my weight on one leg. But I snapped to after she said that.

"When I went up to tell him you were coming home with me. He said okay, and then he leaned out the window and kissed me. On the lips."

She expected me to say something then, I'm pretty sure. But I took too long deciding what that should be.

"It was weird," she said, "because I never got those feelings from Marty before."

"Couldn't you have stopped him?" I spat it out, aware of how jealous it sounded. Cloey scanned my face and seemed to take offense at what she found there. She spun away from me and walked off a few feet, then halted suddenly. She had no idea where she was, and it must have been frightening for her. Her head was swiveling in every direction, like one of those springy-necked dashboard ornaments. Abruptly it came to a stop. She moved back toward me.

"There's a creepy guy over there," she said in a low voice.

"I know."

"He's staring at us."

"It's alright."

"Let's get away from him."

I put my arm around Cloey's shoulder and led her up Tremont Street. She put her arm around the front of me. It felt good to be protecting her, especially when there was no real threat. When you wandered like I did, you got a pretty good sense of when someone meant you harm. There were surprises, of course; indifference and even friendliness could turn in a second.

When we reached the big brick plaza in front of City Hall, I looked back. No surprise: the man was not following us.

But Cloey wanted to keep walking. So I took her across Cambridge Street and down Merrimac, then back around to Government Center and across the City Hall plaza again. The whole trip took twenty minutes and Cloey didn't say one word. Her face was drawn and turned toward the ground. A couple of times she seemed to stumble more than walk, and I had to resist the temptation to grab her by the arm; I didn't want to be shrugged off by her.

The man was nowhere in sight—in fact, we didn't see one person along the way—so Cloey felt assured enough to sit and rest on one of the pointlessly placed steps that made the plaza such an obstacle course. She leaned forward and put her head almost to her knees.

"God I'm tired."

"You just need coffee. We have enough money for that. There's an all-night doughnut shop not far from here."

"No more walking for now. I just need to sit." She opened up her pocketbook and took out a small rolled-up baggie. "What I really need is a jibber."

"You're gonna roll it here?" A stupid question. In the last five months I'd seen her roll in the most impossible places: outside during a thunderstorm, in a department store men's room (the ladies' room was closed—she even got a security guard to stand at the door for her). She could roll joints right in front of people without them ever knowing; she just made as if she couldn't find something in that cavernous pocketbook of hers. And no matter what the joints came out flawless, perfectly round, evenly dispersed and packed to a quarter-inch, with the sweet green weed showing at one end and the smoking end closed just a little so you didn't get pot in your mouth.

She rolled on a crumpled brochure for the Statue of Liberty she kept in her pocketbook. I gave it to her the last time I came back from New York with Gus. I never saw the Statue of Liberty. I found the brochure on the bus seat next to mine.

In no time she was done and had it lit.

"I would have thought there'd be more people out at night in Boston," she said. She took a hit and held it and continued to talk, croaking out the words. "This is as deserted as Brackett."

It was true. Boston was hushed by night. Even the leaves on the young trees, planted at intervals along the sidewalk, declined to rustle in the same light breeze that lifted the strands of hair from Cloey's forehead. But beneath the staid surface, I could sense what she could not: the activity, in the darkened parks and alleyways, in the cars with tinted windows.

She passed me the joint, letting the blue smoke out through her nose.

"So what is it exactly that you do all night?" she said.

"Walk around mostly. Go to the doughnut place if I have extra money. Sometimes I meet someone and we play around."

"You mean you have sex?"

"Yeah."

She looked as though she intended to nod, but was too taken by her thoughts to follow through.

"Right on the street?" she said.

"No. I mean, you have to know where to go."

The nod came then. "I'm sure you know all the places." She added a smile.

"Some."

For a minute we silently passed the joint back and forth. When there was only a nub left and it singed the skin of our thumbs, Cloey extinguished it on the ground and deposited it in the baggie. Then she propped her huge pocketbook against the step so we could lay down with our heads against it. We nestled against each other, and the city became our cradle, our bed. We looked up. It was a perfectly clear night, yet no stars were visible.

"Do you like being gay, Victor? I mean, does it make you happy?"

"I don't know. Does being straight make you happy?"

"I don't know. It seems to me I'm happier when there's a man in my life."

"That's just wanting to be loved, Cloey. That has nothing to do with straight or gay."

We turned to one another and I recalled seeing Mom and Dad do the same thing in bed when we were little, on Sunday mornings when they slept late. I remembered thinking at the time that they were really in love.

"Is that what you want too?" she said. "To be loved?"

"Yes. I want that too," I said.

"But you had that, right? At one time. With Gus."

I agreed without indicating it in any way.

"What happened between you two, Vic? I got Don taken away from me. But you and him I never understood."

The sky, I realized, was actually clouded over. Cloey laid her hand on my chest.

"The few times I saw you together, you seemed to be really in love," she said.

I nodded the briefest, most insubstantial nod. It was almost not a nod.

"Him too," she said.

"I know."

"So?"

"My feelings changed. Or I thought they did. I was twenty-one when I fell in love with Gus. I started to feel like one of those girls who marries the one guy she dated in high school. I felt like I was missing out on something."

She started playing with the flap of my jacket, fingering it.

"And then Gus went to a conference in New York and I met this other guy. At a bar. He took me home. We had really hot sex and then we talked for hours. We seemed to really like each other. It was new. He asked me to see him again. When Gus got back the next day, I told him it was over."

"What was the new guy's name?"

"Fred.—No, Frank."

"What happened to him?"

"I don't know. I rushed to him that night. I was going to tell him everything. I was going to break down crying in his arms. But he was a different person, distant, almost like he was embarrassed by what went on between us."

"I've known men like that."

"It wasn't just him. I was different too. I realized I was sort of repulsed by him. I never saw him again after that."

"So when the new guy fell through you wanted Gus back."

"No. I wasn't sure if I wanted Gus back."

"But you do now?"

"I'm not sure. Somewhere I lost the ability to know what's important."

I wondered if she could understand. She had been in love with a hundred guys, it seemed, since she was a teenager, and definitely not in love with the first guy that had taken her. I looked at her. Her face looked swollen with tiredness and yet wide open, and there welled up in me a desire, a desire to know, and suddenly the questions burned in me. I didn't wonder what Conrad saw in Cloey. I could see that clearly: her vitality, her strength, her openness, the broad, beautiful swath she cut through life. That I understood completely. What I wanted to know, what I burned to know, I could never before ask. I felt her fingers stirring the hairs of my chest through my shirt. *What did you do together?*

"Conrad and you," I said. "Now there's something I never understood."

Her fingers stopped.

"You know what happened," she said.

"I don't." *How far did you go?* "Not really, I don't."

All I ever knew was what I heard. *Did you enjoy it at all?* I was asleep when Felicia, our oldest sister, caught them, and it all came into the open. Earl, the youngest, burst into my room and supplied me with those first lurid details as I struggled in my half-sleep to put my pants on. Cloey was fourteen and already a big drinker. She had come home drunk and passed out on the living room couch. Conrad came in a short time later. *How big was he?* Felicia got up in the middle of the night and went downstairs and flipped a light switch. She caught Conrad with Cloey's pants and underpants down around her ankles. He was shining a flashlight up into her asshole. Conrad went frantic, stammering and stumbling around, begging Felicia not to tell anyone, begging for her forgiveness. Cloey sat up, groggy, when the light came on. Felicia told both of them to go to bed, but only Cloey did. *Did you lead him on?*

By the time I got downstairs, there was only the aftermath. *How could you not know your tits came out of the tube top?* The phone book open on the dining room table, the blood on the page listing the suicide hotline, the blood on the table, on the floor, on the wall by the phone. Conrad had slit his wrists and was being loaded into an ambulance. Felicia was on the phone to Mom and Dad, who had to cut short their Cape Cod getaway from us kids. And Cloey was in the kitchen, surrounded by the other siblings, who all cried as she sat quietly twisting and untwisting a Kleenex. *Did he fuck you?* I liked to believe she was being stalwart about it, but there was a sense that it didn't matter much to her, that this may have been awful but it wasn't going to break her. Even after Mom and Dad arrived and fawned over her like they never did over any of us before and asked her if she wanted to "talk to someone," she said no, that she'd be fine. She was glad it was over, I guess, but she wasn't going to waste anymore time thinking about it. And anyway, after the call came from the hospital saying Conrad had lost too much blood to be saved, the family's attention turned to grieving and burying him. What happened to Cloey was eclipsed, and the family rarely spoke of it again. *Did you throw your head back?* At the funeral and afterward, we all behaved as if Conrad's suicide was an utter mystery, which perhaps it was, and Mom and Dad told everyone that he had always been troubled, which also was true enough.

No one was more silent than Cloey. All she said was that it had been going on for years. *Why did it go on so long?* She hated Conrad, I supposed, but he was dead now and there was nothing more to be done about it. The rest of us were simply left to wonder. *Couldn't you have stopped him?* But the wondering was not enough for me now. I struggled to find a way to say it, to say all the things I somehow needed to know, without sounding vulgar or prurient or jealous or in love.

Cloey rolled away from me and looked at the sky. When I turned to her, *If you were passed out drunk, why'd you wake up when Felicia turned the light on?* she was angry.

"You know what happened!" she said again.

I put one leg up in an attempt to hide my erection. I embraced her. "I'm sorry, Clo. I love you, you know."

She softened like anyone would at the sound of those words. "I love you too," she said.

For the time I was content to be holding on to her, to have her hold on to me, so close that the shudders in her chest rippled through me too. I wondered whether the arousal between my legs was echoed between hers, and I might have found out had it not been for the approaching footsteps. We quickly pulled away from each other and got up. My erection strained painfully inside my jeans.

It was the man who eyed us earlier on Tremont Street. He approached with his long tan coat buttoned from neck to knees, like he was concealing something. The white cigarette was in his mouth now, though not lit. His pace was deliberate and did not change even as he saw us bracing for his arrival. Cloey held my arm and moved behind me. "It's okay, baby," I said.

He stopped in front of us, rocking where he stood, a little back and forth, a little left and right. Occasionally he got up on the balls of his feet. Even more familiar was his expression, which said he had something very particular on his mind, though it was so private that possibly only he could truly understand it. Still, he regarded us like we were his last chance to share it with someone. I was not directly afraid of him, but Cloey gripped my arm.

"You got a light?" he said. His voice sounded weakened, as by disease or exhaustion. The cigarette in his mouth barely moved when he spoke. Cloey pushed her body against mine.

"All I want is a light for my cigarette." His hands started moving inside his coat.

"We don't have one," I said.

"You lie. I saw you both smoking. You passed it back and forth. You lit it over and over."

A gasp came from Cloey. "How long have you been watching us!" she said.

"Long enough to know you're a liar," said the man, looking directly at me.

Right then I thought: I should take Cloey by the arm and move away as fast and as far as possible. That's what I should have done. But I didn't. The man's dead pale stare was exactly how I remembered Conrad. If Conrad were alive, he would have been about his age.

The man's hands were still rustling under his coat. Then he began to draw something from his pocket.

"I'll give you a hit of this," he said. He produced a crude pipe. It had a clear glass cylinder burnt black at one end.

Tentatively Cloey stepped from behind me. She was looking at the pipe.

"All I need is a light," the man repeated.

Cloey opened her pocketbook and produced a lighter. "Cloey," I said. The man said "Yeah" when she handed it to him. He slipped the cigarette back behind his ear and lifted the pipe to his mouth. He stuck out his jaw as he lit it, and again he reminded me of Conrad. My most sustained memories consisted of him smoking, or lighting a smoke, while talking on the street to his hoodlum friends, who seemed so much older to me.

He drew smoke through the pipe and then handed it to Cloey. She didn't even ask what she was smoking. Probably she had a good idea. I wasn't at all sure. I watched her light the pipe like an old pro. She handed it to me, but I refused. She had always been more daring than me. I watched as she smoked. She seemed to regard the feeling as something she'd felt before.

Suddenly a police cruiser came barreling around the corner. It screeched to a stop with its headlights pointed at us. Cloey broke into a run and I followed her. I looked back. One of the cops apprehended the man. The other was coming after us, but then went back to help his partner with the man, who was struggling to get free and screaming, "It's the girl's! She's got a whole stash of it in her pocketbook!" The way Cloey was running down Tremont Street, I almost believed it. I'd never seen her move so fast. She crossed Park Street and was headed for the Commons. I wanted to call to her to slow down, but I didn't want the cops to know her name. It was just a feeling I had. At some point I managed to look around. No cops. Finally I caught up just before she entered the Commons. I grabbed her by the strap of the pocketbook. She swung around and tried to break free but I said, "It's me, Cloey! Hold up!"

"We have to get out of here!" she said. Her eyes were wild, but she seemed aware of who I was. "You have to take me someplace!"

At the end of Tremont we could see headlights slowly creeping forward. As they neared, a band of unlit lights became visible across the vehicle's roof, as well as markings on its side. It was the police cruiser.

"Oh my God!" she said.

"What's the matter with you?"

"I can't get in trouble with the police, Vic. I just can't!"

"This way." I led her down a dusky pathway into the Commons. I knew the Commons was a dangerous place at night, but it would get us out of view of the police. There were a few lamps here and there that let off a faint orange-yellow glow. Everywhere else was nearly pitch black. We walked forward together, nearly blind, never slackening our brisk pace. Just as I was sure we were passing a bench along the pathway, I couldn't be sure if there was a person on it—no, two people, one sitting on the back of the bench with his feet on the seat, the other with his arms and legs sprawled. They were really only the blackest of outlines against the blackest of backgrounds. Were they really there, watching us hurry past? And the trees, as we neared them, formed as huge cobwebs, big enough to ensnare a man. All that kept us from running into things was the light gray pathway that seemed to glow to our light-starved eyes—that, and my memory. I had walked the Commons countless times, with Gus and without him, and at least had that comfort. Cloey, clinging to me with both hands, must have felt she had fallen off a precipice and was still waiting to hit bottom. I held to her as well. We seemed to understand that if we let go of one another, we'd both be hopelessly lost.

And right then the most outrageous thought occurred to me. What if I *were* to let Cloey go, to shake her off and let her fend for herself? *Why do you hold my hand?* Then she wouldn't know where I was, to the left or the right of her, or maybe behind her. Yet I would know *Why do you touch me and hug me and kiss me?* where she was because she would be saying, "Victor, where are you? What happened? Why aren't you saying anything?" And then, if she were to be grabbed and pushed to the ground and beaten into cooperation if need be, and if I would feast upon her body until I had my fill, *Why do you love me?* she would never know it was me. Ahead loomed a lighted white statue. It lit a small circle on the cement path directly beneath it. We stopped at it. It was some Revolutionary War hero. We turned to each other in the white light, which reflected off the statue and made us both look a little stone-like ourselves. We were holding each other by the arms. My hands clasped her almost to her shoulders. Her fingers curled around the knobs of my elbows. There was nothing in the world to stop me from kissing her.

"Why are you so afraid of the police?" I said.

"I'm on probation."

Which, I understood, meant that she had been arrested and convicted, for something.

"Grand larceny," she said.

"What?"

"That's stealing."

"I know that."

"I didn't know if you did or not."

"What did you steal?"

"Actually, nothing. Don did the stealing. I just drove the car."

She sat down at the base of the statue. I stood above her. She told me about a job she had last year as the night cashier at a health and beauty aids store. Eventually she was made night manager. As soon as she started closing the place, she began taking things home with her. At first they were just small things: a couple of packs of cigarettes, a bottle of shampoo. Then, she went into work one day and they told her she was being let go at the end of the week. They didn't even give her a reason, and she was afraid to ask for one.

"When I told Don, he started ranting and raving. We really needed that job. He said we should steal the store blind. He said I still had keys to the place and that would make it easy."

I sat down next to her and put my arms around her.

They drove to the store at three in the morning. She gave the keys to Don and told him the code to shut the alarm off. "I just expected him to take a few things, but he came back with his arms full. Then he went back two more times. The car was really loaded up."

"What did he take?"

"You name it. A hair dryer. A rack to hold CDs. And weird stuff, like a big box of adult diapers. I asked him, 'Why did you take that?' He said he just got carried away. A few hours later the cops showed up at our door. It was so stupid. We had all the stuff piled up in the living room. We hadn't even taken anything out of the boxes yet."

"Jesus, Clo. Why didn't you tell me?"

She shrugged and looked away. Then she turned back. "I didn't want you to hate me," she said.

"I could never hate you, Clo."

She leaned into me and I embraced her.

"I took the blame," she said. "I said it was all me. Don had priors and I was afraid he'd go to jail and I'd lose him. So I told them Don didn't have anything to do with it." Cloey figured she had only minor stuff on her record—Drunk and Disorderly, DUI—and she'd get off easy. Since all the merchandise was returned unharmed, she was given two years' probation. "The judge was really hard on me. He said because the total value of everything stolen was over seven hundred bucks, that made it grand larceny, not just petty larceny, and that was much more serious. It came out to like seven hundred and one and change. Just my luck."

"Too bad Don grabbed those adult diapers," I said.

"The judge said if I so much as jaywalked, he'd land my ass in jail."

A siren sailed through the darkness over our heads.

"We have to get out of here, Victor."

"The park is the safest place for us right now. We'll leave in a little while."

"I don't mean out of here. I mean off the street. I can't take it out here anymore, Vic. I'm not like you." She shook her head and closed her lips tightly. I heard the moisture pop when she opened them again. "How far is Copley Square from here?"

"Aways. Why?"

"Can we walk it?"

"In twenty-five, thirty minutes, maybe. Why do you want to go there?"

"Do you know a place called"—she furrowed her brow—"the Chesterwood?"

I did. It was one of three identical high-rise residential buildings set back from Boylston Street. Both Gus and I hated them. We agreed they looked like rat boxes piled one on top of the other in some laboratory. Gus said they cost a fortune to live in.

"Why do you want to go there?"

I could see her hesitating, or at least trying to figure out how to say it. "Because," she started, "I know someone who lives there. I think we can probably crash at his place."

I tried not to seem flabbergasted. I considered myself Cloey's sole liaison in Boston. That she knew someone who lived in Copley Square, knew this person well enough even to crash at this person's place, and this person's place was the Chesterwood of all places—it made me feel betrayed. For chrissake, I lived in Boston for almost four years and even *I* didn't know anyone we could crash with.

"Do you remember Larry Smalls? He was Don's lawyer."

The one who paid Don's bail. The one who Cloey hated. I remembered him.

"Don told me he lived in Copley Square, in a building called the Chesterwood."

"Why didn't you mention this guy before?"

"I didn't even think of him until I ran into him in the bar."

The old lech, I thought. In the aquamarine turtleneck. It had to be him.

"He was waiting for me when I came out of the bathroom."

"Is that why you wanted to leave so suddenly?"

Cloey nodded. "The guy gives me the creeps. Plus, it was time for us to leave."

"Did he say anything to you?"

"He offered to buy me a drink. I said I was there with someone."

"Did he say anything else?"

"He asked me if I heard from Don."

"Oh." I fidgeted a little. "Anything else?"

She looked at me a little funny, I thought. "He said, 'I see it didn't take you too long to find a replacement for Don.'" She mimicked his effeminate style when he said that. "What an asshole," she said.

"What did you say to that?"

"Nothing. I just walked off. The guy's a dickhead."

"So why do you want to go there?"

"Because it's better than staying out here. I am not going to jail, Victor."

"So you want to just show up at his door and ask him to take you in?"

"I'll explain what happened. That we need a place to crash."

"What if he says no?"

"At least it's worth a shot."

"I don't know, Clo . . ."

"Please, Victor. Please take me to Copley Square."

So I agreed. She took my arm and we walked again the unseeable path. We had to go deeper into the park to get to the other side, and to Copley Square.

When we emerged onto Boylston, Cloey became spooked by every sound. So I took her down the smaller Newbury Street. We passed coffee shops and art galleries, all closed up. Once she got the feel of the deserted street she began to ease up. She let go of my arm and we held hands instead. Our arms swung together at the most light-hearted moments. We didn't say much. The times I glanced her way, her eyes had the relaxed but focused look of someone who had successfully fought back her drowsiness. The knowledge that we were going someplace, that her interminable evening might finally be ending, put her in a serene mood.

We turned up Dartmouth Street and the Chesterwood came into view. It and its two counterparts were as ugly as ever. I pointed out our destination to Cloey, but from the way she was hurrying across the street toward it, she seemed already to know.

Before we got to the glass doors that led into the lobby, she stopped. She brushed back her hair with her hands and shook the uncertainty from her face. We went forward. The doors were locked. A security guard sitting at a raised semi-circular desk buzzed us in without hesitation. He even seemed pleased to see us—or at least Cloey.

"We're here to see Larry Smalls," she said. "He's expecting us."

"Your name?"

"Cloey Farren," she said.

He looked at me.

"He's Vic," she said.

The guard picked up the black phone that was the only thing on his desk and punched three numbers. As we waited, I stood there feeling stiff and guilt-ridden; Cloey gazed into the shiny gold pillar that shot up next to the desk and fussed with her hair.

"Mr. Smalls wants to know if you're the boyfriend from the club," the guard said to me.

It was a question I didn't know how to answer, and when I faltered, Cloey said, "Yes, he is."

A moment later the guard hung up, winked at Cloey, and pointed us in a certain direction. "Apartment 23A," he said. For someone who thought I was her boyfriend, he wasn't being very discreet.

I put my arm around Cloey's waist as we got on the elevator. I wanted to say something about being her boyfriend, but everything stopped at the bottom of my throat. The best I could manage was, "I can't believe you got away with that."

"The guard was cool, thank God." The wall of the elevator was a giant mirror that not only made the box seem twice as big, but made its occupants look thinner. Cloey seemed suddenly disappointed with her appearance. She straightened the tube top, tugging at the top of it. She put two fingers on the puffiness around her eyes. She looked beautiful to me, and I wanted to tell her so. She said, "God I'm tired," and I was reminded of the child who was always the hardest to get up in the morning, who had to be shoved in her bed to be aroused.

The doors opened to a luxurious hallway with seascapes on white walls and fresh flowers in vases on small tables every ten feet or so. We found the apartment and rang the bell.

The old lech opened the door, corpulent in a terry cloth bathrobe. His hair was wet and parted neatly. He seemed almost backlit by the deep blue opulence of the room.

"Cloey darling!" he said. "What a pleasant surprise! Please do come in. You too, Vic." He thrust his hand at me, and I was in no position to turn it down. As we shook he looked me up and down in a frank way. His hand was tiny and hot and left a powdery smell lingering on mine. He then leaned in to kiss Cloey on the cheek, which she allowed. You'd have thought they were the closest of friends.

"I know it's late," Cloey said. "I hope you weren't in bed."

"Not at all. I require very little sleep."

Smalls implored us to sit on the sofa. It was very comfortable, a kind of plushness that gripped you all around; it would have been much easier to sleep on than Mom's. "Cloey, you look absolutely lovely. When I saw you in the bar I thought how that outfit really suits you. Wouldn't you agree, Vic?" He winked at me knowingly.

"Yes," I said. "She's beautiful." I put my arm around her and kissed her on the cheek. I *was* supposed to be her boyfriend. I should have cleared that up with Cloey on the elevator, but in a way I was glad I hadn't. I kept my arm around her there on the couch and she didn't mind at all.

The obvious question was, what were we doing there? But Smalls seemed content not to ask it. I got the feeling that late-night drop-ins at his apartment were not that uncommon—which would account for the lack of suspicion from the guard downstairs.

"Cloey," he said. "If I remember, you're fond of white wine." I couldn't escape the feeling that Cloey had been in this apartment before. "Vic?" I took scotch. He prepared them at an elaborate bar that took up most of one wall. The apartment too was huge, cavernous almost, with a dimly lit corridor that led to other rooms. The wallpaper was dark blue, with vertical curlicue patterns of an even deeper blue running through it. The painting that hung over the bar was a real painting—a tasteful city scene—not just a reproduction. White lacy curtains partially obscured an arresting view of the Hancock building. The television, adjacent to the bar, was enormous, and next to it an open cabinet housed an array of electronics: stereo, tape deck, CD player, and a VCR that was flashing PAUSE in bright squarish letters.

The lawyer handed us our drinks. "Let me just shut this off," he said, going to the VCR. He pressed a button and the image of a couple fucking filled the huge screen. "Oops," he said, turning to us, laughing through his teeth. I glanced at Cloey. She seemed to be staring toward the window. Smalls let the video run a few more seconds before shutting it off.

"I have to compliment you on your taste in men, dear," he said. "Vic here is very handsome."

Cloey downed her drink in almost one gulp and asked for another. Smalls eagerly obliged. She sunk into the sofa very deeply and looked nearly wiped out. "We missed our train home to Brackett," she said.

"Really?" He returned with the fresh glass of wine. "So you decided to pay me a visit. How sweet."

"Actually, we were wondering if you'd let us crash here for the night. I know you have that extra bedroom." Cloey *had* been here before.

"Yes I do." He went back to the bar, this time to fix something for himself. "That would be a favor, wouldn't it?" He dropped the ice cubes into his glass one at a time, seemingly to make as much noise as possible. "You remember, Cloey, the last time you were here? You said some not-very-nice things to me."

"I know. That was a hard time for me, with Don going to prison and everything." It wasn't an apology, but Smalls wasn't really fishing for one. It was clear he was working his way to a point, but only he and Cloey knew what that was.

"Yes. I know you were very attached to Don. But let's not bring up the past. Frankly, I think Vic here is better for you. He's closer to your age. And I dare say he's more in love with you than Don was. I can tell by the way he looks at you."

Cloey emptied her glass and Smalls hurried to fill it again.

"There's nothing like the sight of two young people in love," he said. It was the only time he sounded sincere. "Does Vic know about Don, Cloey dear?"

"Yes, I do." I figured it was time for me to say something. "I know all about it." I looked at Cloey. She was looking into her glass, her lids half-closed.

Smalls went on: "Including our little arrangement concerning Don's bail?"

Suddenly Cloey got up, with some assistance from me, and announced that she had to go to the bathroom. Smalls helped her down the dimly lit corridor. Then he returned and asked me if I'd like my drink freshened. I told him no. He sat down on the couch next to me.

"What was the arrangement?" I had a creeping sense of it, but I needed to know for sure.

"In exchange, Cloey and Don agreed to let me watch them have sex," he said matter-of-factly.

I was not surprised. The man practically oozed lechery. I was surprised, however—maybe titillated is the better word—that Cloey would take part in such a thing.

"I'd like the same deal in exchange for you two staying here tonight. And I'll even take you both out for a pancake breakfast in the morning."

"Oh, I don't know . . ."

"It's not that big a deal, Vic. You would have fucked her tonight anyway, I'll just bet. Am I right?"

"Possibly."

"But you have reservations."

I looked to the corridor and wondered where Cloey could be.

"What *is* taking her?" Smalls said. He got up to find out. A minute later he returned. "Cloey has made herself comfortable in the guest bedroom," he said. "Why don't we join her?"

I made a tentative move toward standing up, but stayed seated.

"What's the matter, Vic? Is it because you're gay?" I wondered if he was just guessing at that, or if he was reading it into me, or if he was daring me.

"No," I said. "That's not the reason." Which was true.

"What then?" He was growing impatient. "Is it because you're her brother?"

I looked at him hard.

"That's right, I know all about it. The brother who fucked her and then killed himself. Don told me. He told me about you too. So what? If she let one brother do it, she'll let the other."

I felt utterly stripped before him. My cock was hardening fast. "I'm not sure if this is what Cloey wants," I said.

"Oh, come now, Vic. Do you think she would have come here— do you think she would have brought you here—if she wasn't willing to do it? She knew right from the start."

It seemed to me there was a certain truth in that. Smalls made me another drink and handed it to me. I thought about all the touching Cloey and I did, the hugging and kissing and hand-holding. *Did you bring me here to fuck you?* I thought about the aura of love we must have given off—Smalls sensed it, so did Marty. We were practically there. We never spoke of it. *Did you bring me here to love you?* Maybe we didn't need to.

"Go ahead, Vic. She's waiting for you."

I got up from the couch, and just stood there.

"Is it me?" Smalls said. "I promise I'm only interested in watching. Let's go."

Slowly I walked toward the corridor with him. I could hear the carpet crushing under my sneakers. I turned and looked at him. His eyes were open as wide as possible, yet still tiny. He had a drink in one hand, the other was massaging his crotch through the bathrobe.

"Give us a few minutes alone first," I said.

Smalls let out an offended breath. "Okay," he said. "Just a few minutes."

I entered the room and shut the door behind me. It was lit by only a small red bulb in the far corner. Cloey lay on the bed, fully clothed. Next to the bed was a nightstand and a wooden chair with a neatly folded towel on it.

As I approached I could see her eyes were closed. *Will you tell me how you like it?* Her arms were up over head, her hair was all splayed out, and the underside of her breasts, which weighted to the sides a bit, showed from beneath the tube top. I was trembling as I reached out *Will you tell me what makes you feel good?* and put my finger on the bottom hem to pull it up even higher.

Her eyes opened.

I froze. I couldn't even pull my arm back. I was caught. I was Conrad. *Do you hate me?*

"You know," she said, "we can do this if you want. I suppose we've been leading up to it."

I still couldn't move or speak.

"It wouldn't make much difference to me," she said, still laying with her arms over her head. "I'm already a lost cause. But you, Vic. There's still a chance for you."

I withdrew my arms and sat down on the edge of the bed.

"I don't know, Clo," I said. "I don't know what I'm doing anymore. I made a mistake once. I've been lost ever since. I don't know how to find my way back . . ."

She drew herself up on the bed. I wanted her to put her arms around me, comfort me. But she didn't.

"You never used to be this way," she said.

I questioned her with my pathetic eyes. Five months we'd known each other for real. I had always been the same. Five long months of nothing but the same.

"What I mean is, you never used to be . . . here. You were always off somewhere. Living in Boston. Going to New York. You were always doing something. Now you don't do anything that I don't do. You're better than me, Vic."

"That's not true, Clo."

"It *is* true. You're the only one of us that wasn't born either dumb as a stump or an out-and-out mental case. And you know that, Vic, but you've just lost sight of it." I started to object but she hushed me down. "I love you, but if you stay around me—around here and around Marty and that bar—you'll end up no better. And you'll always hate yourself for that. And I'll hate you too. Don't make me hate you, Vic."

Smalls, outside the door, said, "Knocky-knocky."

"Go away, Vic. Leave Boston even. Go find Gus or whatever you want but just get the fuck out of here."

Just then Smalls opened the door and poked his fat head in.

"My," he said, "we haven't made much progress, have we?"

Cloey got up and sat at the side of the bed. She looked exhausted. "You're a revolting pig, Larry," she said.

"Now, Cloey, that mouth of yours is going to get you in trouble someday.—Have you been crying, Vic?"

Cloey stood up. "I'm ready to go, Vic. I just needed to lay down a minute."

I got up and followed her gratefully. The old lech looked stupefied.

"What's going on?" he said. "I thought we had a deal!"

"We don't have any deal, Larry," she said. "For chrissake."

"Okay, okay," said Larry, following us to the door. "A hundred dollars apiece. But I won't go any higher."

We left him at the door like that, spouting his sums, unaware that the front of his robe had come undone.

Cloey and I walked to the elevator. She put her arm around me and I put mine around her.

"I've always pictured you in New York City," she said. "I'd love to be able say I have a brother who lives in New York."

I nodded and laughed.

"Just keep me posted, baby," she said.

"I will. I'll leave Boston this morning. I'll hitchhike to New York and we'll see what happens. But first I'll wait with you for the 5:45 train to Brackett."

"You don't have to do that. And you don't have to hitchhike."

Once the elevator started moving, she pulled a wad of cash from her pocketbook.

"Jesus Christ," I said.

"I took it from Larry," she said. "When I said I wanted to go to the bathroom, I actually went into his bedroom. Don told me he kept cash in his sock drawer." She counted out over $1500 in twenties and fifties. "This should get you started," she said, handing me half. I stuffed my cut into my jacket pocket. On the way out, the security guard told us to have a nice night.

I hailed the first cab that came along Boylston Street. I opened the door for her and she got in.

"God," she said. "I think I'll call in sick today."

I closed the door and leaned down to the window. "You deserve the rest," I said. "Bye, baby."

"Bye bye, sweetheart."

I watched the taxi until it was out of sight.

I turned and started the walk to South Station, where the trains came and went. I took a leisurely route, through the South End. I made a point of not passing the apartment where Gus and I had lived. Then I turned a corner and there it was. I laughed at myself as I hurried by; me, lost on the street where I lived.

ICE MACHINE

Vi lifts her pocketbook from the floor, unzips it and pulls out a round plastic container. She got Chinese soup in it once, but now it holds quarters, dimes, nickels, pennies, some fifty-cent pieces and even a silver dollar or two. It seems to her heavier than usual, but when she holds it up eye-level and shakes it, she sees that it's never been emptier.

    what's that endless humming
    vibrating
    through the floor the walls tinkling
    dust from the chandelier into the bowl of chips

Sonny comes back with a bucket of ice from the machine just outside the door

    churning
    generating
    load after load muffled thumping
    freezing
    cubing
    clinking

and heads for the marbleized countertop to make two whiskey-and-waters. "I caught Allen going through our closet again yesterday," he says, bending to measure the whiskey as he pours. "He said he was looking for shoe polish.

    cracking
    trickling

tinkling
ticking
Seems to me I never see him in anything but sneakers."
ticking
clicking
Vi puts her hands over her ears, though she can still hear perfectly well. "I told you," she said, then she takes her hands away to peel the scotch tape she puts around the container's lid to keep out filchers, "I'm not talking about the kids or the house or anything like that until we get home tomorrow night!"

"Okay, honey. Calm down."

"Well, I did tell you that. Where are the drinks?"

"They're coming. Try to relax now, Vi."

"I just need some quiet. Hit that switch before you sit down, will ya?"

There's a black switch on the kitchenette wall, just above the stainless steel sink. When Sonny flips it a fan in the vent over the stove starts to whir, dimming the chandelier, which already has a bulb burned out, and moving the air all around the tiny room. Vi's various tense spots are already easing; the whir has the effect of shutting out irritating distractions from the outside, even the scrape of a key in the lock of the door, so that when it swings open suddenly she is startled. Owen, who as manager of course has a key to every room, always makes a point of knocking first. But this is Owen's girlfriend, Fran.

Fran looks daring this week in freshly pressed green pants and a white blouse with green-edged ruffles up and down the low-cut neckline. A packed purse dangles from her shoulder on a long thin strap as she tries to balance in her arms a bottle of vodka, the small metal strongbox she keeps her money in and an open bag of low-cal pretzels, which she drops in the struggle to unstick the key from the lock. Vi and Sonny watch.

"Owen should fix that," Fran says, more to herself than anyone in the room. She frees the key, and picks up the pretzels.

Owen comes in behind her. "Hi, all," he says.

"How ya doin', Owen," Sonny says.

"Hi, Owen," Vi says.

Owen's craggy face looks somehow more handsome than usual to Vi, less eroded than it's becoming. He has a stack of six-packs under one arm.

"That lock sticks," Fran says. "You should fix it."

"Get off my back." He rips a beer from one of the six-packs and stuffs the rest into the mini-freezer to chill them faster. "Did you buy new cards like I told you?"

"No," Fran says. "Why spend the money when I have two perfectly good decks in my purse?" She takes a seat in the collapsible chair nearest the bathroom. In the two months she's been dating Owen and joining them for cards, that has become her seat. She puts the vodka and the strongbox on the table in front of her and drops the bag of pretzels into the bowl of chips. She zips open her purse and pulls out two blue-backed decks of cards, still in their boxes.

"Why isn't there one red one?" says Owen.

"What difference does it make?"

"We can't play the same color cards all night. Someone'll get saddled with all the bad luck." He says this with a nod toward Sonny and Vi, as if he's apologizing for their recent losing streak. He seems to want to explain it to them somehow, pin it on something. "Run to the gas station across the street and get a red deck," he says.

"Don't be an idiot," Fran says. She tosses a deck on the table and puts the purse on the floor by her chair. Owen crimps his lips and cracks open his beer, lifting a leg over his chair and lowering himself into the seat.

The players are all in their places now: Vi with the air rushing gently around her head, Sonny to the left, Owen to the right, and directly opposite is the girlfriend of the moment, Fran what's-her-name, supposedly to be the first Mrs. Owen Turgett though Vi doesn't believe that will ever happen. Owen's had a tractor-trailerful of girlfriends over the years that at one time or another he claimed he was going to marry. But each time, almost as soon as the engagement was announced, the girlfriend's absence from the weekly card game would be explained as illness or overtime and before long Owen was bringing around someone new.

"He likes his fun," Vi once observed to Sonny about Owen and his parade of women. It doesn't surprise her. In eleven years of playing cards with Owen, and watching him struggle to keep the motel afloat, with its locks and stoves and lighting fixtures breaking down faster than he could fix them, she thinks any man in that position would want a little fun at the end of the day. And nothing is more fun to Owen than a fresh girlfriend. It is with an unexpected fondness that Vi remembers Esther, who used to propose a toast every time she won a hand, and Marlene, who got them playing strip poker more than once, and of course Kitty, who Owen went with for six months nearly a decade ago, and who first suggested that he give Vi and Sonny a free room so the four of them could play together all weekend.

Sometimes Owen picks a bad apple, like Leila, who burst into tears at the slightest ribbing, or Fran. When Owen is laughing and Sonny and Vi are laughing along with him, Fran is biting her lip while arranging her cards or making the ice cubes in her drink bounce up and down with her finger.

Fran takes the deck out of the box and starts shuffling. She works on and off as a blackjack dealer on a gambling ship that sails from Boston to Bourne and back, and she shuffles with an agility that is astonishing to see. She knows all sorts of card tricks too, according to Owen, though she refuses to do any for Sonny and Vi.

"Wait a minute. Why do you get to deal first?" Owen says. "I say we draw for it."

"It doesn't make any difference," Fran says. She starts to deal.

"Hold it, I said!" Owen grabs her by the wrist. Fran pulls away and the cards fly out of her hand and all over the table and the floor.

"Now look what you did!" says Fran. "The way you can be sometimes!" Sonny bends down and starts picking up the cards but Fran says, "I'll do it!" and gets down on her knees. Vi takes a sip of whiskey to hide the smile that's coming on. She is happy to know Owen is well along on his latest breakup, which is long overdue in her opinion, only she wishes she didn't have to witness it. The way she sees it, she works all week sweeping the floor and keeping creditors off the phone at Sonny's plumbing parts shop, she makes sure the kids are fed and clothed and delivered to Mass on Saturdays, she drives with Sonny for three hours to the Cape despite the Friday traffic—all just so she can come to Room 2B at the Sandy Day Motel for a little relaxation, some cards and maybe a few laughs. She doesn't come to watch Owen and his girlfriend fight, or, for that matter, to lose a bucket of dough to someone who plays only to win and not for fun at all.

Fran retakes her chair, brushing the knees of her pants. "This is nice," she says. "I just spent nine ninety-five to have these dry-cleaned." She fashions the pile of cards into a rectangular solid, then shuffles several times with her usual lightning speed. The table is quiet. All that can be heard is the whir from the vent over the sink. For a brief moment Fran pauses, looking into the air as if she sees something there. Then she slaps the deck down, rattling everything on the table. "So draw," she says to Owen, then she stands up to get some ice for her glass from the bucket in the sink. On her way back, she flips off the black switch and the rushing air dies away.

Vi blinks. "We usually leave that on," she says, looking back toward the switch.

"Electricity costs," Fran says flatly. She sits down, opens the vodka, and pours it

crackling

tinking

kinking

clinking

over the ice in her glass. "So are we drawing or not?" she says. She grabs the top card off the deck. Owen and Sonny do the same, followed by Vi.

ticking

clink click clicking

The cards are laid; Sonny shows a four, Owen a nine, Vi a two and Fran the queen of hearts. The dealer sighs through her nose, grabs the cards and shuffles them three more times. She starts the deal.

"Wait!" says Owen. "I wanna cut the cards first. It's bad luck if you don't," he says to Sonny and Vi.

"Oh shut up already," Fran says. "We'll start off with a little five-card stud."

"I said wait!" Owen goes to grab the cards from her but she pulls them in toward her chest, batting at him with her free hand.

"Gimme those cards!" he hollers, reaching deep into the ruffles of her blouse. He gets his hand around the deck and yanks it from her, at the same time ripping the fancy neckline so that her bra is exposed.

"Owen! My good blouse! You fucking bastard!"

ticking
tricking
cricking
some hard-of-hearing
old couple waiting
watching
the tv news in the next room announcing
declaring

"What the hell is that?" Vi hears Owen say. He's pointing at Fran, at her revealed chest. Fran seems suddenly to remember something and quickly covers up. But Owen lunges at her, tears the blouse even more and now even Vi understands: out of the left cup of Fran's bra several playing cards with blue backs are sticking up. Fran screams "No!" as Owen pulls the cards out. He drops them on the tables. They are aces and kings of various suits.

"She's cheating!" Vi realizes. "I knew it!"

Owen grabs Fran by the wrist. There is a sense that he will do something terrible. "You're ripping off my friends?" he hollers.

"Owen," says Sonny. "Calm down, buddy."

Owen nearly knocks Fran from her chair when he lets go of her. He says "You're ripping off my friends?" even louder than before.

"I only did it because I love you!" Fran hollers back. "And these two people over here, Owen,—these two people are not your friends!"

warning
blinkering
at the drivers rolling
rippling
on the pavement of the road outside speeding
screeching

"Shut up!" hollers Owen.

But Fran won't shut up. "They've been ripping you off for years, Owen! Taking up this room practically every single weekend of the summer and never paying!

screaming

Never once even offering to pay, with money as tight as it is! What kind of friends are that!"

"I'm warning you, Fran!" Owen says.

Fran turns away and cups her face with her hands. "I just wanted to win a little of your money back, baby," she says. "I got tired of seeing you

then crushing twisting collapsing
metal and puncturing
glass

get taken advantage of."

Owen brings his fist down on the table, collapsing the legs on Vi's side, though Sonny grabs it in time and quickly fixes it.

"Are you deaf?" says Owen. "I said shut up!"

"Fine then," Fran says. She gets up and grabs her purse, money and pretzels. In one gulp she finishes her drink, then caps the vodka bottle and takes that too. "Stay here with your pals and get ripped off some more.

and moaning
wailing
swearing to God

I'm leavin'." Even with everything she's carrying, and holding closed her blouse, she manages to slam the door on the way out.

Owen stands looking at the door.

"Owen," says Sonny.

"I'm sorry about all this," Owen says in a low voice.

"It's alright," says Sonny.

"I had a feeling she didn't like our card games," he says, trying to laugh. "Although she's awfully good." He looks at them, then looks away. He says, "I should go see if she's alright. She normally doesn't go off like that.

sirens burbling
approaching
overhead pouring
through the cracks in the ceiling
running
from the plastic chandelier

She's really a very nice person. Did I tell you she's cleaning the rooms now? It was her idea. So I won't have to pay the housekeeper anymore. And she's helping me balance the books—Christ, what a mess. I mean, she's good to me. I wouldn't have married her if she wasn't."

"Married her?" says Vi. "Did he say he married her?"

"Yeah," Owen says. "We were gonna tell you tonight. We did it today. She's already moved into my place."

Sonny is genuinely pleased. "You sneaky Petes," he says.

"We had to be up in Brockton this morning anyway," says Owen, "so we stopped off at the JP." He pauses, then looks at the door again. "I should go see her."

"You should," Sonny says. "And tell her congratulations from us."

"I will." Owen is at the door now, his hand is on the knob, his back is to Sonny and Vi. He seems to be waiting for something to happen before he can leave. He says, "We'll be away next weekend. We're driving to Boston for a little honeymoon. Imagine me on a honeymoon. But you two can still come use the room if you want."

"No," Sonny says. "We have things to do at home next weekend."

"Alright," Owen says. He is gone.

Sonny looks at Vi.

"The switch," Vi says. "Turn it on, please."

Sonny gets up and flips the switch. The fan starts to whir again, filling up the room. He sits down again.

Vi collects the cards left on the table and shuffles them. She deals. "Let's play hearts," she says. "Nickel a trick."

CLEANSER

1

Every year there was one Dot couldn't help but be nice to, one whose polite open face made it sort of painful for her to behave the way she normally did. She actually liked Ed Teabern, even if she doubted that he cared about her any more than anyone else at Bradenton State did. It probably wouldn't matter to him at all if he knew that she was feeling a little dizzy this morning, for instance. Or that her supervisor Carolee—who was only supposed to be sitting in while her real boss was recovering from thyroid surgery— strutted around like she owned the place. But on the other hand, when she was talking with Ed it was easy to pretend those problems didn't mean very much. Ed was all toothy hellos, picking up a sponge that had just fallen off her cart, or saying, right out of nowhere, "Thanks for doing such a great job on the bathrooms, Dot."

She smiled as she remembered that, pushing her cart off the elevator and wheeling it down the corridor of Ed's floor in Eppley Hall. The smile widened when she noticed his door was open. By the time she peered in, she'd mustered a full and actual grin, just for him.

But Ed wasn't there. Of course his roommate was. He was always there, lying on his bed with his feet propped up on the headboard, watching some sports game or other on the TV. The name taped on the door next to ED was ANDREW, but the first two letters had been carefully blacked out with a magic marker so that it read DREW. Ed had told her that his roommate wanted people to call him that and not the other, though he wouldn't say why. As a result, Dot didn't know what to call him. She wouldn't bother breaking his bubble by using his real name, but neither would she play a part in his foolishness by using his chosen one. At any rate, Drew or Andrew, she didn't see much difference, or why it should matter.

He glanced from the TV long enough to say, "Ed's in the shower."

"Oh," she said. She was a little surprised that he knew she was looking for Ed. She wondered if all the boys on the floor connected her with him like that, maybe even teased him about it. The wondering made her linger a moment, which Drew not Andrew noticed. Dot covered by gazing at a poster of a giant vodka bottle hanging on the wall over his bed. He was probably not even of age to drink. He grinned when he saw her looking at it, no doubt happy that someone suspected not only that he drank, but that he was doing something illegal by it. He was really just a little boy, Dot thought. Most men were when it came to alcohol and petty criminal behavior.

Dot turned back toward her cart and started to push it when she saw Ed, lumbering down the hall. His hair was wet and a wet towel was balled up in one of his large hands, but he was fully clothed. That's the way Ed took his showers. He went into the bathroom with all his clothes on and came out wearing the exact same things. Dot figured he did it because he didn't have the body that some of the others, like his roommate, did. Ed was a big guy but soft and slouchy, with love handles, and pimples on his chest. Dot saw them once when she burst into the bathroom, suspecting he was in there and forgetting for some reason to call out her usual warning of "Housekeeping!" Dot liked Ed's modesty. It was nice that he wasn't like the others, who trotted to and from the showers she scrubbed every day wearing only their towels, stopping to talk at the open doors of their friends, their wet, naked arms raised against the door frames.

"Hello, Ed," she said.

"Hi, Dot." He smiled in his open-mouthed way. "I hope you're doing good today."

"Oh, I can't complain. And you?"

"I'm good." It was their usual greeting. But something was different. Ed wouldn't quite meet her eyes. Instead he looked at the dirty socks on his feet. He kicked the heel of one foot with the toes of the other. Then he came out with it.

"I'm really sorry you have to clean the bathroom today," he said. Drew not Andrew did not turn his head from the TV, but suddenly seemed as though he was listening carefully.

"Why, Ed?" said Dot. "Is it real bad?"

Ed looked deeply embarrassed. "Someone threw up all over one of the stalls," he said. "It's pretty disgusting."

"Oh," said Dot.

"I'm really sorry. The guys on this floor," he said, shaking his head "—they're pigs."

"It's alright, Ed."

"People who can't hold their liquor shouldn't drink," he said. "They're just ignorant."

Dot couldn't exactly disagree. In her nine years of cleaning up after them, none of the students impressed her as particularly smart. They gabbed on their phones and played their music too loud and left notes on their doors saying what party they were at and how many kegs were involved. In short, they behaved like they were stupid.

Suddenly Drew not Andrew got up from his bed and pulled off the shirt he was wearing. He had, Dot had noticed before, a well-muscled back. He began picking through a pile of clothes in the corner of the room until he found a new shirt and pulled it on. Then he turned to Ed, muttering, "I'll leave you lovebirds alone," and made his eyebrows go up and down a couple of times before walking out of the room. So it was true, Dot thought. The others *did* make fun of Ed for being friendly with her.

But Ed acted like he didn't even hear it. "You'd think whoever did it could've at least tried to clean it up," he said.

"He was probably too drunk, Ed." said Dot. "Besides, it's not the first time I've had to clean up vomit," and in fact there was a special vomit cleanser the cleaning ladies had to use. It was sprinkled on and it could either loosen up vomit that had hardened overnight or make wet vomit congeal.

"You shouldn't feel so bad about it," Dot said. "It is not your fault."

Ed sat down on the corner of his bed. Despite the shower, his tan complexion made him look dirty. Dot thought if she ever touched his skin it would feel like a new-bought towel, soft but rough.

"Guess I'm not getting used to all of this very good," he said.

"Don't let the others bother you, Ed. They're no better."

"I don't mean just them. I mean the whole place. The whole school." He swiped a hand across his forehead to catch a trickle from his damp hair. It was stark blond, and always in need of a good combing. "I'm starting to think maybe college is not for me."

"You have to give it time, Ed."

Ed shrugged. "This is the third school I've been to in the last two years. I just don't go for it, all the reading and writing. My parents, though. They keep sending me to school."

"They're just trying to do what's best, Ed."

"Best for them, I'm starting to think."

Dot had heard some of the others talking and pieced together that Ed came from a relatively well-to-do family. His father supposedly owned a string of dog food plants across Nebraska, including the one right here in Bradenton, just three blocks from Dot's house. When the wind was right, the thick malty stench of sorghum being processed blanketed her neighborhood. Dot had always hated it. It didn't matter if she shut all the doors and windows and put air fresheners in every room, the odor still seeped in. And she could never hang anything on the clothesline for fear her sheets and towels and her husband's shirts would also smell that way. But lately, it made her think of Ed, of what a nice boy he was, and why if his parents had so much money he wasn't going to a fancier school down in Kansas City or even Chicago. Now she knew.

"Maybe you're right, Ed," said Dot. "College isn't that big a deal. These kids here, they'll never amount to a hill of beans."

Ed smiled, if only with one side of his mouth, and Dot would have smiled back if she hadn't heard the elevator opening at the end of the corridor.

2.

Even from the corner of her eye Dot knew it was Carolee coming toward her. She could tell by how she walked too fast, leaning forward a little, and how she held that godforsaken clipboard against her like it was some kind of bulletproof vest. Carolee never went anywhere without it.

"I'm sorry to interrupt you," Carolee said to Dot, casting a sarcastic glance at Ed and around his room, "but there's a special meeting in the office in ten minutes."

That made Dot turn her head. The only time the cleaning ladies were called to the office was when complaints were made against them. In the lobby of each dormitory was a small wooden box with a slot in the top and a sign on it that read SUGGESTIONS. The cleaning ladies knew the students were encouraged to write down any complaints they had and slip them in there. The boxes were emptied daily by the custodial supervisor. It had been three years since Dot was last called in; she was grouchy to a boy who asked her if she scrubbed the floors or only mopped them. She was pretty sure similar complaints had been made against her since then, and she considered it a victory of sorts that Olive, her real supervisor, had given up trying to get her to change. At the same time, she wondered if her behavior was the reason that Carolee was given Olive's position, despite Dot's having seniority. But if Carolee was going to make an issue of her attitude, Dot would welcome the opportunity to remind her that, really, Carolee was just a cleaning lady like the rest of them and not a true supervisor.

"It's nothing to worry about, Dot," said Carolee. "The meeting is for the whole staff. A special announcement. So finish up what you're doing here"—she gave Ed another disapproving glance—"and we'll see you in my office, okay?" She hurried off like she never expected Dot to answer.

Dot looked at Ed and said, "*Her* office, she says."

"Guess you two don't get along," said Ed.

"It's nothing," said Dot, resuming her smile. Again she was reluctant to let her problems interfere with her good feelings for Ed. "I'll see you later. And ease up on yourself, okay?"

She pushed the cleaning cart to the end of the corridor and locked it in the custodial closet. Now that she knew she wasn't being reprimanded, she was worried about what the "special announcement" was really about. Carolee did have a peculiar glow about her, and it wasn't her new perm, which did nothing for her in Dot's estimation.

She met up with the other housekeepers, Trula and Mary Kate, outside the Main Building where the custodial supervisor's office was. They buzzed over the meaning of the meeting.

"If you ask me," Dot said, "she's let being acting supervisor go to her head a little. I mean, she's only supposed to be sitting in for Olive."

"Well, Olive's been gone for more than two months now," said Trula.

"Poor Olive," said Mary Kate.

"And she's not coming back," Dot said. "That's what this is about. Carolee's gonna be our new boss. Wait and see."

"Worse things could happen," said Trula.

"Olive just won't seem to heal," said Mary Kate. "That's what Carolee said Mr. Weeks told her."

"She's just licking her chops," said Dot. "Have you seen the way she walks around with that clipboard? You'd think it was glued to her hands."

"She's just doing her job," said Trula. "And at least we don't run out of disposable gloves in the middle of the week the way we did when Olive was here."

"Carolee even got me the kind without the powder," said Mary Kate. "Those always make my knuckles itch."

"And I always had to fight with Olive to get an extra bottle of disinfectant on my cart," said Trula. "You should have tried that lotion I told you about, Mary Kate."

"I never said Olive was perfect," said Dot. They got on the elevator and rode to the third floor. "I just hope whoever they hire to do Carolee's dormitory is nice."

"Do you really hope that, Dot?" said Trula.

They walked to the office in silence, Dot straggling a bit. The door was open when they got there. Carolee was standing behind the desk and talking with Mr. Weeks, a thin man with an easy way of speaking who wore wire-rimmed glasses and had hair like steel wool. His suits were always a little too big for him, but within them he moved freely. His presence made the cleaning ladies a little nervous; he was the one who hired and fired people.

"Come in, girls," said Mr. Weeks.

They went in, hanging together, staying close to the open door.

"Good morning," he said.

"Good morning, Mr. Weeks," said Mary Kate.

Trula said, "Good morning."

"Good morning again, Carolee," said Mary Kate.

"Good morning, Mary Kate. Morning, Trula. Hi, Dot." Dot glared at Carolee, then turned to Mr. Weeks and opened her mouth to say "Good morning" but nothing came out.

"The reason we called you all here," he said, "is because, as you know, Olive is still recovering—"

"Isn't she doing any better, Mr. Weeks?" said Mary Kate.

"I'm afraid not. She just won't seem to heal."

"What a shame."

"That is too bad," put in Trula.

"As you know, Carolee here has been taking over some of Olive's duties in her absence—ordering supplies, stocking the cleaning carts, and so on. But now we've learned Olive will be out indefinitely, and we need someone to take over the whole job until she's back on her feet. So Carolee here will be doing that, for the time being." Carolee blinked twice and didn't even bother trying not to smile. "That means she'll no longer have time to clean the bathrooms in her building. So we're splitting her dormitory among the rest of you. Mary Kate will take the bathrooms on the first floor, Trula will take the second floor, and Dot will take the third and fourth floors."

All eyes fell on Dot, who felt as if yet another get-well card for Olive was being passed around for signatures, and when it came to her she simply let it drop to the floor.

"The reason we gave you two floors, Dot, is because Carolee here informs me the bathrooms in your dormitory are smaller than the ones in the other buildings, and therefore take less time to clean."

Dot glanced Carolee's way, but Carolee was completely focused on what her superior was saying.

"Are there any questions, girls? Good." He looked at his watch. "Remember now," he added, "this is only until Olive comes back." And with a smiling nod he was gone.

For a moment, the three cleaning ladies and Carolee stood in silence.

"What a shame about Olive," said Mary Kate.

"Yes it is," said Carolee, who nevertheless continued to smile. "I want you girls to know that if you have any problems you can talk to me."

Nobody said anything. None of them were happy about the extra work, but if Dot wasn't going to complain, then Trula and Mary Kate weren't going to either.

The same was true on the elevator. Trula and Mary Kate waited for Dot to speak. But Dot seemed lost in thought. No one had ever before mentioned anything about the bathrooms in her dorm being smaller. Of course, she knew it was true, and she assumed Trula and Mary Kate knew it as well, although she wasn't sure about that. But she also assumed everyone knew her dorm was all boys and, as everybody knows, boys are filthier than girls. And since she had to work harder to clean their bathrooms, she believed, it all balanced out in the end.

But obviously Carolee thought differently. The whole business made Dot so angry she went dizzy, and in the custodial closet she had to turn over a trash basket and sit on it for a minute.

3.

Dot resolved not to talk to anybody for the rest of the day. She was glad Ed's door was shut when she pushed her cart by. She didn't want to have to be rude to him too. She stopped her cart at the bathroom and fished out the doorstop. She knocked at the door, pushed it open a little, and called, "Housekeeping." Someone in a stall responded, "Um!—I'm in here!" They always sounded so panicked, as if they'd been caught doing something they had no business doing. Dot stepped back and let the door close, waiting. There was a notice taped there:

> YOUR CLEANING LADY'S NAME IS
> Dot
> PLEASE HELP HER OUT
> BY CLEANING UP AFTER YOURSELF

The signs were Carolee's idea. Dot wondered what name would be there when she got to the bathrooms in Carolee's building.

After a minute Drew not Andrew came out, looking a little embarrassed. Dot ignored him. She pushed at the door and bent over to put the stop in. He really stunk up the place. She glanced at the trash basket. It was overflowing with brown beer bottles. She checked the line of stalls until she found the one with the vomit. Ed wasn't exaggerating. A lumpy orange-yellow spew clung to every-thing—the bowl, the seat, the flusher, not to mention the floor and the stall walls and even the back wall. Dot had never seen so much vomit in all the years she'd been cleaning it up.

She returned to her cart and dug out the can of vomit cleanser. It was then that she realized it was empty. The discovery stunned her at first, then made her neck tighten, and brought back her dizziness before she even had the chance to realize it had gone away. It was, after all, the duty of the custodial supervisor to make sure the clean-ing carts were fully stocked every day. She had half a mind to march right back to that office and tell off Carolee for it—better yet, she'd go straight to Mr. Weeks and inform him of the situation. But right at that moment she couldn't do anything but sit down a minute, on the small damp bench next to the showers, until the dizziness passed.

She had to get up before she really felt recovered. There was lots of work to do, especially if she was to get to Carolee's bathrooms by the end of the day. Dot nurtured the thought of confronting Car-olee, but for now she cleaned. And she did an especially good job too, she thought, except for the vomit-covered stall. That she re-fused to touch. It was true she might get some complaints—in fact, as it occurred to her, she hoped she would. She would be called to the office and that would give her the chance to tell Carolee what she really thought. She imagined the words she'd say: "I can't be ex-pected to clean vomit when there's no cleanser on my cart, Carolee." "If you'd do your job, I could do mine." And even, "This never would have happened if I was supervisor!"

During her afternoon break, Dot stepped outside to smoke a cig-arette. The wind was strong and warm for late September, and she could smell the sorghum, and that made her think of Ed. Today was the first time she had seen him so unhappy. She recalled his re-mark about the people on his floor being pigs—and suddenly she was struck. What if nobody complained about the vomit? What if, pigs that they were, the boys on Ed's floor simply stopped using that stall? If no one complained, her chance to confront Carolee would be shot.

She hurried back inside and locked herself in the custodial closet. She searched the bottom of the cart for the small pad of paper and short pencil that they were supposed to use to write down anything that needed repair. She would write the complaint herself and slip it into the box.

She took pencil in hand and thought for a long while. She always had a difficult time when she had to write things down. The right words seemed to come to her only when she wasn't trying to think of them, and besides, she was a bad speller. With a lot of concentration she forced out the first word, VOMIT. Her penmanship was terrible. Carolee once called it "chicken scratch." And suddenly she realized that Carolee would recognize her terrible penmanship, and she despaired as again her plan seemed to fall apart.

But then she thought of another way.

Quickly she locked the closet behind her and hurried across the campus, looking around to make sure no one saw her. She entered Eppley Hall and rode the elevator to the fourth floor, holding the pad and pencil in both hands. When she came to Ed's door, it was shut. She felt a little strange knocking.

"It's open," she heard Ed call.

Dot poked her head inside. Ed was sitting at the desk, his long arms dangling between his legs. In front of him was an open book. Dot could see that the top of the page read CHAPTER ONE.

"Hi, Dot. How're you?"

"I'm fine, Ed. How're you?"

"Oh, alright."

"Are you busy?"

"No," he said, flipping the book closed.

"Your roommate's not around?"

"He said he was going to the bathroom an hour ago. Then he never came back."

"Ed, would you do me a favor?"

"Sure, Dot."

"You know that complaint box that's down in the lobby?" Ed looked puzzled. He didn't seem to know what she was talking about.

"Well, it's there," Dot said. "I wonder . . . I mean, I'd like you to write something down for me, if you could, and put it in there."

Ed blinked. "What do you want me to write down?"

"Well, that no one cleaned up the vomit in the bathroom."

Ed showed no glimmer of comprehension.

"Why would you want me to do that?"

Dot hesitated. She still didn't want to introduce her problems into their relationship.

"It's for a joke, Ed. On the custodial supervisor."

"That woman who came up here this morning?"

"Yes, that's her."

Ed's eyebrows pushed together. "She didn't seem like the type who likes jokes."

"Oh, she loves them. All the girls are doing it."

Ed seemed to need a minute to think about it. Dot wondered if he just didn't like the idea of jokes. Maybe too many had been played on him.

"It's not a mean joke," she added.

"Why don't you write it?"

"To tell you the truth, I'm not so good at writing down things."

Ed nodded. He took a notebook from the top desk drawer and opened it to the blank first page. Dot thought that was even better than the pad she brought—now there would be no way to trace the complaint to her. Ed looked around on the floor for a pen. Dot handed him the short pencil. "So what is it you want me to write again?"

She told him, and Ed stuck his tongue out one side of his mouth as he wrote. When he was finished, he ripped the page from the notebook and handed it to Dot. She read it a couple of times, then felt sort of disappointed. It was just a sentence on an otherwise big blank page. And in a scrawl not a whole lot better than her own; it started off big and got small and slanty as it moved to the right. It seemed like the kind of thing Carolee might glance at and throw away. She needed more.

"That's real good, Ed," she said. "Now write me another one?" This time she directed a complaint about the shower curtains being mildewy. And after that she had him write one about there not being enough toilet paper left, and then, feeling four would clinch it, one about how the cleaning lady just barged into the bathroom one day without announcing beforehand that she was coming in. She held in her hands the four complaints. She really had something now.

"Thank you, Ed," she said. "And don't worry. You won't get in any trouble. No one will know who wrote these."

"It'd be alright if they did," Ed said. "I won't be here much longer."

Dot looked up. "What do you mean, Ed?"

"I'm leaving here. Quitting. Tomorrow. I've just decided."

"Oh," said Dot.

"College isn't everything, like you said. I'm leaving with the first light in the morning."

"How'd your folks take it?"

"Haven't told them yet. I will though. Need time."

"What are you gonna do, Ed?"

"I've been thinking. I'm gonna be a truck driver."

"Oh."

"There's a school up in North Dakota. A truck-driving school."

"That's a good job."

"Yeah."

Through the air vent came the sound of a flushing toilet. Dot didn't realize he could hear that in his room.

"You driving up?" she said.

"Yeah."

Ed looked around the room, at the desk with the unread book on it, at the bed, at his blank half of the wall. He looked like he wouldn't miss the place at all.

"Well. Thanks for writing these, Ed."

"Sure."

"I'll see you then, Ed. Drive safe."

"I will."

Dot turned and left the room, closing the door behind her. She clutched the complaints to her chest. Unexpectedly, they had become the last things she would know about Ed Teabern. In the elevator she folded them into neat quarters and hid them in one hand.

At the lobby, Dot poked her head outside the elevator. She saw no one. The complaint box hung next to the bulletin board listing school activities. She walked quickly to it. The complaints disappeared into the dark slot. She almost didn't want to let them go. She turned and walked out the door and halted suddenly. But even if she had made a mistake, she couldn't turn back now; the boxes all had padlocks on them. And even if she'd gone overboard—four complaints instead of one—she'd just tell Carolee to go see the shower curtains for herself. They were spotless.

She worked out the remainder of the afternoon, and when she saw what a poor job Carolee did on her bathrooms, it only confirmed to her that she had done the right thing. Carolee deserved a good telling-off.

By punch-out time, Trula and Mary Kate already had their timecards and were waiting for the minute hand on the clock to snap forward two more times so they could go home.

"Where've you been, Dot?" said Trula. "You're usually the first one waiting to punch out."

Dot smiled mildly. "I like your hair up like that, Mary Kate," she said.

Mary Kate nearly blushed. "It's just to keep it out of my face," she said.

"Why are you so happy?" Trula wanted to know.

"I'm not," said Dot.

The minute hand snapped once.

"Did either of you see Carolee this afternoon?" Dot said, casually of course.

Trula shook her head, but Mary Kate said, "She came up to ask if the toilet on my first floor was still backed up."

"Is it?" beamed Dot.

"It's been that way over two weeks now," said Mary Kate.

"Did you have to clean the spillover?" said Dot.

"Oh no. It's not backed up that much. But the whole thing stinks."

"What exciting things we have to talk about," said Trula.

"Did Carolee say anything about, you know, anything else?"

"No," Mary Kate said, though she appeared to be trying to remember.

"You mean about this morning, Dot?" said Trula.

"Not necessarily," said Dot.

"I figure if Olive doesn't come back within two weeks," Trula said, "they'll have to hire a fourth girl for Carolee's building."

"More than likely," said Dot.

Trula looked at Dot as if she wasn't expecting her to be so agreeable.

4.

The clock finally arrived at 5:30 and they took turns sticking their cards in the clock, first Trula, then Mary Kate, then Dot, who'd waited politely behind.

At home, too, Dot's unusual mood did not go unnoticed. Her husband Will was genuinely heartened when during supper he asked how her dizziness was and she said, "I'm not dizzy at all." Instead, a kind of heady buzz had descended on her, which felt a little like a virus. It tickled her insides and gave everything she sensed a plushness not unlike that of the carpet in the custodial supervisor's office.

While she was cleaning up after supper, her husband told her she looked beautiful and snuggled her from behind. He smelled a little like sorghum. Dot smiled and said, "I'm trying to scrub this pan, Will."

They spent the unusually mild evening sipping bourbon on the front porch, Will's transistor radio tuned low to a talk show he liked. The smell of the dog food plant was in the breeze, and Dot wondered how long it would take Ed to drive to North Dakota, whether he'd go straight through or have to stop for the night somewhere along the way. Will talked about the things he had seen on television that day, about tornadoes down in Kansas and a program on people who recovered from catastrophic car-wreck injuries. Will himself had been hurt lifting fifty-gallon steel drums at his warehouse job, and had been on disability for going on three years now. Dot did not really care about tornadoes or car injuries, but she listened to the way he said things, the warm cracking of his voice that was the first thing she liked about him when they met. She laughed when he laughed, even though nothing about what he said was funny. It just felt good to be doing something with him again, to be together with him. She found there was something in just acting it out, how that helped her to almost feel it. It was not unlike what happened when she talked with Ed, how their being pleasant with one another helped create pleasantness.

"Will," she said after some time, "what would we do if I ever lost my job?"

Apparently the idea had never occurred to him. She watched his face contort in several directions before coming to rest in a downward cast.

"Did you get fired today?" he said.

"No."

"Do you think you're gonna get fired tomorrow?"

"No, Will."

He let out a breath and settled back in the porch chair.

"Why'd you ask that then?" he said.

Dot shook her head slightly. "I don't know." She realized she was hoping for a different response—she didn't know what exactly. Maybe that he'd say they'd be alright, that they'd get along somehow. She didn't say much else for the rest of the night.

At bedtime, Will wanted to make love. "You want to do that a lot for a man with a bad back," she said, adding that she was too tired from working all day. So Will went out to the living room to watch TV.

In the morning, Dot woke up before the alarm clock went off. She tiptoed around the bedroom so as not to wake Will, who usually didn't get up before eleven. It was not so much that she didn't want to wake him up, she just didn't want him awake.

5.

She arrived at work earlier than she had to. She thought maybe Carolee would be waiting at the punch clock. But Trula arrived, and then Mary Kate showed up, and soon it was time to start work—and there was no sign of Carolee.

But a short time later, Dot emerged from a stall she was cleaning in Eppley Hall to find Carolee standing at the stopped-open door.

She of course had her clipboard, holding it tight with both hands, as if to say, "Sorry, but these hands have much more important things to do than clean. Like writing down things. Possibly about you." And there was the pencil to do it with, freshly sharpened and poking out from between her ear and her stiff curls.

"Dot," she said, "could you stop by the office before your 10:15 break?" She didn't seem angry, but then, she was good at faking niceness.

Dot thought she might say, "You mean by Olive's office?" but she found herself tongue-tied. She pushed open the next stall door with the tip of her toilet bowl scrubber. She entered the stall and let the door slam behind her.

"Okay?" she heard Carolee say.

"Yup," Dot called, bending over to squirt disinfectant into the bowl. The bending made her a little dizzy. She heard Carolee walk away.

As her break approached, Dot managed to keep all nervousness at bay. She felt confident that Carolee would finally get what was coming to her. She knew she had to go into that office without flinching. But by the time she walked over to the Main Building and rode the elevator to the third floor, the effort at confidence began to take its toll.

She arrived at the office door and took a deep breath. Unfortunately that only made her dizziness worse. She knocked lightly a couple of times. "Come in," she heard Carolee say—as if she had the right to say who could come into that office and who couldn't. Dot regretted knocking. She should have just barged right in. So she tried to enter that way. But she was stopped in her tracks when she discovered Carolee wasn't alone. Mr. Weeks was sitting in a chair set up next to the desk. They were both looking at her.

"Hello, Dot," he said.

"Come in and sit down," said Carolee. Dot focused in on her. She stepped up to the desk but did not sit down.

"I know you want to get to your break, Dot," Mr. Weeks began. "This won't take long. We'd like to know if you're having any problems in the building—your building, that is, not Carolee's."

Dot lifted her eyebrows and turned down the corners of her

mouth and shook her head no. It was never easy to talk to Mr. Weeks, what with his ties and his glasses and his unexpected presence, though he was always around somewhere.

"What we mean is, are you having a problem with one of the students in particular?" he said.

Dot indicated no in exactly the same way.

"The reason we ask is, yesterday we found these in the suggestion box," and he nodded toward the desk. There were the complaints Ed had written for her, all four in a pile. They were more crumpled than she remembered them, but the creases along which they were folded were still visible.

"Would you like to know what they say?"

Mr. Weeks read all four of them aloud, though not word for word. As he did, Dot snuck a glance at Carolee. She was seated behind the desk, on the very edge of the plush chair, paying rapt attention to Mr. Weeks. Her clipboard was nowhere in sight. Probably it was in one of those desk drawers she had no right to be using. Dot turned back to Mr. Weeks, who had just read the final complaint, the one about the vomit that was never cleaned up. He laid them on the desk again and sat back in his chair. "That's quite a litany," he said, pretending to suppress a smile.

Dot didn't care if Mr. Weeks was there. She could say it in front of him. In fact, that would be even better: to embarrass Carolee in front of her boss.

He went on: "The thing is, Dot, Carolee here checked out these complaints and found them to be absolutely untrue."

"It was obvious they were all written by the same person," Carolee put in—"the handwriting."

"That's why we wanted to know if you'd had a run-in with one of the students," Mr. Weeks said. "It looks like somebody was trying to get you in trouble."

Dot nodded like she understood, and thought she might say, "I don't know who would want to do that," but her dizziness was now accompanied by a crushing revulsion that came upon her as soon as Carolee opened her mouth.

"So Carolee here did some asking around. She found the young man who wrote the notes."

Dot felt her eyes widen, though there was no discernible change in her expression.

"His roommate recognized the writing when I showed it to him," Carolee said. "It turned out to be that young man I saw you talking with. I thought there was something going on between you two."

"We brought him in yesterday afternoon," said Mr. Weeks, "and asked him why he did it. He said it was just a joke. But when we asked him what was funny about it, he said he didn't know."

Mr. Weeks stopped. He seemed to be waiting for some kind of response from Dot, but she could only blink.

"As it happens, he's failing all his classes and is planning to drop out today. We figure he was just taking out the frustration of his failure at Bradenton in any way he could think of." He laughed gently, and Carolee laughed with him. "Some of the kids here are rather dim-witted. At any rate, he won't be bothering you anymore. Like we said, he's gone."

Dot stood awkwardly a moment. She could not have said anything at this point even if she wanted to. She looked at the door, which she had left open, and wanted to go. She looked back at her two superiors.

"Dot," Carolee said in a somewhat annoyed tone, "don't you have anything to say?"

She looked straight at Carolee, who maybe was waiting to be thanked, but who had actually loused up everything again. Ed's complaints were still on the desk in front of her. Dot wanted them. They were to her mementos of him. She opened her mouth to ask for them, leaned forward a little, and suddenly threw up on Carolee's desk with such force that the complaints were completely covered over. Carolee let out a small shriek and tried to backpedal in her chair, though the wall wouldn't let her go any further. A second convulsion immediately followed, spewing vomit even farther, right into Carolee's lap. After a third and final heave, Dot glanced toward Mr. Weeks, who had apparently gotten splattered because he had hopped up and was checking the front of his suit with a disgusted look. Dot quickly turned and headed for the door. Her head was still spinning, but she thought she heard Carolee yell, "Come back here, Dot!" Dot staggered from the office. Somehow she managed to close the door behind her.

She made her way to the elevator, which was thankfully empty. By the time she arrived at the first floor, she felt much better. In fact, her dizziness was completely gone. For a moment she stood dumbfounded in the lobby. She simply didn't know what to do, so she went back to work. Her only regret was that she hadn't got Ed's complaints before she'd thrown up on them.

6.

Back in her building Dot unlocked her cart. She felt the tartness of the vomit in her mouth and wished she could brush her teeth.

The elevator opened to the fourth floor and she pushed out the cart. She realized she was on Ed's floor, and noticed his door was open as she approached it. She was surprised to find him there, standing next to a suitcase and three cardboard boxes stacked one on top of the other. On the bed were other items waiting to be packed. "Ed," she said, "how're you?"

"Fine, Dot. And you?"

"I can't complain. I thought you'd be gone by now."

"So did I. But late yesterday, I got called to some guy's office about those complaints I wrote for you. Kept me there a long time, all afternoon. By the time they let me go, the registrar's office was closed. So I couldn't officially drop out until this morning. But I'm leaving now."

"I'm sorry about that, Ed."

"It's alright. And don't worry. I didn't mention you at all." He grinned, like a child would grin at another child when they'd gotten away with something. Dot grinned in kind.

"It would have been okay if you had," Dot said. "I don't care anymore." She looked at his luggage. "I wish I was driving to North Dakota." She paused a minute. "Was it you that cleaned up the vomit in the bathroom, Ed?"

"No. Didn't you do it?"

Dot shook her head.

"I guess whoever puked it must've finally cleaned it up," Ed said. Suddenly he halted his packing. He seemed to have spotted something on the front of her. Dot looked down to find her shirt stained with vomit.

"I threw up," she said, holding out the shirt to get a better look at it. "I don't know what happened."

"You should go home if you're sick," said Ed.

"I don't really want to go home," she said with a laugh.

"You shouldn't go around wearing that," he said. He took a box off the stack and tore open the sealed one underneath it. Inside were clothes, all neatly folded. He pulled out a sweatshirt, a brand new Bradenton State sweatshirt. "Here," he said. "Wear this."

"Oh no, Ed. I can't wear your shirt."

"You can't wear that. Go ahead. I have to use the bathroom anyway." He left it in her hands and headed for the door. He pushed the lock in the middle of the doorknob before closing it behind him. Dot looked up and saw herself in the long mirror that hung on the back of the closet door. She watched as she unbuttoned the stained shirt and took it off. It was exhilarating to stand in Ed's room in just her bra. She pulled on the sweatshirt. It felt against her skin the way she thought he might feel—soft but rough. In the mirror she thought it looked a little tight on her. She heard the toilet flush and a minute later, two gentle knocks came at the door. Dot opened it.

"There you go," said Ed, sizing her up in the sweatshirt.

"It's a nice color," said Dot.

"I've never even worn it," he said. "Don't know why I ever bought it. Keep it."

"That's nice of you, Ed." She looked in the mirror again. She stretched it down over her hips, and then it didn't look too bad. She'd keep it from shrinking, she thought. She'd wash it in cold water, and hang it in the wind to dry.

FELLOW FEELING

1

"**P**hilip. Philip Allan Flatley.—Why are you doing this?"

He just told her why.

"No," she said. "That's a crock of shit, God forgive me. Made up to make yourself feel good about doing something that you know is bad. It's not enough that you're abandoning your faith, and condemning yourself and probably your whole family, but to blaspheme the entire priesthood. You're not man enough to say, 'I'm too weak to take it.' You have to blame everyone else for your own faults, just like you always have! 'Oh, everybody there is so awful' and all that, and 'I'm too good for them!'" She turned to her husband. "Imagine that, Chester! We raised a better person than all the other priests in the world! Who'd've thought!" She turned back. "Let me tell you something, Philip. You've never understood the difference between being good and being a goody-goody!"

it's important to keep in mind that she's speaking out of pain and that people in pain do not see or think clearly I believe therefore that your words while somehow devastatingly candid still aren't exactly truthful but it's a painful thing I know to realize that your son after all really isn't meant for a life with God that he's meant instead for one involving things you never even dared to think about "I'm not abandoning my faith, Mother," he said, while holding back his tears.

"You just said you didn't even want to be a Catholic anymore, didn't you?"

there are some things that cannot be said

"Yes, but I meant I'm not abandoning my faith in God."

"Oh!" She sat back. She'd been clipping coupons when he arrived and they were spread before her on the kitchen table. She
folded her hands against her chest, her fingers still lodged in the
holes of the scissors, the dirty black blade sticking up at an angle
parallel to her jaw. "Well," she said. "I'm sure God feels a lot better
knowing that you've decided to still believe in Him *some vows cannot be broken* You're very arrogant, Philip. Picking and choosing
what you want to believe in."

"But isn't God the important—"

"So you believe in God, big deal. So does the devil."

Phil could see now that it was only that he'd been far enough
away for a long enough period of time to forget how his parents really were *how Mother really is* he remembered them *her* as *a* caring
people *person* who wanted only what was best for him *I must have
fabricated that memory wished it* he relied too willingly on objects:

**15 Love not the world, neither the things that are in the world. If
any man love the world, the love of the Father is not in him.**

the deep blue parka sent for his birthday, worn on the train home;
the Christmas geranium, dead now; the ten-dollar donations made
to his parish when she could, the check made out to him and not Sacred Heart Church.

But they *she* had to be told. At least now they *she* knew, even if his
reasons did seem feeble *cannot be told you don't believe me because I
haven't told you the half of it*

cleanse thou me from secret faults.

*when I was at seminary one of the students formed the Catholic Call-
ing Circle*

A WEEKLY DISCUSSION GROUP
First meeting: Thurs., 8:00 pm, Shine Hall
Purpose: to provide a setting where students can
give and get support, and talk about the problems
that face aspiring clergymen.

*loved the student Arthur Antez everyone did faculty students me too
Costa Rican he'd lived in the United States since he was one spoke flawless English he was as American as any of us really probably more so he
hated to be called by his Spanish name Arturo still his origins in a foreign*

land were emphasized enough to make the rest of us believe his piousness was truer than ours I went to Shine Hall that Thursday mostly because I had no one to talk to I didn't say a word but I did feel better just being around the ten or twelve others that showed up listening to their problems several said seminary work was much harder than they expected it would be one man Gerard pale with greasy red hair I recognized him from my Church History class confessed that it was hard keeping his focus with his mother very sick back at home she kept calling to say how proud of him she was and in the next breath she'd say she was dying of loneliness I went up to him after class a few days later and told him I was praying for him and his mother it's not that unusual a thing to say at a seminary he thanked me by the second meeting I was ready to talk the Circle had shrunk to six or seven Arthur called the meeting to order with an opening prayer a few people spoke then it was my turn I raised my hand Arthur said this isn't class just speak so I did I started with a forthright confession that I am a homosexual

Chester reached and put his hand on her forearm, his way of asking her to please calm down. She put her hand on top of his and gripped his bony knuckles *I doubt she can say you never suspected* "I know, hun," she said. "But when I think about the money." Seminary cost nothing but his first year Phil "borrowed" $2000 from them *her* to adjust to living on his own. They *she* objected at first but that was just reflex; deep down there was a knowledge of Phil as oblivious and vulnerable, a blind child who was not yet old enough to know it. "We would have done just as well, Chester, if you'd taken it all up to the Pit and thrown it all in." Phil's father ran the town incinerator until his retirement the year before, the same year Phil was ordained. Since then his lungs, always a problem, rapidly began to break down. He could wheeze out sentences between infusions from an oxygen tube stuck up his nostrils, but usually he chose not to. "We were so proud," said Mother, speaking to some invisible person between her husband and her son. Then she looked Phil straight in the face for the last time and said, "I'll never forgive you."

I've never confessed this to anyone before but I've decided to now because since coming here the struggle with my feelings had become a daily torture it's not that I'm afraid I'll act on my feelings I know the Church position on that I just worry about the presence of the feelings

inside me I wonder why God has chosen to torture me this way what did
I ever do I'm sorry I didn't intend to sound like that but I was conscious
of hush falling over the group as I was speaking

    the meeting broke up quickly no one came up to me no one looked at
me finally in the corridor Arthur Antez pulled me aside God he was
handsome square face black eyes very thick very black hair I was hopeful
he'd have something helpful to say

what you had to say was very interesting Phil I just want you to know
that if you ever stand in my way in the future I won't hesitate to use that
information against you

    they're like that aspiring or not Father Binney excepted he would
never try to make God an accomplice in his crimes as if that were possi-
ble I lived in fear of Arthur Antez and everyone else for almost a whole
year I was too scared to find out if the seminary could do anything to me
I avoided everybody when I didn't have to be at classes or the library I
stayed in my room I ate all my meals there instead of going to the
cafeteria

hello

will you accept the charges

hhhhhyes I will what's the matter

I think I mean I'm having problems here Mother I'm in trouble

what kind of trouble I can't believe you're flunking anything

I'm not it's just I mean nobody here talks to me

that's the trouble that's all Philip that doesn't matter you're not there to
talk to people you're there to learn how to be a priest if other people are
snobby and all that just ignore them it doesn't interfere with you one bit

    shortly after that Arthur Antez graduated and went away forever and
that helped too (they had a big party for him in the chapel basement he
was assigned to an important parish on the lake in Chicago I didn't go to
the party but that day I ran into him on the stairwell to the library good
luck Arthur I said I extended my hand God bless you I said) by the sec-
ond year everybody seemed to have forgotten about it

Phil did not know how to tell them *her* the rest: that, just as they
were *she was* shutting him out, he needed to move back in with
them *her* he had no choice. He had very little money saved and no
friends he could stay with. Divining that essence, Mother stiffened
in her chair and looked straight down. She threw her scissors down,
got up from the table, and left the room.

Phil sat alone. His father was across the room in the rolling recliner in which it was easiest for him to breathe. Phil could hear his straining lungs. "I'm sorry, Dad," he said. "I just didn't belong in the order like I thought I did."

Phil's father reached up and slipped the Y-shaped tube from his nose. His head rolled back a little and he shut his eyes. Phil got up and knelt next to him; he'd worked with emphysema patients before and knew they did this when they wanted to speak. His father was slowly drawing air through his clogged passages, building up energy. "Your room," he said finally, faintly, "Mother uses it for her sewing now."

"Oh." He paused. "I could sleep on the couch."

"No," his father said. "Sleep in your room." He couldn't go on. He slipped the tube in again. He seemed to fall asleep immediately after that. Phil at once felt a swelling of cruelty toward the old man *he never spoke even when he had the chance* and wanted to hurt him in some way.

Phil went upstairs to find Mother moving her sewing things out of his old room. She would not accept any help from him, she would not even talk to him. She wheeled her old Singer out by herself. She collected under one arm the three or four half-done macrames that were laying around. The only thing she left behind was a calendar with the dates her sewing circle met checked off. It hung on the wall like a memorial plaque to the sewing room that was. Phil did not dare move it.

On his third day home, he was gazing through the window in his room, which overlooked the driveway, when he saw Mother pull up with several bags of groceries. He decided he would go down and help her carry them in. She was just coming in through the back door as he arrived in the kitchen. She looked at him as if startled, then turned away with that same wordless hostility. Phil suddenly felt very heavy, and for some reason he did not get the rest of the groceries like he planned. Instead he stood there and watched her as she went out and came back with two more bags, placing them on the counter with the others. At the top of one of the bags was the receipt, a curling white slip with purple print. She picked it up, scrutinized it, then filed it carefully away with some other papers in a drawer in the counter.

Phil nearly jumped when she broke the silence: "Your father and I can't support you indefinitely. We're old." She started to put away her purchases.

"I plan to get a job," Phil was prompted to say. She finished with the groceries and left the room without another word.

As it turned out, every two or three days, she would break her silence in that same, unexpected, tersely precise way. It was as if she couldn't help but speak, and she always seemed peeved with herself afterward. The second time, she said, "Electricity isn't cheap" (there happened to be two lights on in the room) and the time after that: "You should pay room-and-board here. It's only right." Her words were pointed and aimed precisely at Phil's heart. Once he was there long enough to detect Mother's pattern, he abandoned his policy of looking out for opportunities to be kind to her and began avoiding her whenever he could. He stayed in his room and did not keep it up. The little he ate he ate up there, leaving food-encrusted plates and bowls on the floor and half-filled glasses and cups along the windowsill. Tipped-over stacks of books and papers also made any movement a precarious undertaking. He came to feel as though he was at the seminary again. He spoke to no one. No one knocked on his door and wanted to come in, nor did he think he could let anyone in if they did. And there was the same searing loneliness that afflicted him at all times, even when he was sleeping.

He honestly tried to take the steps that would lead to his getting a job. Every day he'd start off hopeful. Every day he took the morning paper up to his room and spread it out on a cleared away space on his bed. But when he got to the want ads, a strange and irresistible tiredness would come over him and he'd have put the paper aside and take a nap *the truth is I've never paid rent before that was always taken care of when I quit as a priest I thought vaguely that I'd find other work but I had no idea how hard it would be and my clothes everything down to the dull black shoes was provided by the Church and the shirts and pants sent for Christmases and birthdays filled the gaps but now a small hole is forming in the crotch of my pants I did go to one interview a sheet music company over in Troyaka I took the bus they were looking for an order-picker to work in their warehouse I told myself it was important I told myself I wanted the job I believed it too sort of right up until I got to the place then I suddenly felt very listless by the time I sat in the straightback hardwood chair by Mr Gilwicki's desk I felt as though I'd burned up every last ounce of myself I had one leg locked over one knee to hide the hole all I put down under Work Experience was ROMAN CATHOLIC PRIEST*

that doesn't seem like much Mr Gilwicki said looking the application over

you left it blank here under Wage Earned I hadn't seen that column I apologized and told him how much I made

is that all priests earn

he flipped the application over and wrote some comments that I could see but couldn't make out two minutes later we were on our feet and shaking hands he told me honestly I don't think this is the right job for you

I'd been in a stupor since I walked into the place and failed to respond to even that as I was leaving I heard him say

if you don't mind my asking why did you leave the priesthood

a good question but I walked out as if I never heard it

outside in the cold sunshine I seemed to recover my capacity for thinking I immediately recalled Father Binney God rest his soul I remembered how when I was an altar boy at St Francis of Assisi Father Binney used to see to every aspect of the parish from the well-being of the parishioners to the sturdiness of the pews he was so involved with everything that I asked him once what the main job of a priest was

being a priest requires attending to a lot of things more earthly than spiritual I'm telling you this because I see in you that you'll probably enter into this vocation someday unless something drastic happens if you do you should keep in mind that above everything else the main job of a priest is the salvation of souls

and so I always believed totally unaware until right then that the market value of soul-saving was a lot lower than that of fishing out copies of the marching band version of the lemon tree song in some filthy basement

I could never go to another interview several times I'd left the house intending to go to one but I never quite made it then I started leaving the house with the intention of making Mother believe I was going to an interview whenever he did that he was sure Mother was on to him. Through some glance or gesture, she seemed to say, "We both know you're a liar. Go already."

On the morning of the thirtieth day back in his old room, Phil awoke to realize that the entire time he had not even thought of going to Mass once. He wondered if perhaps Mother was right. Maybe he really had abandoned his faith. So he cleared a spot amid the mess on the floor, got on his knees and prayed to God to help him. Afterward, he felt better. He had not abandoned God. He did not feel so alone.

2.

But the feeling fluctuated. As the weeks went by Phil would repeatedly flash on the idea that he needed more than God—he needed people—and he was ashamed that God wasn't enough for him. As much as he had come to despise the Church, he did miss a little his particular parish, Sacred Heart, in a small town in the remote north of the state. True, the pastor there, Father Connell, had a reeking disposition. And the parishioners acknowledged tepidly if at all the new assistant priest, a sad-looking and uncertain young man with medium-brown hair parted jaggedly on the left side *there was one man gentle friendly devout name of Broom first name Marty the father of seven children before he was forty all of whom unfortunately for them took after their untrusting pig-nosed mother rather than him amiable handsome father Marty the volunteer around the parish carried the collection baskets shoveled our walkway Marty the snowman gave up an entire Sunday night at home with his seething pig-nosed family to fix the rectory furnace I spent the time with him in the basement watching him working bringing him hot tea he was a printer who ran a failing business not learned but had the sadness of the genuinely devout*

we became friends

or at least friendly he was working I noticed a tattoo of a woman lower right arm kept it covered up in church

he saw me looking

a little embarrassed

it's a stupid thing he told me I was a kid in the Army I was just doing what everybody else was doing and not thinking too much

thoughtless grunt handsome humanity sprawled out on the basement floor legs open in front of me our furnace had to be attacked from underneath I liked the tattoo and I told him not to be embarrassed we had a se-

cret laugh over Father Connell totally inappropriate Marty reliever of solitude now all I do is read

He had several Bibles in his room and would often switch from one to another in mid-passage. The Church had always insisted on the King James Version, but on his own Phil gravitated toward the Revised Standard, which was less mystical while retaining the spiritual power.

15 Do not love the world or the things in the world. The love of the Father is not in those who love the world;

He read other books. For pocket change, he bought used theology books in laughably good shape. For a quarter and a nickel he got one about the Hinayana Buddhists and read how their attainment of God came essentially through isolation. That was something he could never do. The loneliness would kill him. It was killing him now *each meaningless if not impossible without the other I put the host on Marty's thick smooth pink tongue and watched it disappear*

One afternoon, Phil suddenly put down his book and stood up. He felt if he didn't talk to someone, or at least see a sympathetic face, he would burst. He pulled on his sneakers and grabbed his deep blue parka. He listened at his door for any indications of Mother and, hearing none, quickly made his way downstairs and out the back door. He took Mandemer Street, which wound clandestinely behind the house into a thicket of overhanging trees, and opened up into a wide flat thoroughfare on which much of the town's business was transacted. But it was a cold Sunday afternoon and no one was around, although he saw people up and down Mandemer Street, from windows and tinted windshields. He walked fast, hands thrust into the pockets of his parka and his upper body bent forward, as if headed somewhere important. He talked to himself.

He passed a bus stop just as the bus was arriving there, and hopped on. He did not know where the bus was going, but it was heated. He paid no heed to what he was staring at out the window, but instead looked for his own expression in the warped thickness of the windowpane. He was able to catch his eyes once, and saw in them Mother's eyes. He sat back, recalling her latest near-telegraphic communication *delivered just that morning and already I've almost forgotten about it* "Your father talked to some people down at the incinerator. They can get you work. Be there tomorrow at nine." *I hate the incinerator I've always hated it even as a child the constant hot roar the large cement pit the foul-smelling choking fumes the people of the town backing their station wagons up to the treacherous edge and throwing their garbage in the loud cliquish workers stupidly pretending the white masks they breathe through are protecting them but I'll go if she wants me to but I'll go to the Pit tomorrow and throw myself in* Mother would hear about it if he didn't.

He became aware of a voice calling to him. It was the bus driver. This was his last stop. Phil apologized and hurried off. It was only when the bus was pulling away that he realized he didn't know where he was. Night was falling. The air was colder. He zipped up his parka and rushed to the nearest corner. He saw with a flush of panic that he was no longer on Mandemer Street—judging by the odd colors of the street signs, he didn't think he was even in the same town anymore. Around him he saw large, well-groomed houses with attached garages. Behind him was a meticulously trimmed wall of vegetation that towered over passersby.

He heard voices. He suspected hoodlums at first, but then he listened carefully and heard gentle, reassuring voices. They came from behind the wall of vegetation. Phil quickly followed the perimeter of the wall, in search of an opening. He turned two corners until at last the bushes gave way to an open gate. He peered in.

It was a church. The voices he heard were of the pastor, fully dressed in white surplice and a tippet of navy blue, and of the worshippers he was welcoming to the five o'clock service. Phil didn't know this church or this priest, but he was humiliated at having to ask for help from either. He made his way up the paved walkway. He learned from the sign that this was not a Catholic church, but an Episcopal one, and he felt a little better.

But the priest, a tall, white-haired man with a puffy face, had apparently welcomed the last of the worshippers and was now heading into the church himself, shutting the door behind him without ever looking Phil's way. Phil dashed ahead, caught the handle, and pulled at the heavy, intricately carved wood. He made it inside just in time to call the old priest back before he disappeared irretrievably into the nave.

The old priest turned, regarding the entirety of Phil's six-foot being. The visitor was panting and sweating despite the cold. His clothes were shabby and smelly.

"Yes?" the priest said. One white tweezed eyebrow was arched.

But Phil was looking past the priest now, into the most magnificent church he'd ever seen—or if not, then at least something worlds removed from old Sacred Heart, which was tiny and had, especially in winter, the dim, dank atmosphere of a basement. This church was lighted exultantly, so that not a shadow was cast in any direction. On each side wall there were seven enormous stained-glass windows that all together depicted the Fourteen Stations of the Cross. He looked across the nave. On each side, a massive pillar made of a cream-colored stone rose from amidst the pews to the vaulted ceiling. Directly ahead, the sanctuary in the distance loomed. Raised several feet from the pews, it almost seemed to float above them. It contained an enormous altar of white marble and, hanging on the wall behind, a vast painted-wood carving of a Christ nailed to the cross that overlooked the proceedings not with an expression of suffering, but understanding. The flames at the ends of the towering altar candles stood as solid slivers of light—there was no draft in here to blow them around—and they were reflected everywhere, in gold linings and casements and fringes.

"I have to begin," he heard the priest say, adopting the gentle tone that had apparently served him so well. "Please," he took Phil by the arm to the backmost pew, "have a seat." Phil knelt, crossed himself, and sat down. Even the pew, a shiny shellacked wood, appeared to him exceptionally beautiful. It was not scratched up by keys like the pews at old Sacred Heart—why they did that, he never understood.

The service began, but not in the way Phil expected, with the priest and the altar boys emerging from the sacristy. Instead, a single organ note sounded, alarmingly loud, and soon the air was thick with other organ notes, and then those were joined by an up-swelling of voices in unison, a choir. Phil looked up and behind him, to where the music was issuing from. He saw them up there, men on one side, women on the other, all dressed in white robes and holding hymnals. Behind them was an organ with enormous rising golden pipes, being played by someone Phil couldn't see. The music they made was so beautiful that Phil wept.

The service was almost exactly like the Mass that he was so intimately familiar with, except for the intervals of choir music, which were not the norm in the churches he had grown up and served in. He went through the service, doing and saying everything as it should have been done and said, and taking comfort in it. All the while he managed to talk privately to God as well, asking him to relieve his loneliness, and feeling perhaps that God had answered him already in bringing him to this magnificent church.

He listened when it came time for the homily. The white-haired priest talked about charity, the importance of giving freely to others, a common theme for priests as Christmas approached. He invoked in part the famous Chapter Thirteen of Paul's first letter to the Corinthians.

13 And now abideth, faith, hope, charity, these three; but the greatest of these is charity.

Then he moved away from the microphone and engaged in a minor fit of coughing. The altar boy, who from Phil's distance reminded him of himself, poured a glass of water from a pitcher that was ready there. The old priest recovered himself quickly and returned to the microphone. "Sorry 'bout that," he chuckled, feeling his neck beneath his Adam's apple. "That reminds me—throat-blessings are coming up!" The congregants burst into laughter. Even Phil smiled. The old priest continued with a cunning grin: "But as I was saying, seriously," and he went on about how charity included being charitable to one's church, their beloved Holy Trinity. He said they'd been trying to raise funds to complete repairs on the back fence after it was knocked down by last month's "unfortunate incident" (they all seemed to know what that was). As it was now, the fence provided easy access to anyone who wanted to come in, "including prowlers and other miscreants." He directed the parishioners' attention to the small envelopes that had been placed at the end of each pew. "Whatever extra you can give at collection time would be greatly appreciated in the eyes of God."

Then came time for Holy Communion. Phil watched carefully as the old priest carried out the preparatory duties. He spread his hands over the bread and wine. The choir sang. He lifted the shining chalice above his head. He closed his eyes and moved his lips in silent prayer. It reminded Phil of the ostentatious way Father

Connell would say the Secret, a prayer said inaudibly. It was a time when a priest could say anything he wanted to.

I have grievously sinned in thought word and deed through my fault through my fault through my own great fault I can never tell you how though already I'm a lawbreaker a killer an innocent killer yet I still want love

Phil did not refrain from taking the sacrament because of the way he was dressed, although he did notice how well-attired most of the other worshippers were, in suits with ties, in dresses. As he was in the last pew, he was at the end of the line to receive the Eucharist. The white-haired priest seemed dismayed when he saw him, but he smiled and placed the host on his tongue.

At the end of the service, Phil bowed his head to pray again as the others filed past him. The old priest was the first to go by, frowning on his way outside to bid the worshippers goodbye. Next came the congregants, silent except for a cough or the call of a child. Some took notice of him as he sat contentedly in his pew. Some did not look at all.

He was just standing when the pastor returned, rubbing his arms against the cold. They eyed each other at the same time. The priest smiled his gentle smile. "The service is over now," he said. "Thank you for coming."

"It was lovely. And what a beautiful church."

They fell silent. Phil did not move. The priest noticed he'd been crying. He said, "Is it that you don't have a place to go?"

The members of the choir, dressed now in lay clothes, were noisily making their way down the middle aisle. They stopped to receive the praises of the priest, tactfully avoiding Phil's eyes. Having figured out who they were from the conversation, Phil suddenly came alive. "You're all wonderful singers!" he said. "Thank you all so much!" They returned his thanks and he shook two or three hands, much to the old priest's annoyance. As they were leaving another person came in, a man with a long, asymmetrical face, a bit distorted-looking as if immense heat were rising in front of it. He could have been a few years younger than Phil, and wore a soft-looking brown beard. He apparently came to talk to the priest, but seeing him engaged, he stayed back. Phil watched him as he occupied himself with viewing the stained-glass windows.

The priest again turned to Phil. He waited a moment, to see if Phil would leave.

"My friend," the old priest said, "I'm going to call the city. They have agencies, places where you can stay."

Phil turned to him. "You won't let me stay here?" he said. "Not even just a little while longer?"

"It's not safe."

"I'll be alright."

The old priest held his tongue. He had a countenance for every occasion, and now adopted a stern-but-concerned one. Under this new, harder gaze, the last traces of Phil's tears evaporated from his face.

"What, exactly, is the matter with you?"

The slight smile Phil had been wearing since he entered the church died. He was suddenly overcome with the desire to leave, to run out of there, yet he continued to linger. He asked, "How long have you been pastor here?"

The old priest lowered his eyelids. "Thirty-one years."

"Were you assigned to this church right out of seminary?"

"I was hired by this parish, right out of seminary. But the service is over now. Everyone's left and you have to go too. I'm going to call the city—"

"When you say you're going to call the city, do you really mean the police?"

Now the expression was anger. His delicate eyebrows merged. The excess skin above his lip pushed together in a pleated fashion. "I'll call the police," he said, "if that's what it takes!" He moved off.

"Mercy triumphs over judgment, Father," Phil called out. The priest paused and turned around again. The soft-bearded man was also looking now. Both Phil and the old priest seemed conscious of the man's presence, though neither acknowledged him. The priest took a few steps toward Phil again, extending his nose like a sniffing dog. "Remember the letter of James," Phil instructed in a gentler voice, a voice he used when admonishing parishioners while trying not to alienate them. It was a way of speaking he learned initially from old Father Binney.

"You're a priest? Why would you behave this way in a church? Why would you come here in the state you're in?" The old man spoke slowly, the words smoldering in his mouth awhile before he verbalized them. "You're a disgrace to the vocation."

"I'm not in the vocation anymore"—he was going to say "Father" but didn't.

"Why not?—Never mind, it doesn't surprise me. I can see how unsuited to it you are. What parish would hire you?"

"I was assigned to a church, up in St. Cloud. Sacred Heart."

"You're a Roman Catholic?"

"I was."

"Have you converted?"

Phil looked down at the red-carpeted aisle. "I thought I might for a while there. But now, thanks to you, I doubt it very much." He moved to go, nearly pushing the old man aside. He halted, turned. "And by the way, you completely misinterpreted the passage you read. By 'charity,' Paul was referring to love, the love we have for other human beings, and that God has for us *is it wrong to talk so angrily of love* he didn't mean it in the self-serving material sense that you just reduced it to." The old man now looked frightened, but Phil couldn't stop himself. "And the way you softened them up for it with that comedy routine! Doesn't preaching mean anything more to you than tawdry showmanship?" With that the old man made a wheezing sound and proceeded to hurry toward the sacristy. Phil did not like the image of himself as a bully. He turned and left the church.

He hustled up the paved walkway and out into the street, kicking something ahead of him with the tip of his sneaker. He looked down: it was a jagged rock. He toyed with the idea of picking it up and throwing it through one of those glorious stained-glass windows. It pleased him that he was still young enough to entertain such a thought *but in truth I've never been so young as to actually do something like that I was too busy indulging my sentiment for symbol and pageantry a boy an altar boy a seminarian a priest and again this afternoon indulgent idolatrous fetishistic you remember how I washed by hand the white lace of my vestment I promise to hold the world I see in greater disregard* he tripped on the curb. He still had no idea where he was going. There was no light left in the sky, and the air was colder still. He passed from streets to roads and was frightened by the far-off sound of a barking dog *what if the old man probably over his shock by now called the police anyway no one's more spiteful than a decrepit clergyman must be something a person can do* the wind gusted. The parka Mother had given him was not enough for cold this severe. He felt as though his face was cracking and falling away piece by piece. Ahead he saw a couple in a compact car parked at the side of the street. The car's interior light was on. The man and woman had their gloves off and were turning their hands over the vent in the blue plastic dashboard. Phil broke into a run. Then suddenly the interior light flashed off, the taillights blazed red and the car abruptly sped away. He stood and watched until it disappeared around a corner.

He knew it would be better to keep moving, but he didn't know which way to go.

Then the knocking of boots made him aware that he was not alone—and that whoever was behind him was gaining fast. He bolted ahead, refusing to look back. But when the stalker was so close that his breathing could be heard, Phil turned his head. It was the young man with the long face and the soft beard who he had seen in the church.

"Wait up!" he called.

"Why are you following me!" hissed Phil.

"Take it easy!" He added, "That doesn't sound like love for a fellow human being."

help me please he slowed, letting the man catch up. "I'm sorry . . ."

"I'm glad I caught you. Do you realize how fast you walk?"

I wanted to talk to you about what you said back there in the church, about Paul's meaning of charity. I think you're right. The old goat should have known that. Even I know that, and I haven't read the Bible since parochial school."

"I think he did know it *I went too far treated him much too harshly there were times when the parish was in need that Father Connell did exactly the same thing Father Binney too* besides," he said, "charity in the sense that he meant it is important too. It's good to give freely."

"Maybe so," said the bearded man, "but I know the old guy pretty well and it doesn't surprise me at all to hear his sermons are soft, although the people who go there seem to love him."

his eyes are bright you don't go there?"

He shook his head. "I did some carpentry for them. They had a stockade fence that ran along the back of the church until some drunk driver knocked it down last month. The old guy's been putting me off. So I finally told him I wouldn't finish the job until he paid me what I was owed. That's why I was there."

"Did you get your money?"

"After he settled down, I did. At first he was too upset to talk. He locked himself in his little room back there. I pounded on the door a couple times, then he came running out and said we should get our business over with. He paid me everything he owed and rushed me out. He was embarrassed that I heard what you said. What were you doing there, anyway? I know you don't go there."

"How do you know that?"

"The way you're dressed, for one thing. That's important to them. And the way you were laying into the old guy, you didn't sound like one of his adoring flock."

I was lost I don't know what I was doing there. I never should have gone in *how much did he hear how much does he know* they walked slowly and silently awhile, and Phil did not mind the company. The wind had died down and the cold was less painful. Then the bearded man said, "That is a beautiful passage though, if I'm remembering right,

4 Love is patient;

that one from Corinthians.

love is kind;

I have to admit it,

love is not envious or boastful or arrogant 5 or rude

as much as I can't stand Paul."

8 Love never ends.

Phil glanced up quickly. "Why can't you stand Paul?" he said. Up until then, the bearded man had been easy and forthcoming *look now how he's a little uncomfortable keeps his eyes on the street won't answer I doubt there's a gay man alive who knows Scripture who doesn't have mixed feelings about Paul*

27 and in the same way also the men,

a scrawl slid under my door a day after my confession

giving up natural intercourse with women,

having memorized its contents forever

were consumed with passion for one another.

I Men *took* committed *it* shameless acts *outside* with *and* men *burned* and *it* received *in* in *the* their *weedy* own *lot* person *behind* due penalty *the* for *seminary* their *chapel* error.

They came to the corner and the bearded man said, "Stop a minute." He appeared to be mustering his courage. "I live nearby here. I was just wondering.... maybe you'd like to come home with me?"

I do I want to but I'm in trouble I'm lost I'm cold Dad's dying and I'll end up the same if I go to the Pit tomorrow tomorrow I'll throw myself in the long-faced soft-bearded carpenter looked away *I want to go with him even more when I see that forlorn look that reveals such sensitivity a stranger is pursuing me* yes," he heard himself say. "Let's hurry."

The man gave his name, Sam. It was too cold for them to take out their hands and shake. They walked a block and a half and entered a building that looked run-down even in the poor street lighting. Sam's apartment was a fifth-floor walk-up. The steps sagged to one side as they climbed them. Phil couldn't tell where the faint light was coming from—it just seemed to float about the stairway like mist.

"The heat's a problem here," Sam warned, and indeed, the apartment was not much warmer than the stairs. Phil could see all three rooms from the tiny hallway just inside the door where he stood: a bedroom to the left, a small kitchen to the right, and directly ahead a room with no recognizable purpose aside from housing stacks of unpacked cardboard boxes and books. The floor was strewn with newspapers and rags that had what looked like white plaster all over them. Several green trash bags were stuffed and tied and heaped against the far wall. It was close to squalid *I wish I had a place like this myself*

Sam said, "This way," and they moved into the bedroom. He shut the door behind them and turned on the three space heaters that were set up around the bed. They lit up gradually, humming, casting the room in a toasty orange glow.

Sam undressed; Phil followed suit. Sam climbed into bed but Phil remained where he was, standing naked in the warming air. Even at thirty-one, Phil was fairly innocent sexually. His life in the service of God had afforded him a few opportunities, but he was mostly too scared to take them. Since then, Phil hadn't exactly intended to be chaste, but chastity by this time had become a bad habit. So he was a passive creature in sex, following the lead of the other, taking Sam's hand when it was extended. He was almost like a clay figure being molded, the way Sam was pushing and steering the direction of his body on the bed, a pleasing breathless blend of gentle instruction and passionate insistence. He was in the hands of someone who knew the uses of the hands, what rough and subtle pressures they could apply, when they should lift *breathing* or hold down *shuddering* or clamp shut. Phil abandoned himself.

sleeping

3.

In the middle of the night, Phil sat up in a panic.

"What's wrong?" said Sam. He had been awake.

Nothing was familiar. "My mother . . . I mean, I have an appointment tomorrow, this morning . . ." He rubbed his eyes to hide his embarrassment *here I am after all a man with a few white hairs on my chest already the mirror leaning against the bedroom wall shows me still worried about*

"You're a strange one, Phil," Sam said. "You're so bright, so handsome *handsome he said* you obviously believe in God. But you seem so nervous. What's wrong?"

Phil turned away, a little hurt. "You're funny, too." He looked around at the books that were stacked against the wall and tumbling from beneath the bed. "I never met a carpenter who read so much."

"I'm not a carpenter. That's just what I do for money. Come with me. I'll show you what I really do." Sam leapt out of bed. Phil followed. The cold air rushed to surround them and they clung to one another, naked, scampering across the littered floor, into the darkness of the apartment. Phil stepped on something slippery and nearly went down, but Sam's strong hands kept him up. He was led to a room in the back that he had not seen when he first came in.

"This is not the light they should be seen in," Sam explained.

"Daylight is ideal." He snapped a switch and a series of large over-hanging lamps flickered to life.

The room was much larger than the others. One wall was lined with large curtainless windows that showed the sky. Against the other three walls were what Phil figured to be abstract sculptures, some as small as a hand, one or two as large as a refrigerator. Most of them were covered with plaster and seemed to sweep upward, resembling frozen white fire. "It's not plaster," the sculptor ex-plained. "It's a more moldable mixture I make myself. It doesn't dry as fast and it gives me the bulk and texture I need—Please don't touch!"

"I'm sorry. They're beautiful. Have you ever made any money from them?" Phil regretted the question as soon as he asked it. The sculptor shivered and Phil embraced him.

"Not so far," Sam said, "but I'm hopeful." Together they noticed the dawn arching overhead. Then Sam led Phil back to bed.

"So what do you do, handsome?"

how much does he know how much did he hear nothing. I had a job, but I quit. The appointment I have this morning at nine is an inter-view. It'll be my last interview ever."

"You sound confident." He paused. The walls snapped inexpli-cably. "Why did you quit the priesthood?" Sam said.

I just told you why

"So you do know. You did hear."

"You seem so unhappy. Do you regret leaving?"

"No. I regret it for others, maybe, but not for myself. I do miss it at times, but only because it's the only life I've ever known."

"Why would you leave the only life you've ever known?"

Phil took a long breath, the way his father did when he wanted to speak. He proceeded to tell Sam everything, about Arthur Antez, about the passage from Romans slipped under his door, about how they made him a priest only with reservations and how they exiled him to St. Cloud with the ornery Father Connell.

"I still don't get it," Sam said *I just told you* they didn't stop you from doing your job as a priest, did they? They didn't interfere with that, did they?"

Phil trembled in the cold. Sam held him tighter.

"Don't you miss your parishioners?"

"No, I don't *it's not because I think I'm better than they are it's because I think I'm worse* except for one *Marty Broom* him I miss *you wouldn't think a man like that had sins to confess*

"I wouldn't think a man like you would."

confession purges you're absolutely right

"I was hearing confessions. Marty came in *there are some things that cannot be said* there were these screens that were supposed to keep penitents anonymous, but I could always tell who it was. I hated that."

I'd never heard a confession from Marty some vows must be broken I could see through the screen that he was disturbed his flinching face he told me he was attracted to men he'd always been attracted to men ever since he could remember he always tried to ignore how he felt but lately the feelings were growing in him every day since I'd come to town he broke down in tears this big handsome burly man this father of seven married twenty-two years

"Tears are fine," Sam said. "Go ahead."

"He said he never told anyone before. I was the first one he told *it seemed like I should have said something then but I didn't I sort of froze it was the last thing I was expecting* he said he knew the feelings were wrong. He begged me for forgiveness, as if he'd ever done anything at all to me *but he wasn't talking to me I realized* he was talking to every priest he'd ever known. He was talking to the Church. He was talking to God even. It was a very uncomfortable position to be in *God's position I mean I knew I couldn't tell him what God thought* so I told him what every priest he'd ever known thought, what the Church thought. I told him to be a man and to fight vigilantly against the feelings that he knew were wrong *I knew even as I was saying it Marty had confessed my sins not his and I panicked a little I got paranoid somehow I thought he was really talking about me he knew something* when he saw my coldness, he composed himself and apologized. I said there was no need to apologize to me and I gave him his penance *a harsh one* and he left. At Mass that afternoon, I noticed he didn't help with the collection, and afterward he didn't hang around. I tried to catch him *even though I knew I had done what I should have as a priest I wanted to show him some of the friendliness that had seemed so natural between us I even during the Secret confessed to a fantasy I had about taking him back to the rectory and making love to him*

"Fantasies are nothing to confess," said Sam.

"But he brushed me off *avoided looking at me* he said his family was getting ready for a trip to his wife's parents up in Canada and they wanted to make it before nightfall. Apparently, though, it was only his wife and kids that went, because he gassed himself to death the next day in his sealed-off garage. Carbon monoxide poisoning. His kids found him when they came back that night. One of them broke lose from his mother and ran screaming it down the street. 'Our Daddy's dead! Our Daddy's dead!'"

Phil nestled his face into the space between Sam's arm and his chest. He pushed his face into the wetness there.

"I'm afraid," he said brokenly, "that sometime soon I'll have to join him."

"Quiet," Sam said. He slid down and put both arms around him, letting Phil rest his head on his chest. In a short time they were both asleep.

quiet you

quiet

They awoke several hours later, exactly at the same time. The small digital clock across the room flashed 9:01, 9:02. They remained still and silent a minute, watching their breath dissipate in the frigid air. Then, without saying a word, Sam got up, put on his robe, and went into his studio. Phil stayed in the bed, edging into the warm impression his lover had left him.

THE HOST

1

When he opened the door, I was smiling. I shouldn't have been. I wasn't happy, God knows, or amused, or even nervous. But somehow I thought that even though I was arriving at this man's door on only the scantest pretext of acquaintanceship, with no money and no indication of where I was coming from or going to, he would think I was a perfectly normal person if only I showed up smiling.

I walked in like I owned the place. Months before a man in a bar was very impressed with the way I entered it. He said, after taking me home, "Always walk in that way, wherever you go." So I always did.

My first impression of Meyersohn's apartment was that it was warm and safe, with walls and a floor and a ceiling. Later I would notice other things. Like the overall cramped feeling of the place. And the impractical arrangement of the furniture, which put you in constant danger of being jabbed or tripped up by some edge or corner. And then there were the houseplants that crowded every window, all of them with the same brown disease creeping up their leaves.

A meal was all laid out for me on the table. That gave us something to talk about.

"Take more of those delicious peas!" he said.

"Thanks."

"Help yourself to that wonderful bread!" he said.

"I think I will."

"And there's plenty more chicken!"

That voice. Lilting. Severely sibilant. Over the phone it had given an impression of culture and refinement. In person it came off as a sort of British-sounding affectation, probably adopted to dress up an inexorable homosexual's lisp.

"Let me get you some more milk," he said.

The chicken was dry and hard to chew and the peas were shriveled. The milk he poured me was warm and a little sour. Still, I ate an awful lot, being much hungrier than I realized. Meyersohn watched me as I ate, saying he'd already had his supper. He was sitting straight up in his chair with his hands folded on the table.

"What do your parents do, Neal?" he said.

"Not much. They're dead." (That was only half-true.)

"Oh. Well, what *did* they do, then?"

I wanted to say I was an orphan, just to end the whole investigation, but I didn't think I could pull off that lie, not right then anyway. So I just told him the truth.

"My father was a printer."

"I see!" he said. "That makes perfect sense."

"It does?"

"Absolutely. I could tell even over the phone that you were of the working class. The accent. The bluntness of your answers. And now, the way you keep your elbows on the table when you eat. Oh, no! I didn't mean to make you self-conscious about it, Neal. Put your elbows back! I find it charming! Here, take another chicken leg. Now tell me. What's your background?"

I thought I understood then. This was the initial interrogation. He wanted to know if I planned on stabbing him and stealing his wallet.

"I've always managed to stay out of trouble," I said. "I've never been arrested. I've never even had a run-in with the police." That was the truth.

"No, I mean what's your *ethnic* background."

"Oh. Well—"

"Irish?"

"Um. Yeah." I didn't know that for sure, but if it made him happy. Which it seemed to.

"I knew it! It's written all over your face. The pug nose. The crooked mouth." Then he adopted an Irish brogue and said, "Ay! He's got a bit of the old sod in 'im, he does!"

I smiled and brought the glass of milk to my lips. I thought, Okay, a little eccentric, but he'll do.

"Tell me about your old Irish mother, Neal."

I had had enough of this prying. "All these plants," I said, looking around suddenly. "They're so nice." A plain contradiction of fact. But if I'd learned one thing about childless unmarried men in their fifties, it's that they loved to hear their plants complimented.

"Why, thank you, Neal," he said. "I think they add a bit of life to the place. Most of them were castoffs, the poor darlings. I found them and brought them home. My parents were farmers, so I have a special affinity for things that grow in the dirt. Do you know what affinity means, Neal?"

"Sure."

"Really?"

"It's a liking for something. Or someone."

"How impressive! The way with words you Irish have. And your father a printer. It all makes such sense! Do you have any brothers or sisters, Neal?"

"It was your word, not mine," I said, trying to deflect the attention away from me.

"But it was your definition. And you came up with it instantly, as anyone of your kind would have."

I swallowed the piece of chicken I was chewing and smiled good-naturedly. I had no desire to contradict him, but he seemed to need correcting on a few points. I said, as innocuously as I could, "But you can't just say that. What if someone said to you, 'Oh, you're just saying that because your ancestors were whatever they were.'?"

"But you know, Neal, there are some things I would say just because my ancestors were what they were."

"Like what?"

"Like, 'Run, Ben! It's a group of Irish hoodlums!'" He laughed hysterically. He choked himself off when he saw I wasn't laughing with him.

"You shouldn't stereotype people," I said, smiling pleasantly.

"Now he's using the word stereotype! Amazing! But you know, Neal, in all stereotypes, there's a grain of truth."

"If there's only a grain of truth, then there must be much more to them that isn't true."

"Oh, no! I won't get into word games with you! I've been beaten up enough by Irish kids—the ones in my town while I was growing up. They were terrible."

"They used to beat you up?"

"Well, no. Not me. But my brother Eli got beat up. I always knew when to run. Eli never did."

"Did he get beat up a lot?"

"Well, there are lots of ways to get beaten up, Neal. There's the jeering and the taunting, which I admit I also never experienced firsthand, though my brother Eli did. And then there's the exclusion, the snubbing. The feeling that you're not worth wasting the punches on in the first place." And for the first time since I arrived, the smile left Meyersohn's face and he looked at the air in front of him as if he was seeing again the hatred he inspired. It gave me the sensation that it probably was him, and not his brother, that had suffered everything he'd been describing.

But the next instant he was grinning stupidly again. "Eli's big mistake," he said, "was that he always tried to make the gentiles like him. And there was no way that they ever would. Eli wouldn't even go out with the Jewish girls in our town. He said they were all trash. He was right about that. He ended up marrying an Irish Catholic, you know. Our mother had a conniption fit."

"I guess he persuaded at least one of them to like him, then," I said, finding myself with the strange burden of having to elevate the conversation.

"Jeannie," he said, apparently referring to his brother's wife. "She just pitied him. I don't think she ever really loved him. I don't think she ever loved anyone. And she herself is a real cunt."

I was a person who liked to swear. There was a certain visceral release that came with uttering those kinds of words. But that word, cunt, at least as it came out of Meyersohn's mouth at that moment, disgusted me.

"You two don't get along?" I said in a level tone.

"I doubt she'll ever be able to get over those ancient Hibernian teachings."

I couldn't help chuckling at that. There was nothing left to say, besides. I was being treated to a clown-like display to which there was no appropriate response. I half-expected him to ask me if I knew what Hibernian meant.

"Oh, don't laugh, Neal," he said, laughing himself. "If my mother ever got a look at you she would have said to me, 'Stay far away from that one and his friends, Benjamin!'"

"That would've been easy," I said. "I've never had any friends."

We both laughed. Now I was grateful, strangely enough, to be talking about me rather than him.

I stood up and announced that I would do the dishes.

"Absolutely not, Neal. You're the guest and I'm the host."

"No, Ben. I insist." I started carrying the plates into the kitchen before he could say anything more. From the glance I stole he seemed as impressed as I hoped he'd be, probably thinking it was my old Irish mother that taught me my manners.

That night I had sex with Meyersohn because I thought that's what he was expecting. To this day I don't know if he really was expecting it, but I do know it was a revolting disaster.

We went to bed not long after I finished the dishes. Meyersohn insisted I looked "a little ragged" and that a good night's sleep would "do wonders" for me. That struck me as the most thoughtful line anyone had ever used to get me into bed. But I really was tired. I stripped to my underwear and jumped under the covers while he was in the bathroom. I laid back on something hard. I pulled from beneath me a remote control, presumably for the TV in the corner of the room. Then there was something else, under my shoulder blade. It was a peach pit, brown and shriveled though still a little moist. I flung it away as soon as I figured out what it was. It bounced off the wall and fell back behind the TV somewhere.

Meyersohn emerged from the bathroom wearing nothing but a terry cloth wraparound and a four-inch bumpy pink scar that bisected his chest from the sternum to the top of his stomach. I was quietly horrified. He told me later the scar was from a heart operation he had three years earlier. He snapped off the light and, thankfully, I couldn't see anything anymore.

He climbed into bed next to me. For several minutes I waited for him to make a move on me. When he didn't, I began to think he was devising a way of asking me to leave the next day—we never discussed how long my visit might be. That worried me. Because I didn't need Meyersohn to tell me I looked ragged. I was aware of that already. What I needed more than anything was a rest, a place to just stop and think, and now that I was warm in bed with a full stomach, this place seemed as good as any.

I had a hard-on, usually the case when I laid down to sleep, no matter where I was. I could get a hard-on at almost any time, even when thinking of the most unsexy things—that scar on Meyersohn's chest, for instance. He was lying on his side, facing away from me. I threw the blanket away to expose my cock and said, "Ben." Meyersohn didn't move. Again I said, "Ben." He turned around. Looking back on it, I think he may have been asleep already.

I waved my cock at him. I said something like, "Why don't you take care of this for me?" He leaned over and without a word he put his mouth on it.

The rest should have been simple. He should have sucked me and I should have cum. But he wouldn't suck. He just held his mouth on my cock, not moving, not making any sound. I kept waiting for him to start. We must have stayed in that position for a good minute before I felt a cold trickle run down past my balls to the crack of my ass—he was letting the saliva escape his mouth. It sort of disgusted me. I was close to bolting from the bed when I felt another cold wetness, this time spreading down my left leg. Meyersohn had cum. He took his mouth off my cock and said, "My my." Then he got out of bed, appearing a little disoriented but pleased. He disappeared into the bathroom.

I waited for him to come back, laying in bed in a mortified state, before I went to the bathroom myself. At the sink I scrubbed my cock and balls and ass and left leg as if they'd been contaminated somehow. When I wasn't satisfied with that, I drew the curtain and took a shower, a scaldingly hot one. The whole time I was saying to myself, Who cums cold? All the cum that had ever touched my skin—and there had been a lot—was always steamy hot at first, and then grew cold. I kept scrubbing and examining the spot on my leg the cum had touched, not knowing what I'd find there and in fact not finding anything. I stepped out of the shower and fished from the closet what looked like a fresh towel. I draped it over my head and just held it there a minute. I was sort of at a loss as to what to think, and I even felt like crying. On the one hand, the old guy seemed to be satisfied with what went on. On the other hand, I wasn't, and I wasn't talking about sexual satisfaction either. That I would never have expected from him in the first place. What I meant was a contentment about where I was and where I planned to remain for the foreseeable. Meyersohn's place was warm and had food, like I said. A real shelter. But there was also this malignant feeling that I just couldn't shake. Something about this place and this person—not something, but everything, from the food and the talk to the sex and the damp medicinal smell of the towel I was us-ing—all of it was off somehow, it was warped and sickening, like the tilt-a-whirl. And it wasn't me. It would never have occurred to me to think it was.

When I came out, Meyersohn had the TV going and was flip-ping the channels with the remote control.

"I hope you don't mind that I used your shower," I said.

"Certainly not." He smiled. I smiled back. He threw back the covers on my side and invited me to lay down. A shudder went through me and I told him I didn't think I could sleep just yet and would rather stay up awhile, if that was alright with him. I turned and went into the main room and sat at the table there. Being actu-ally very tired, I rubbed my eyes. When I opened them again, Mey-ersohn was standing in the doorway in his little terry cloth skirt. His chest scar seemed almost to be throbbing with the way he breathed.

I realized now that he must have been nervous about a stranger being awake in his apartment while he slept. He used the pretext of needing something to drink. He went into the kitchen. I could still see him and he could still see me. He took a glass from the cabinet above the sink, a glass I had washed and put there myself. He opened the refrigerator. There was no light in it, and no other light was on, but I could see everything clearly. He poured himself some orange juice and sipped it in front of the open door. He went, "Mmmm . . . ," very loudly, like it was some sort of goddam TV commercial.

He said, "Would you like some juice, Neal?"

"No. Thank you."

I continued to sit at the table and he continued to stand in front of the refrigerator, leaning on the open door, sipping very slowly. It didn't take me long to realize it wouldn't do any good to wait him out. So I said I was tired and, though I was, I could only pretend to yawn. I went into the bedroom. He followed me less than a minute later.

I kept waking up throughout the night, wary of one thing, afraid of another, unable to move for fear of touching that wet spot somewhere on the bed, very near me. One of the times I woke up famished, which I thought was odd since I'd eaten so much supper. Meyersohn was snoring away. Carefully I crept from the bed. In the kitchen, I gorged on the leftover chicken legs and orange juice. I ate in the dark, standing up in front of the open refrigerator. With my stomach full, it seemed it would be easier to get back to sleep.

Meyersohn wasn't snoring anymore when I returned to the bedroom, but he was laying in the exact same position. Carefully I climbed back into bed. When I was settled in, he turned toward me and said, "Feel better?" I was suddenly enraged at being deceived like that. I wanted to kill him. He put his hand on my crotch then, and I flinched if I didn't actually cringe. He said, "If we're going to do that again, we'll have to get some prophylactics."

Meyersohn had a job doing God knows what at some kind of non-profit organization. When he got up the next morning—we seemed to get up at more or less the same time because I was laying there waiting for him to awaken—I said, "So what would you like to do today?" I wanted to be the first to speak.

"There's nothing I'd like better than to spend the day frolicking with you, Neal. But unfortunately my workload is so heavy that I have to bring some of it home with me on the weekends."

He was kicking me out already, I thought.

"But you're welcome to spend the day reading if you want. There are shelves just full of books in the study. Or you can watch television, if you keep the sound down. And tonight, I promise we'll do something together!"

So I guess he hadn't grown tired of me yet.

Over breakfast I asked him what was the work he had to do.

"Oh. I have to write a grant proposal. For an exhibition we want to do."

"What's it about?" I said. He answered. But since I asked only because I wanted him to think I cared and not because I was actually interested, I don't remember the answer exactly. Something to do with American history. And as he elaborated on the topic, I kept nodding my head and smiling and the whole time I was thinking, These are the runniest fried eggs I've ever had in my life.

"You probably have an instinctive understanding of that," Meyersohn was saying, "being an Irishman."

I nodded. I had no idea what he was talking about.

Then Meyersohn got an idea. I could tell by the way his face looked as though it was about to say something but was holding it back on purpose, savoring it a little.

"Neal," he said, "why don't you help me write the proposal?"

I was a little surprised—I mean, someone like him asking someone like me to do something like that.

"Come on," he said. "You were smart in school. You know the meanings of words."

"I don't know anything about what you're writing about."

"It doesn't matter! What do you say, Neal? It'll make it a lot less boring for me."

So I said yes, not being in a position to say no.

After breakfast I did the dishes and then we settled ourselves in front of the computer on Meyersohn's desk. I'd never seen one before, but Meyersohn said he'd do all the typing. He wore a delighted expression as he set everything up. "Now let's just pull this over here . . . there! Now, you can sit in this chair and I'll sit here and that way we can both see the screen. Can you see? Good. Now. Maybe we need a fresh pot of coffee to get us started. Would you like some nice coffee?"

After a lot of that sort of thing, we got to work. I didn't think I'd have much to contribute, but Meyersohn was convinced I was a valuable asset. He punched up whatever he had to on the computer and let out a heavy sigh.

"So," I said, "what's this about again?"

"It's about me getting the shitty assignments, thanks to that cunt at work."

I paused to digest that. "No, I mean what's this project supposed to be about?"

He made a face to show his utter boredom with the whole business. Then he said, "Oh, it's just about how the established fucking asshole immigrants in this country reacted to the boatloads of new fucking asshole immigrants that were arriving in the 1800s."

"Why were they all fucking assholes?"

"Oh, I don't know."

"So how did they react?"

"Well. The ones that were already here helped the new ones in a lot of ways. They let them into their network of institutions—businesses, hospitals. They gave them places to live"—here I flinched a little but I don't think Meyersohn noticed; he actually seemed to have tapped into a reservoir of knowledge he had somewhere in his head and was rather impressively listing its contents—"but then, in other ways, they hurt them. They gave them the dirtiest jobs. They held them back socially. They looked down on them and made fun of them privately. They really thought they were the scum of the earth." Meyersohn glanced over at me, then turned back to the computer screen and said, "I wish I didn't have to do this."

"You seem to know what you're saying."

"Ha! It's all him!" He pointed to a book open on the desk next to the computer.

"Who?" I said.

"Ephraim Zain. Have you ever heard of him, Neal? Ephraim Zain probably wrote the history book they used in your public school. He's one of the greatest living historians—until he died last year, that is." Then he showed me the exact place in the Ephraim Zain book where he lifted what he just told me.

"You're stealing from this book?" I said, just to clarify.

He adopted a haughty, smiling expression. "That's exactly what I'm doing. This is just one of those things that everybody does but no one talks about, like wiping your ass. Besides, Zain's dead. And no one will ever know."

"*You'll* know," I said, rather incidentally.

He waved his hand in front of his face as if to say, Now that's something that really doesn't matter.

"There are no new thoughts, Neal," he went on. I guess he felt the need to say more after I failed to congratulate him on what he told me already. "Years ago, I taught history at a community college in the Bronx. All freshman survey classes. I hated it. But the point is this: At first I tried to follow the department's guidelines, but it got to be too much, day after day. So eventually I started making things up as I went along. Just a little embellishment of the facts, to make it more interesting to them and to myself. And then one day, one of the students challenged me on something I said—I forget what, some interesting tidbit I'd made up about how the slaves were treated on the galleys. Do you know what a galley is, Neal? So the student said to me, 'That's not true. You made that up.' And do you know what I said to him? I said, 'You're absolutely correct. I was bored and I made it up.' And then I went right along teaching the class. No one ever said anything about it again. Not the students, not the school. Nobody cared, and the same is true of this."

What struck me most about Meyersohn's speech was not the extent of self-degradation he went to, but the big smile he had on his face while he did so. He seemed to be dying to demonstrate what a fucking asshole he was. And he did it with such energy and articulation I couldn't help but sense a considerable, if seriously malformed, intelligence. Up until then I had thought of him simply as a buffoon. Now I saw just how impossibly complex a buffoon he was.

The writing of the proposal was torturous—for me, anyway. Meyersohn had no ideas of his own. He'd copy a little from the book, then ask me a question about it. I'd give him some feeble answer, adding that I knew nothing about the subject, and Meyersohn would copy it down anyway, saying, "That's good! What else?" Not once did he contribute an original thought. He pulled out a couple more Ephraim Zain books and a couple of books by some other people and, opening one up, said, "Let's see what we can take from here." It was shameless, yes, but so bizarrely overt. He seemed to want to think that it was not so bad as long as he was being so open about it. Or maybe he thought that if he let someone else in on it, thereby distributing the guilt, then he was less guilty. Or maybe he truly didn't care. In any case, to me, Meyersohn's honesty about his dishonesty made the original deed that much more appalling, and him that much more repugnant.

Early in the afternoon, the work was completed. I was dazed. I hadn't said anything more than one or two words long in the last hours, and had been reduced to dictating parts of books to Meyersohn as he typed into the computer. But now the computer was shut off and Meyersohn stood, stretching.

"It's past lunchtime," he announced. "Why don't we go to the grocery store together!"

But I couldn't stand to be around him another minute.

"I'm really tired," I said, inducing a yawn. "Can't I stay here and take a nap while you do that?"

I could tell he had doubts about that. But I just walked into the bedroom and climbed into bed. I put my face in the pillow and made like I was nodding off. When I didn't move at all for a few minutes, he leaned over and kissed my neck and left for the grocery store.

First I heard his keys jingling outside the door. He locked the heavy top lock, which seemed to rumble in the walls, then the flimsy bottom one, which gave off a light snapping sound. The keys jingled again as they were taken away. Ever so slightly, I heard the footfalls in the corridor as they headed for the elevator. I waited. Then, just as I expected, the keys jingled outside the door and the bottom lock snapped and the top lock rumbled in the walls and Meyersohn burst back in, his footfalls coming in the direction of the bedroom.

I hadn't moved a muscle. I could feel the disturbance his head made in the air when he poked it into the room. I was snoring lightly.

Then, satisfied, he went to the goddam store.

I jumped out of bed. I knew I didn't have much time. There were several places to look. I went to the desk where the computer was in the bedroom. It had three drawers. I pulled the top one open and started to pick through the junk. I took anything I could get, pennies, subway tokens. Then I went through the second drawer but the only coins I found there were foreign ones, strangely shaped and colored and utterly useless. I opened the third drawer, which would only open slowly due to a partly fallen-through bottom. It was filled with all sorts of scattered papers and envelopes. I went through them carefully, looking under each one. I found a little more change, but nothing like I was hoping to find, not even enough to get a drink with.

The papers in that drawer were mostly official-looking. I was making a conscious effort not to look at them too carefully. I was getting that sick, tilt-a-whirl feeling again. I felt I knew too much about Meyersohn already, much more than I wanted to know, much more than was healthy. Just sifting through his stuff this way was giving me the sensation of being contaminated. But when I came across a small piece of yellow notebook paper, which looked so different than the other papers, I couldn't help but read the few handwritten words on it:

I am a liar and a plagiarist and a bore.

Underneath that was the signature of Ben Meyersohn.

It was bizarre, this little scrawled confession, the purpose of which I couldn't understand. But in a strange way it made me feel better. I thought, So you *do* have some shame, some knowledge of the limits you transgress. I took a little comfort in that. And I was actually able to feel a little sorry for the guy.

My ears pricked up: footfalls. I slipped the note back and eased the drawer into place. Already the second lock was unlocked by the time I got it in. I leapt for the bed but I was breathing too hard to pull off sleep. So I awoke just as Meyersohn walked into the room with a grocery bag. Now that I thought of it, I was kind of hungry.

2.

The organization Meyersohn worked for wasn't in New York but in Washington, D.C., where he kept another apartment, living there Monday to Friday. I reacted with uncertainty when he told me this news the following morning, a Monday. To my great relief, he didn't ask me to leave but instead made me "promise" to take care of the plants until he got back on Friday. I said, "No problem," smiling for real for once. He left me keys and a certain amount of money—not a whole lot, just enough to make my eyes bug out—and said it was for food and to leave whatever I didn't use in the top drawer of the bureau. I said, "You bet."

Meyersohn was dressing in a suit and hurriedly packing a small bag. He went to the computer and printed out the proposal we worked on together. "I'll call on Wednesday," he said.

I was sitting at the table with my hands together, practically in prayer formation. Unfortunately he felt the need to lean down and kiss me on the lips before he left.

The door closed. The top lock was locked, then the bottom. I sat at the table, still quiet and still not moving. I heard the elevator in the hall opening and closing. Still, I waited. After a minute I got up and went to the study. This room had a sofa, a stereo, lots of books and records on shelves lining the walls, and a window that looked directly down on the lobby door. I threw the window open and peeked my head through. I saw Meyersohn in his long coat and briefcase emerge onto the street. He hailed a taxi and got in. I watched the taxi drive away until I couldn't see it anymore.

Whatever goals I might have had in life seemed right then to have been suddenly achieved. I had an apartment all to myself, in the middle of New York City, with money in my pocket, and I was not yet dead.

I realized how hungry I was, and went to the kitchen. There wasn't much in the refrigerator except for a few raw potatoes on the bottom shelf. I recalled faintly how my mother used to peel them, boil them, and mash them. That struck me as way too much trouble. So I took the money that Meyersohn left me, about sixty dollars, and went out.

I admit that I'd become something of a wild animal before I arrived at Meyersohn's, skulking and scavenging and sniffing around, trying to fulfill whatever the needs and desires of the moment were. But I'd never felt wilder than I did right then when I walked out the lobby door and hit the street. It seemed to me that for sixty dollars the whole of Manhattan was mine. And I must have been looking exceptional because not one person I passed on the street failed to look me over. I turned the corner and went into a diner and had myself a breakfast of pancakes, bacon, sausages, ham, toast, orange juice and two cups of coffee. The waitress regarded me with suspicion and talked about me with the cook. I couldn't hear anything but she was moving her lips like a bad ventriloquist as she made coffee, while the cook cast sidelong glances at me.

I thought that maybe it wasn't that I looked so exceptional. Maybe I looked crazy. It made me a little angry. I thought of making a dash for it without paying, but decided I was sitting too far from the door. They both looked relieved when I went up to the cash register. The waitress even smiled a little and said, "Thank you" as she handed me my change. Right then I leaned forward and spit in her face. It was unexpected for me too, having thought of it and done it at exactly the same moment. And as soon as I did it, I turned and ran out the door. For a split second I looked back. I saw the waitress standing in front of the open cash drawer. She was holding her hands the way she might hold a baby but her fingers were curled. She had on her face a twisted expression of pain, as if a knife had been plunged into her back. I turned away and hurried through the crowd on the street in a wildly excited state. After a couple of blocks, I calmed down and started walking at a more normal pace.

That night, I was seeing what was on the videotapes Meyersohn had stacked behind the television. I put the first one in and pressed PLAY. The image of a woman screaming flashed on the screen. Instantly I recalled the waitress' face with my spit hanging off it and it greatly upset me. I shut off the tape. I became very sad and sunk down on the bed and cried about what I had done. I wanted to run to the diner then, find her, apologize to her, give her a really big tip. It was at that moment that I realized what a poor wild animal I made. Because, though I tried, I could never forget what I was doing. There were no moments of pure instinctual relish, no action I took that spoke solely for itself. Everything was tainted, or at least adulterated, by an unforgiving awareness.

For the next few days I felt exhausted and laid low. Actually, those days were, in a way, extraordinary. I watched television, which I hadn't seen in a long time, and let myself become absorbed in it the way I did when I was little. Even when I was not interested in the content, I kept it on for the sound of people talking. When I was tired I slept, and I kept on sleeping until I wasn't tired anymore. When I was hungry, I went to the refrigerator, which I had stocked somewhat, and ate.

Late in the week, I awoke in the middle of the night in a restless state. I dressed and took what money was left and went out, to a bar. There was one in the neighborhood and when I went in I realized I had been there before—probably it was where I first met Meyersohn. I sat at the bar the whole time, not cruising at all. I was content to be able to just sit and enjoy a drink. Several men came up to me. One, a burly, bearded guy with warm eyes, asked me to come back to his apartment, which was in the neighborhood. I said yes.

The sex was pleasing and unrushed, even affectionate. Afterwards we talked with astonishing intimacy. For some reason, maybe a desire for absolution, I told him about the episode with the waitress, although I related it in a laughing, almost proud manner that reminded me disturbingly of Meyersohn. He frowned and told me I shouldn't have done that. I said, "I know," feeling contrite again.

He asked me to stay the rest of the night with him. I said no. "I have to be getting home," I said. Then he said alright, that it was okay if I didn't stay, as long as I didn't go just yet. He told me to lay down next to him and tell him about myself, in particular he wanted to know about my family. He handed me a scotch he'd just poured, and I ended up staying if not the night, then long into it. I opened up to him partly because I liked him, I suppose, but mostly because I knew I would never see him again.

I told him about my father, a hard-working man with a weak constitution. In fact, my father's health was so bad that my memories of him consisted mostly of his evolution from ulcers to heart attacks (two) to, finally, cancer of the intestine, with my mother constantly hovering between him and us kids, fearful that we would aggravate his condition in some way. It turned out the doctor he'd had, the same doctor who'd seen him through the ulcers and the heart attacks, misread an x-ray that showed his tumor in an early stage, failing to notice it and take action until it had reached a fatal size. After a lot of encouragement from Maureen, the oldest of us nine siblings, he sued the doctor. It was hard for my father to do, since the doctor was old and white-haired and genial and had himself a large family to feed. But Maureen, who was very shrewd about these things, kept telling him how he'd never live to see his grandkids the way the doctor would, and eventually she stoked my father's anger to the point where a lawyer was brought to the house, one she had waiting in the wings. The lawyer seemed delighted to see so many kids. The rotten condition the house was in pleased him too.

He brought with him a man who operated a video camera. The

cameraman taped every pathetic gurgle my father could emit as he sat slumped at the kitchen table. Whenever my father came up with anything really juicy, usually involving either wrenching physical pain or the loss of some trivial joy—a highball during a game of horseshoes out in the yard, for example—the cameraman would turn the lens and the lawyer would nodded encouragingly.

We younger children, who were told to leave the kitchen while all of this was going on, huddled at the kitchen doorway to watch. The only thing my father would look at while he spoke was the table. My mother sat adjacent to him, trying to avert her eyes from the blinking video equipment set up on the table next to her. She seemed almost ashamed of the whole business. Maureen sat very businesslike with her hands folded, across from my father. The lawyer completed the square.

At the times when my father broke down, everyone was quiet and still and all eyes were riveted on him. His face was bony and had an inky pall cast over it due to an absurdly dark hairpiece.

When he finished with my father, the lawyer asked my mother, and then Maureen, to say something for the camera. "The court places a high value on the suffering of the family," he said. My mother spoke of how unfair it was that she would be left to carry on by herself, becoming more red-eyed and broken-voiced as she went on. Maureen, who was dry-eyed during the most wrenching of my father's testimony, promptly burst into sobs when the camera turned her way.

Then the lawyer turned to us kids and said, "It would be good to get a word from the younger ones. That always gets at the emotions. One boy and one girl." He wasn't encouraging any certain two of us, but waited instead for a couple of volunteers. We fidgeted. There were a couple of false starts. Then my mother said, "Patrice. Why don't you?"

My sister Patrice stepped forward. She was blubbering a little bit. The man turned the camera on her face. She spoke unsurely, looking at the floor. "Well. I just think it's lousy that, you know, we have to be without a father from now on," she said, as if Dad was already dead, "and that Mum'll have to carry on by herself and that Daddy won't grow up to see his grandkids." Patrice ended her statement by running from the room sobbing. My father during all of this had his face buried in his hands and was not moving at all, as if he was listening very carefully. The lawyer was beaming.

"And which of you boys would like to say something?" he said.

We fidgeted some more. I wanted to be the one, but I felt I should wait for my mother to say, like she did with Patrice. I kept looking into my mother's eyes and looking away again. And I really thought she would pick me. Patrice and I were only a year apart, and she was standing right next to me when she was chosen. But my mother picked Vincent, who was four years younger than me and hardly ever said anything. Vincent, though, didn't want to do it. He started wailing. The lawyer tried to coax him to step forward from the bunch but he wouldn't budge and only cried harder. Then my mother told him he didn't have to do it if he didn't want to. That was when I stepped forward. The lawyer smiled at me. To him there was no difference between Vincent and me. My mother, though, looked angry, and Maureen looked uncomfortable.

The small red light on top of the camera blinked on. The man said that meant, "You're on." I was suddenly overcome with embarrassment and could only smile stupidly, which appalled the adults at the table. I had wanted to say something about the discussions my father and I sometimes had, usually about items that appeared in the newspaper. I was a bright kid and my father liked to make me show it, even when our discussions escalated into arguments, as he would often encourage. But I didn't know how to say it. The lawyer encouraged me to, "Go ahead. Just say what you'll miss most about your dad." He said it very gently and kindly, and that put me more at ease.

"Well," I said, still unable to stop smiling, "what I'll miss most is the fights we used to have." The whole table looked at me strangely, except for my father, who still hadn't moved. "What I mean is, I'll miss arguing with him all the time"—that didn't seem to clear up anything. Everyone started squirming. I had to give it one more try. I actually turned to my father, smiling so hard it hurt, and said, "You're so wrong about so many things!"

The red light on the camera blinked off. The lawyer said, "I think I have enough for now."

Less than two years after that meeting, my father died. During that time I began to feel as though I had no obligations to him, since my mother rarely let me or anyone else see him. The times he wasn't in the hospital, she kept him squirreled away in an upstairs room, where she herself spent most of her time. So there was little left for the rest of us to do but go on. Besides which, my awakening sexuality was drawing me further and further away from the house, away from the little Massachusetts town where we lived, and into the city of Boston. The day I turned seventeen I caught the morning show at the Ladylove Cinema. The man in the ticket booth didn't even ask me for my ID, though I had it ready to show him. There, in the bathroom, I had my first sex, with a man just about my father's age.

Before long I was returning to the house a little drunk or with hickeys on my neck. It was only then that my mother called me into my father's room. The sight of my father shocked me. The disease had eaten him into a frail, bald creature who was so pale he was almost translucent. He was laying in bed but was lucid, and had a worried look on his face. I was accused of hanging out with "bad people." I shouted back that the people I was hanging out with were "better people than the people in this house." They failed to appreciate that. More was said, and all of it at top volume, and I left for good that night, checking into a rooming house in the city. The next time I saw any of them was at the funeral.

And it was another year and a half after my father's burial before the doctor agreed to settle out of court. I was working as a drugstore clerk when my mother's call came (I didn't have a phone in my room). I was told to be at the lawyer's office first thing in the morning. That was quite the ceremony. The ten of us packed into that small space. The lawyer making a fuss that enough chairs be brought in from the other offices. Only Maureen dressed up specially. It was never said but was generally understood that each of us kids got roughly the same amount, Maureen substantially more, and our mother the most, which was enough so she wouldn't have to worry for the remaining years of her life. After the checks were handed out, the family commiserated, though not too much. It was hard to feel sad with those checks in our pockets and, besides, we all seemed privately and unthinkably disgusted with one another and wanted to get back to our lives. In the departing mingle, my mother and I found ourselves facing one another. She put a hand on my shoulder, something she'd never done before. She smiled slightly and said, "It's all for the best," as if she knew something I didn't. Then we parted.

On the train back to the city, I looked at the check—almost $11,000—and said to myself, This will go toward something useful. Yet the first things I did were call in sick to the drugstore and go on a bender. But as drunk and high as I got, as lost as I became in the smell and the feel of sex, I kept always in the back of my mind this thought: Soon I'll get down to business.

The problem was, I really didn't know what that entailed. I had no understanding of how $11,000 might change a person's life beyond the most immediate and obvious ways—like being able to call in sick when I wasn't. So, after my initial bash, I began to settle into the patterns that would define my existence for the next year or so. I called in sick to the drugstore more and more, so they fired me. After that, I started dipping into the money to pay the weekly rent at the rooming house. For the first time I discovered what bars looked like in the middle of the day. I found them warm and homey and comfortable, usually there was a television playing, occasionally I would meet someone. I began to go on mysterious walking treks through all parts of the city, excited by something too vague to make out but which nevertheless left my heart with a fluttery feeling. The walks went on for hours. The longer I walked, the more exhilarated I felt. The outer halves of my boot soles wore down. (In this way, I learned my walk was bowlegged.) The few pants and shirts I had were starting to fray, but I scarcely noticed. With all the money I had, it never occurred to me to walk into a store and buy new clothes.

Gradually but inevitably, like the moon moving across the sun, I was losing touch with the things that anchor a person in the world. I slept later and later in the day, sometimes until early evening, and when I woke up I always felt horrible, like I'd done something I shouldn't have and couldn't remember what, or like I hadn't done something I was supposed to. Walking at night, I began to experience the distinct sensation—or nonsensation—of not feeling the ground beneath my feet, and this phenomenon increased the more I walked. The few acquaintances I had dropped away, and the only people I talked to were the men I tricked with and the tellers at the bank I visited every few days to replenish the money I was pissing away. My isolation, the three walls of my room (it was triangle-shaped, adjacent to the furnace in the basement), the vanished burden of having to work to survive, all increased my sense of unreality. The whims and fancies kept in check by daily routine became my constant companions. My appearance grew scarier, my recklessness more dangerous and more desperate. Women crossed to the other side of the street when they saw me coming their way; when I was behind them, they sensed it somehow, clutching their handbags more tightly and picking up the pace. Their reactions made me angry, and I would sputter childish obscenities after them, since I thought it should have been obvious to everyone that I was as incapable of hurting anyone as I was of helping myself.

As unattached as I was becoming, however, I was still aware of my deterioration, and that worried me more than anything else. I went on this way for a period of time I could have measured only if I'd had a calendar.

Then, late one afternoon at one of the bars I was now a regular at, after having failed to snare a curious businessman who wandered in after work, I suddenly felt very ill and had to hold on to the bar for support. When I looked up, the bartender, who had always been so much like a friend, was wearing a disgusted expression. He said, "Christ, go home already—if you have a home. You look like hell." The others at the bar snickered. I caught sight of myself in the mirror across the bar and was shocked to see my tired, sunken eyes. I ran out into the street. I decided what I needed was one of my walks. But although I went as far as downtown, I couldn't shake the sad, sick feeling that was threatening to overtake me completely. Suddenly I was overcome with the most urgent desperation, like I realized I had only minutes to live. It began to sprinkle. I walked into the train station and went to a bank of pay phones.

Not since the meeting at the lawyer's office had I been in touch with my mother. But it occurred to me then, and recurred to me now, that at the time she had acted very cordially toward me. I had to call her collect because all I had on me was a twenty.

"Hi, Mum?"

"Neal?"—and here there were rustling sounds, like she'd laid down the phone and was putting something away. Then she picked up the phone again and said, "Neal? My heavenly days."

"How are you?"

"I'm fine. How are *you*?"

"I was wondering if maybe . . . if I could come out there. To visit. To talk to you."

"Sure."

"Oh. Thank you." I really was grateful.

"Where are you?"

"In town. I can get the train and be out there in forty-five minutes."

"Okay."

"Thanks a lot for this, Mum. I mean it. I really need—" I choked off there because I unexpectedly started to cry. I think it was the kindness in her voice. The way she said "Sure" and "Okay."

"Neal?"

"It's just that . . . I feel that I'm . . ." I stammered out a few more words but they were lost in the sudden torrent of tears. I was soon blubbering, screaming into the phone. The people around me were near horrified, but I cared about nothing at that point except the outlet suddenly available to me and the pain that was pouring through it. Even in the midst of it, however, I was conscious of the change at the other end of the line. A silence had ensued, devoid of breathing even. The line hadn't gone dead but became empty, empty as a three-story ten-room house in which only an aging, self-sufficient widow lived. But I raved on, unable to stop myself. Still, I was in control enough to wind up with this saving plea: ". . . if only you could help, if you could drive me somewhere, to a doctor . . ."

"A doctor?" came the low, cool voice.

I was thinking of a mental hospital when I said that, or maybe I wasn't—I had no idea of what was done with people like me. I only wanted them to do it. I blubbered something to that effect.

"Okay, Neal," my mother said. "Calm down now. I need to find out about some places first. Calm down now, Neal. I'm going to help you. Listen. Let me get the phone book and make a few calls. You're at a pay phone? Okay, call me back in ten minutes."

I hung up. I was calm now. I would call her back in ten minutes. I told her it would have to be collect and she said that was okay. Across the street was a digital bank clock alternately flashing the temperature and time. I kept the ten minutes by that. To pass the time I circled the block twice. All four sides of the block were the enormous downtown train station. A begging homeless person was standing by the back entrance. The first time I passed her I ignored her. My eyes were puffy and red from crying and I was keeping my face down in embarrassment. But the second time my head was up and I felt lighter than I had in a long time. I still couldn't feel the street beneath my feet, but I was remembering it clearly now and was convinced it was merely a case of working my way back using that memory as a map. The beggar shook her cup at me. I halted abruptly in front of her, seized with generosity. I took the twenty out of my pocket and stuffed it into the beggar's cup. She began to thank me but I stopped her. She would have been just as grateful for a quarter.

I went back into the train station and headed right to the same phone. I panicked a little when I saw by the bank clock that eleven minutes had passed. I called my mother's number collect. It rang and rang and no one answered. The operator refused to let it ring more than fifteen times. I called up four other operators and pushed them to their limits too.

I hung up for the last time. I looked around the train station. An elderly lady was waiting to use the phone. I stepped aside and said, "Pardon me." Right then, it seemed very clear to me that I had to leave, leave Boston, leave Massachusetts altogether. It would be impossible to make a fresh start here. And I knew it was right because instead of feeling panicked, I now felt serene. I went into the downtown branch of my bank and withdrew all that remained of the $11,000—still a substantial sum. So I had thousands of dollars in the pocket of my leather jacket when I returned to the train station and got on the next train to New York, where I had been a few times before. I imagined I would set myself up in another rooming house there. Getting an actual apartment didn't seem a possibility to me since that required (or at least I imagined it required) too many complexities. As the train pulled out, I thought about how I'd find a job doing anything before the rest of the money ran out—I even thought I'd be able to earn back some of it. I was soothed by the train jostling me, pushing me this way and that, relieving me of the responsibility for my own movements. I became very excited, planning out the steps I would take once I got to New York, my new home. I would be sensible now, thrifty. The conductor came around and asked for tickets. I said I had to buy one. The conductor shook his head like it was a real shame, saying I could have gotten it five dollars cheaper had I bought it at the station.

But despite all my planning, the truth was I had been out of work too long, my hedonistic habits had become a lifestyle, and the money I had on me meant I could always eat. When I stepped out of Penn Station onto Eighth Avenue, I was conscious again of not feeling the ground. I walked straight to the bars in the Village.

In the ensuing days, I found myself reluctant to go through the bother of getting a room when some genuinely nice guy I'd met was insisting I stay with him for the night. On the nights when there were no such genuinely nice guys, I learned to lower my standards. On nights when there were no offers period, I became increasingly skilled at imposing myself on people.

And then there were the nights when nothing worked. At four a.m. the weary doorman made the rounds, calling out, "Let's go!" He checked the bathrooms, then called out again, "Let's go, guys!" We didn't go, not right away anyway. Instead, we shuffled out a few minutes later, thinking somehow that we'd done it on our own terms. Those who had cars got into them, idled for a minute, and drove away. Those who didn't hung around on the street in front of the bar, eyeing the others. Then they turned around and walked off. From a block away, they'd looked back for the last time.

On these nights I would become horribly depressed and lonely, tired to the point of aching, sitting on a curb or a doorstep with a wad of money in my jacket that anyone could have had for a club on the head or a shot in the back. Even the prospect of finding a room somewhere had now become an impossibly complex undertaking. So I would go to the train station and board the first train to the next city. In this way I moved up and down the eastern seaboard— New York, Philadelphia, Washington, Baltimore, even Wilmington, Delaware (I avoided Boston). While en route to the new desti nation, I would again imagine that I would use the rest of the money to get a place to live and a job once I got there. But again my weaknesses prevailed and I would head straight for the bars, which I was able to locate easily with the help of a small pocket guide taken from some trick's dresser drawer. It was called SEE GAY

AMERICA! and had a drawing of two men with backpacks on (but not shirts), looking back and smiling as they went on their way.

Many departures and arrivals later, I was on a stool in a bar in New York, slumped against the mirrored wall at my right. I had in my hand a nearly finished drink that wasn't mine—someone had put it down and I picked it up to make it look like I'd bought a drink and would therefore not be asked to leave. A drink in my hand also gave me license to sit at the bar and my legs were aching. The money had run out weeks before. I was surviving on whatever I was fed by tricks, a little hustling on the piers in the Village, and the occasional fruit-stand theft.

The men in this bar I had all seen before, if not literally, then in a generic way—and they were as uninterested in me as I was in them. It would be time to move to a new city, had I the money, but the last thing I felt like doing was moving. It was nearly four o'clock, but new men were still coming into the bar. Out of habit, I eyed them up and down. Every one of them looked me over and immediately turned away, never to look again. From that I drew the only conclusion possible: that I was unpleasant to look at. I remembered the nights when four or five men vied for me, and the ephemeral, meaningless thrill that gave me. Now I felt lucky if a guy didn't walk off in the opposite direction the instant he saw me coming.

The bartender tapped the bar. Of course, he said, "Time to go, bud."

I left the drink, got up from the stool, and went to the bathroom. I didn't have to go to the bathroom. I just wanted to see what was there.

Sure enough, standing at one of the two urinals was some guy, mid-to-late forties, with a thin strip of beard graying only at the chin, decked out in a leather jacket, cap, boots, jeans, mirror shades, the whole bit. On most men, this looked like either a costume, like trick-or-treaters who decided to go out this year dressed as Manliness, or like a logical extension of something already found in the man. This guy was on the borderline. The boots and the belt and the cap had a shiny, plastic look, but the jeans were worn and slightly too big, and the T-shirt read CAFETERIA and hung on him inconspicuously.

I moved to the sink to wash my hands. His head was turned in my general direction, but I couldn't tell if he was looking at me because of his glasses. Then he stood back from the urinal to reveal a huge, thick cock hanging halfway to his knees. My eyes must have lit up or something because he smiled at me. Then he stuffed his cock into his pants and said, "Follow Daddy."

I did. Out of the bathroom, out of the bar, and into a taxi that seemed to be waiting there for us at curbside. My mood was improving.

He said his name was J.J., but that I was to call him Daddy. Outside the bar, he looked to me a little leaner than he had in the bathroom. I also noticed he walked like he was drunk, but that seemed to me put on. He told me how handsome I was. He laughed gently whenever I said anything.

"You looked so in need when I saw you there," he said, "like you wanted someone to take you over."

The cab stopped somewhere in Tribeca. He pulled an enormous wad of money from his pocket. He went through hundreds and fifties before finding a twenty, which he gave to the driver without waiting for change. Riding up in the elevator, he told me he liked my smile. I smiled for him then, though I could never be sure when he was actually looking at me. He unlocked his door and invited me to go in before him. I walked in, liking the look of the place, feeling very nice, like I was someplace I wanted to be.

But J.J., once inside, seemed to adopt an entirely different personality. He became callous and quick-tempered. He kicked his boots off at me. He told me to come over and suck his dick. I did. He grabbed me by the hair and fucked my face very roughly. He really did take me over. It made me very horny, hornier than I'd been in a long time, and I wanted to abandon all control to him. But as soon as I realized that that what was I wanted, I became afraid of it. The tip of his cock touched the back of my throat, and I vomited, and not just a little.

He pushed my head back and let go of me. He seemed enraged, disgusted, then resigned that I was not as good as he wanted. Then he pulled my head back on his vomit-covered dick and said, "Suck it, faggot!"

I sucked him eagerly. I felt bad about throwing up. I wanted to make it up to him. At the same time, it made me hornier to think he liked me less, and the willingness to let him take me over grew once again. I was jerking my dick like crazy.

And just as J.J. perceived this newfound passion, he backed away from me, his huge dong popping from my mouth. I looked up. He was smiling maliciously. He turned around and bent over so that his ass was in my face. He pulled his asscheeks apart with his hands. A small brown bud began forming in the hole in the center.

"Eat it," he said.

"No, man," I said, backing off. "I don't do that."

"You wanna suck my big cock?"

"Yes!"

"You wanna be Daddy's boy and stay here for a week or maybe longer all tied up and let me do to you everything I think needs doing?"

"God yes!"

"You gotta eat my shit first."

But I didn't move. Something was holding me back. The brown bud hadn't gotten any bigger since we started talking. I moved closer to it, wanting to let go, wanting to stay here and be tied up and taken over. But I couldn't forget myself. I backed away and sat on the nearby couch. J.J. straightened up and took a seat at the other end of the couch. He opened his legs and his cock hung down. He lit a cigarette. Several times I got on my knees and began to crawl toward his cock, but each time he kicked me away, saying I had to eat his shit first. Still I was jerking my dick like a madman.

J.J. turned around and laid on his stomach, thrusting his ass in the air. He said I knew what I had to do and whenever I was ready I should just do it. He put his hands on his asscheeks and spread them, then shut his eyes like he was going to sleep. For a few minutes I hesitated. Then I leaned over and licked the brown bud with my tongue, once.

"Do it some more," he said.

I did it again, two or three more licks. I was holding my nose. The shit tasted very bitter. Stiffening my tongue seemed to help me not to taste it so much. But after a minute I sat back on the couch again, my jerking hand stilled, suddenly feeling sick.

J.J. laughed. He turned around and sat facing me again. Apparently he was satisfied that he had gotten me to comply. "You're not gonna throw up again," he said, noticing my state of queasy exhaustion.

"I just . . . if we could take a break . . ."

"Oh, sure. Let's take a break." He grabbed me by the arm and pulled me into another room, a bedroom with two beds, and left me there, closing the door behind him. I laid down on one of the beds and felt better. I started jerking off and in a minute I came all over the blanket. I felt very strange after I came, all nervous and guilty like after that first time at the Ladylove Cinema. Only this time, there was also the stench of shit in my nose. I sat up and only then realized how tired I was. Despite my instinct to flee, my body did not want to move at all.

Suddenly I noticed there was someone in the room with me. He was sitting on the floor between the two beds. He was very slight and small, and completely nude. His wrists and ankles were so thin they looked like they could be snapped off. His knees were drawn up to his chest. When he saw me looking at him, he said, "So, do you love your Daddy?"

"What?"

"J.J. Do you love him? If you do, it's okay for you to stay. If you don't, you really should leave."

"And go where?"

"That's another issue entirely. So, do you love him?"

"No."

He nodded his head slowly, digesting the grim reality.

"But I only just met him," I said.

"Doesn't matter. You should go."

"But how can I leave if I'm locked up in here?"

"The door's not locked."

So I got up and walked out of the room. J.J. was nowhere in sight. I started feeling nervous and guilty again so I made a dash for the door, not even bothering to shut it behind me. I ran to the elevator, which because of the early hour was still on that floor. I got in and pressed LOBBY. The downward movement made me dizzy. I hit the EMERGENCY STOP and the elevator came to an abrupt halt, knocking me to the floor. I laid there a minute, calming down. In my calmness, I assessed that I was badly in need of a rest. In the pocket of my jacket I had accumulated many slips of paper with names, addresses, and phone numbers on them. I took them out and spread them over the elevator floor. I looked them over carefully. One of the addresses was not so very far from where I was now. The name meant nothing to me. I had no recollection of the person at all. I gathered the addresses and put them all away except for that one. Then I stood up and released the EMERGENCY STOP button. I ran through the lobby and out into the street. I went to a phone and made the call, collect. Just as I had hoped, the charges were accepted. "Ben!" I said, trying to sound as happy as I could. I told him I was coming to New York for a few days and would like to drop by. Meyersohn said he remembered me very well, which scared me a little, and he didn't seem to mind the early hour. He said, "You've got the correct address, right?" I told him my train arrived in two hours, providing there were no delays.

The sun was rising. I turned and walked up West Street until I came to the piers, which were deserted this time of morning. I felt sure that I was on the way to a good long rest, after which I would feel revitalized. I walked out to the end of the longest pier. If there's one thing I hated, it was sleeping outside, but I was just so tired.

As I laid there, I looked out over the river. Suddenly I noticed something in the water. It was a dog, a big Irish terrier it looked like, out there in the middle of the river, being helplessly swept along by the current, struggling to keep its head above the water. I sat up and watched it. I wondered how it got there. Did someone sail him out there and push him in the water? Or was it the dog's own recklessness? I felt for the dog as if I'd played with it at some time—a vital, robust dog with silky red hair, strong but no match for the Hudson. I watched it until it was swept from my sight.

3.

Around Meyersohn I tried always to be good-natured and inoffensive. In reality I lived in fear, constantly on guard against him. The worst scenario was that he would grow tired of me and ask me to leave before I was sufficiently rested. I didn't know what it would take for me to attain the right level of restedness, but I assumed that when I reached it I would be able to tell somehow.

Just as I was becoming more adept at always showing a pleasant demeanor, I was also becoming more conscious that my tolerance for Meyersohn's unbearable personality and his revolting physical being was diminishing fast.

Out of fear, I spent the afternoon before Meyersohn's Friday return cleaning the apartment as best I could. I didn't want to give Meyersohn any reason to be displeased with me. I gave a lot of consideration to where I would be and what I would be doing when Meyersohn walked in. I decided to be sitting at the kitchen table reading one of the books he was always pushing on me. I went and selected one and sat down with it. The book was very old and dusty. Some of the pages crumbled away as I turned them. I didn't read any of it, but I did notice little remarks scribbled in red pen in the margins here and there, things like "That's telling him" and "Stupid asshole" that sounded like Meyersohn, and things like "Uses of tropes" and "Prefigures modernists" that sounded like some teacher. Looking into the book, I realized I was exploring Meyersohn's past even more, and it made me kind of sick. I drummed my fingers on the table, waiting. I looked around; everything was in its place; I even had the table lamp on instead of the overhead light— I believed he would notice I was using less of his electricity. I was ready.

But when I heard it, the scraping of Meyersohn's keys against the lock, a severe pain came to my heart. Then the door swung open and Meyersohn walked in and I saw his face and heard him say, "Hi, Neal!" and something in me recoiled.

"So how did the week go?" he said. He was looking all around, like he was seeing if everything was still in place. I just sat at the table, looking down into the book, feeling very oppressed. Meyersohn took off his coat and laid his briefcase on the table. The briefcase bumped the book toward me an inch or so. It seemed like he did it on purpose. When I thought about it, I agreed that it was a just retaliation for my not saying hello to him.

I looked up and said, feebly, "Hi."

There was a big smile on his face, like he was really happy to see me, or he was thinking about something else completely. Then he said, "Neal, you're reading Rollings! How wonderful! He's my favorite! You know, that book is older than you! I was an undergraduate when I got it. Which story are you reading?"

I mumbled that I was just paging through.

"Oh! There's one in there that I absolutely adore! Can I read it to you?"

What was I supposed to say? I pushed the book toward him weakly. He took it up and began thumbing through it. He didn't seem to know where exactly he wanted to go. He had to stop to put on his glasses. When he sensed he was taking too long and losing my interest, he said, "It's just wonderful!"

When he found it he sat in the chair, but he kept his back poised as if he was standing up. He cleared his throat. It looked to me like something he learned years ago when he was a little Meyersohn and, indeed, he said, "I won the Best Speaking Award in my class in grammar school." So he read. At first I actually tried to listen. But it became clear, halfway through the first paragraph, that his silly attempt to entertain me was not working. He began, " 'She come about'—no, I mean—'She came about in the way'—no, I'm sorry—'in this way . . . ' " By the time he finished, I was totally off on my own.

"So," he said, closing the book. "Isn't that nice?"

"Yeah," I said.

Then he said, "Would you like some supper?" Though I was really hungry, I acted as if the idea of food was utterly new to me.

"Okay," I said. And as I ate, my hostility toward Meyersohn receded a little. Throughout the meal, he prattled on about this and that, the people at his job, all of which he seemed to dislike or dismiss. When he exhausted that, he moved on to other topics. I nodded in between mouthfuls, chuckled when what he said was intended to be funny, and said, "Uh-huh" when he needed acknowledgment. But he seemed able to tell when I was tuning out too much, and out of the blue he'd say something notable only for its extreme crudeness, something apparently intended to make you dislike him before you could dislike him of your own free will.

I insisted as usual on doing the dishes, partly as a way to get away from him, but also because, in my mind anyway, I was trying to "pay him back" for the meal. I was especially worried about that because night was coming and the two of us would be going to bed soon. He might have been expecting his recompense then, and with the disaster of our first encounter still fresh in my mind, I shrank at the possibility of a replay. I washed the dishes as slowly and thoroughly as I could, but I couldn't get the respite I wanted since Meyersohn stood right next to me at the sink the whole time, chattering incessantly. It was as if he had been locked in a cage and not allowed to talk to anyone all week. At one point, fearing I couldn't take it anymore, I said, "Why don't we watch some TV?" The TV was in the bedroom, but I was desperate.

That worked for a while. We watched the tail end of something on the old-movie channel, Meyersohn laying in bed and me sitting on the wooden fold-out chair next to the bed. Even as we watched, we seemed acutely conscious of each other, and Meyersohn apparently felt the need to continually acknowledge me. He talked to me about the two main actors—I forget their names—how they were married in real life though they were playing mortal enemies. But when the movie ended, Meyersohn began flipping the channels madly by remote. The only time he stopped was when there was an image of a man he found attractive, and then he would lick his lips and say, very loudly, "Mmmm . . . yummy yum yum!"

That made TV-watching just about unbearable. I stood up and casually announced that I was going for a walk. Meyersohn protested a little, saying I looked tired, but I insisted a walk was just the thing I needed.

I determined to make my walk a good, long one. But even as I walked and even as the breeze was clean and refreshing, I could not rid myself of the malignancy that was Meyersohn. It lingered in my head, in my body. And yet, I was well aware that I could not be rid of it, not yet. That malignancy was for the moment keeping me alive. It was a tricky matter, I could see, and the trick was not to take too much of him at any one time, or for too long. That would surely kill me.

I returned to the apartment. Meyersohn was snoring. That came as a huge relief. As I'd walked more than I really wanted to, I was exhausted. I undressed quietly in the main room, then slipped into the bedroom and into bed, next to Meyersohn. I fell asleep quickly.

I awoke shortly thereafter to the feeling of a hand trying to get into my underwear. I let him do what he wanted. I tried to think about Monday, when again I would be left alone.

Every Monday morning Meyersohn said, "I'll call Wednesday," and every Wednesday that's what he did.

I was lying on his bed, beating off to the one good porno tape he had. I was glad when the phone rang since I had made plans and was anxious to begin my night. I turned the TV down. I didn't want Meyersohn to think I was so presumptuous as to watch his TV.

"Hi, Neal!"

"Hi, Ben."

"What're you doing?"

"Oh. Just reading."

"Really? Good for you! What're you reading?"

"Oh. Just the newspaper."

"You can see there are many, many books there, Neal. You're welcome to read any one of them. In fact, any book you read you can have!"

"Oh. Thanks."

We chatted for a few more minutes. Mostly he talked about that woman at his job and how "what she needed was a good fuck"— and he said it as if he would be the one to give it to her. I was listening, but only for some indication that he was irritated with my continuing presence in his apartment. I could detect nothing like that in what he was saying, so I began to relax a little. I watched the soundless porno tape while he talked. I could see by the VCR's digital clock that the time for my night's plans was drawing closer. I heard Meyersohn say, "You know what I mean, Neal?" I said, "Uh-huh." Finally Meyersohn said he'd see me Friday night.

"And remember to take a look at those books, Neal."

"Yeah, I will. See you Friday."

I was happy to get through the conversation without there being any direct reference to my existence.

I started straightening up the bedroom in anticipation. Here and there was a sock or a pair of underwear. I refastened the corner of the bed sheet that had come off. All day I'd been jerking my dick without making myself cum. That made me so hot I could scarcely breathe without getting aroused.

The buzzer buzzed. I ran to the intercom. I asked who it was. "Van," came the reply.

Van was fiftyish, remarkably fit, with a silvery beard cut bristle-short. He had a wide, open face spanned by large round glasses. I had met him on the street the night before and invited him up to "my" apartment. He said he had to be somewhere and we made plans for the following night. Still, we fondled each other a bit and eventually ended up in the bathroom of the bar, where I blew him. It was the kind of wild sexual experience that takes less than two minutes yet keeps replaying in your mind, and fuels a whole day's worth of masturbation. When I pressed the buzzer to let Van in, I already had a hard-on.

The knock came at the door. But when I opened it, Van looked a little different to me than he had the night before. He seemed fatter, and instead of a manly flannel shirt he wore a bright pink short-sleeve jersey with an animal embroidered on the pocket. The jersey was too tight for him and made his pecs look like sagging breasts. I might've been able to handle all that, but he also wore this curious expression that broke into an overly polite smile.

He stepped in and I shut the door behind him. He said, "Hey, this is Ben Meyersohn's place, isn't it?"

That brought everything to a complete halt. Even my hard-on went away.

I felt tremendously embarrassed, like I'd been caught in a lie. But I wasn't going to show it. I faked a smile and said, "Yes. Ben's my roommate."

"Oh, really?" Van said, like he didn't believe me. "Ben took a roommate," he said. He weighed the lie like it was a cantaloupe he was thinking of buying at the fruit stand. "So where is he now?"

"Out of town. At work."

"When I was on the elevator, I had this sense of déjà vu."

"You're a friend of Ben's?"

"Oh, no. Not really. I haven't been in this apartment in, oh, ten years at least! So how is Ben?"

Van was smiling when he asked about "Ben" but I could see the very thought of Meyersohn was making him wince a little. He kept asking questions about Meyersohn and I kept answering them reluctantly and with as few words as possible, until finally I had to say, "Look, I don't know. He's just my roommate." Van laughed and said okay and started to kiss me. This alarmed me a little, since he'd shown no inclination toward kissing the night before and anyway, I didn't like it. I wanted him to stop but I didn't want to embarrass him, especially since I'd invited him here in the first place. So I pulled away and asked him how it was he knew Meyersohn.

"Ben? I think we might have tricked years ago, maybe twenty years ago, and then I saw him socially now and then. At people's parties in the neighborhood." As he talked about Meyersohn, that same slight wincing was evident, as if he had just bitten into something bad-tasting but didn't want to embarrass the server. "But I haven't seen him since . . . I don't know when." He put his hand on my knee.

"What was Ben like all those years ago?" I said.

"Ben?" He seemed to need a minute to think up something. What drove me crazy was how careful he was being for my sake, as if I had some vested interest in people thinking only good things about Meyersohn. It assumed an intimate connection between Meyersohn and me that just wasn't there. I wanted to say to him, "Let her rip, pal." But Van leaned into me and said, "Oh, Ben was nice. Very nice. He used to love to give dinner parties. Big ones. The more the merrier, for Ben. He considered party-giving his real forte." He rolled his eyes, then glanced over at me.

I was thinking, Go ahead. Don't hold back on my account.

"But more often than not, the dinner parties were . . . unsuccessful, I guess. Ben always had good intentions, though."

"Why were they unsuccessful?"

"Well." I could see he was picking and choosing his words. "Ben never knew who to invite and who not to invite. He would invite people who were mad at each other or who hated each other, or who hated him. So someone always ended up with a drink thrown on them or a slapped face. And then Ben would act like he had no idea that that was going to happen, and he'd go around apologizing to everyone for it and bad-mouthing the people involved and encouraging everyone else to bad-mouth them too. And we'd say, 'God, Ben. It's not like you couldn't have known.'"

"Did anyone ever slap Ben in the face?"

"Oh, yes!"

This I had to hear.

"Well, if you really want to know. It was the last Ben Meyersohn party I ever went to—it may have been the last one he ever gave. After that one, I personally couldn't put up with the spectacle anymore. Ben at the time had just finished assisting Ephraim Zain on his most recent book. He did some research for Zain, I think. You know Ephraim Zain, don't you?" I said yes, remembering the author I'd helped Meyersohn plagiarize. "Ben had him as a teacher in college, I believe. Anyway, I forget the title, but the book was one of Zain's most successful and it won some kind of history book award. It was in all the papers. Ben's party was shortly after the award was announced. I'm sure he decided to have the party because of the award." Van looked at me after he said that, no doubt to see if he'd gone too far. But I returned his look with a gentle, steady, prompting smile, and he went on. "The way Ben was acting, you would have thought it was he who wrote the book and Zain who was the research assistant. In fact, he got very caught up in himself that night and even went so far as to start bad-mouthing Ephraim Zain, hinting that he had a drinking problem and even that he had plagiarized part of his last book. And he said it so loudly the whole party came to a stop. The silly thing was there was no way he could expect anyone to believe it. Ephraim Zain was a well-known scholar who had written something like twenty books. And everyone in the room that night knew Ben pretty well and had a pretty good idea of what he was capable of. So this friend of mine, Edward—he's still a friend, in fact—actually, he's a she now, named Lynn. Lynn had had a little too much to drink and decided to call Ben on it. She said it was outrageous that he would try to smear Ephraim Zain after Zain had been so nice to him. Lynn said it took a lot of gall. Then Ben began to stammer and get red in the face. He said he never tried to smear Zain, and he accused Lynn of being jealous. 'Jealous!' Lynn said. 'Jealous of what? Of your being a leech? A parasite? I'm jealous because you're a blood-sucking hanger-on?!'"—Van stopped abruptly at that point, as if he just realized what he said. He looked at me, a little embarrassed.

I said, "It's alright. Tell me what happened next."

"Well. After that—let me see—well, after that Ben went up and threw his drink in Lynn's face, I believe. And it was a Bloody Mary, too." Van put his hand on the inside of my thigh.

"And then?" I said.

"And then? And then Lynn left the party, of course. Quite a few people left after that. But Ben went on acting just as he had before the incident. At least he was consistent, we all said later. Now that I think of it, that *was* the last dinner party Ben Meyersohn ever gave."

"But what about the part where he got slapped in the face?" I said.

"What?"

"You said Mey—Ben—got slapped in the face."

"I did? I guess I was wrong. It was Ben who threw the drink in Lynn's face."

I felt mad and disappointed, gypped somehow. Meyersohn really deserved that slap.

Van began running his hands up my legs and squeezing my crotch. I didn't much feel like it anymore, but I had sex with him anyway. Right there on the dining room floor. There was a lot of huffing and puffing, but neither of us enjoyed it much. It was as if the whole meeting, the whole night had been tainted somehow. We had one very perfunctory orgasm each, and then Van struggled to fit his body back into his jeans. For some reason, probably because he was polite, he gave me his phone number and said we should get together again sometime. He told me he thought I was nice and said he had a nice time.

Van turned around at the door and said, "So you're a friend of Ben Meyersohn's? Imagine that!"

I closed the door behind him and locked it. I had a sour feeling in my chest and stomach. I never said I was Meyersohn's friend.

After Van's departure, I went into the study and sat down on the couch. I felt a heavy tiredness coming over me, but I didn't want to lay on Meyersohn's bed. I thought about what Van had told me. The story appalled and horrified me, and made perfect sense. To be a shameless liar was one thing, to be openly and publicly accused of it was every shameless liar's worst nightmare. I felt accused myself, although no word was said against me.

I looked over at the shelves of books and noticed for the first time that they were arranged alphabetically by author. That put Zain at the very end, on the very lowest, dustiest shelf. That shelf alone was filled with Zain books almost exclusively. The titles were rather abstract and meaningless to me, which is why I don't remember them, but from them I gleaned that they were indeed writings on history. One of the books was thicker and taller than the others, and had a gold cover. I could see written across the top of it WINNER —KRIEGER HISTORY PRIZE. I took hold of the binding. Small columns of black powder fell as I slid the book from its place. Apparently it hadn't been moved for a very long time.

4.

I never said anything to Meyersohn about what I had learned. Instead, for the next few weeks we went on just as we had. I was typically elated on Mondays and depressed on Fridays. Then, inevitably, came the Friday that was not so typical.

It was early in the afternoon. I was sleeping after a long and unsuccessful night at the bars. The phone rang. I shot up in bed. Except for Meyersohn's Wednesday night call, the phone never rang. I was sure it was bad news.

It was Meyersohn. He sounded uncharacteristically subdued. "I just wanted to let you know that I'll be home a little earlier than usual," he said. "I'm at the train station in Washington now."

"Oh," I said, and I really knew something was up when he didn't say anything more.

"Is everything alright?" I ventured.

"Yes." Nothing more.

"Are you sure?" I said.

Meyersohn paused and said, "Everything's alright. Considering I just got fired from my job."

What this meant for me, I was not exactly sure. I said, "Jeez, Ben. I'm really sorry."

"Well," he said, "I've been fired before."

"Did they say why?"

Here the tone of his voice changed, as if he'd suddenly decided it was all a big joke that had nothing to do with him. "The grant proposal we wrote together? That cunt spoke up about the few passages we took from Ephraim Zain."

I didn't say anything. I was thinking about his use of the word we.

He went on: "I'm sure if I dug into her work, I'd find one or two things!" He said more but a train was pulling out near him. The next words I heard were, ". . . then the director said to me, 'We'd rather have Ephraim Zain working here, for that matter.'" Then he laughed out loud.

"Don't, Ben—don't laugh." I had decided on a route of serious concern.

"I have to, Neal. It's alright. I can't really say I wasn't expecting it. No one there really seemed to like me. But I'll land on my feet. I've always been good at survival. There'll have to be some belt-tightening . . . but here comes my train, Neal. I'll see you in a few hours." He hung up.

I was devastated. In an instant everything was different. Meyersohn was coming back to New York for good. And for some "belt-tightening." That he put that in just before he hung up seemed very significant. And I noticed that not once during the conversation did he ask how I was. Very unusual. It was clear to me what he was intending to do.

I sat down at the table. I thought, Maybe it was time to go anyway. I was sick of this life of endless stealth, and I was sick of the old queen. I even flashed on the idea of leaving then and there, before Meyersohn got back. I had by this time discovered a stash of a few hundred dollars hidden in a coat in Meyersohn's closet, and had been nibbling at it here and there. But having been fed and clothed and taken care of for over a month now, I was a little afraid of returning to my former methods of survival. I decided that the fear meant I wasn't yet fully rested.

I went about the usual Friday cleaning with a serene resolve. I went over every room carefully—bedroom, bathroom, study, kitchen—and cleaned with an intensity that precluded everything else. I hadn't worked so hard, it seemed, in a very long time.

When I got to the main room, I wasn't sure how much time had passed. I put the chairs on top of the table to sweep the floor. I was sweeping and sweeping—there seemed to be no way to gather together all the dirt and keep it in a single pile—when I turned and, suddenly, there was Meyersohn standing at the open door. What shocked me more than the sight of him was my failure to hear him coming. I jumped back a little and the broom handle caught one of the chair legs. The wooden chair hit the floor in such a way that it smashed into several pieces.

I looked at Meyersohn. "Oh, God," I said. "I'm sorry—it was an accident!"

But Meyersohn was unfazed. All he said was, "It doesn't matter." The words, instead of being a relief, gave me an odd chill, which he exacerbated by leaving the room abruptly to take off his suit and coat in the bedroom. Normally he would have yakked on about God knows what. My heart began to beat fast. I knew the time had come. I listened to him undressing in the next room. I heard the tiny grunts that accompanied each move he made. I heard the shoes as they dropped from foot to floor.

I knelt down and rather frantically tried to fashion together the pieces of the smashed chair.

Meyersohn returned to the main room. "My my," he said, looking at the mess. He stood at the table, going through the week's mail in only his flowered boxer shorts, that hideous scar running down his chest. He took no notice of what I was doing. I was sure now. He had had it with me. He was sick of everything about me, probably my face most of all, which I kept turned away. But that meant I could see myself in the full-length mirror that hung on the inside of the open closet door. What a sight. I was worse-looking, as far as I could remember, than when I first arrived. My skin was sallow. I was unshaven. My hair was mussed and tangled. I did not look at all like someone who was having a good long rest.

"Have you had your supper yet?" Meyersohn asked distractedly, while he opened up his credit card bill and shook his head. That was it. He was attempting to find out how much more I would cost him before it was over. And the worst thing was, as much as I disliked him, I couldn't blame him one bit for feeling the way he did.

I didn't know what to do. All I wanted was for the end to come.

I grabbed one of the broken chair legs and started beating my chest and stomach with it as my knees buckled. Meyersohn ran over. He yelled for me to stop. He succeeded in taking the weapon away from me. He knelt down and put his arms around me from behind. I struggled to get away, but I had suddenly become very weak. I couldn't lift myself off the floor. I was crying so uncontrollably my insides hurt.

"Easy now, Neal."

"I don't blame you! I don't blame you at all!" I tried to break away, but Meyersohn held me down.

"Quiet now."

"Why don't you just say it!" I screamed.

"Shhhhh."

I was too weak to say anymore, too weak to keep up the struggle. I collapsed backward, into his arms.

"I love you, Neal," Meyersohn said then.

"I love you, too!" I cried.

So I ended up telling the worst lie a person can tell. And, as if I couldn't stop myself, I added, "I really do!"

5.

Things started to change after that.

Far from attempting to throw me out, Meyersohn began to assume a greater intimacy with me. He would unexpectedly slip his arms around me from behind and squeeze my torso, laying his head against my neck. He would kiss me anytime he got the notion. For my part I would stiffen and bear it, though sometimes I would break away on some trumped-up excuse. The more demonstrative he became, the more I withdrew into myself. I began sleeping later and later in the morning, and took long naps during the day. I talked less and less, reducing my speech almost to the bare minimum of communication. And I could never seem to get clean. I started taking showers at night as well as in the morning.

Meyersohn never got discouraged by my attitude. He was happy, and conducted himself with a noticeable ease. He breezed from topic to topic at the dinner table while I barely more than grunted in reply. And he kept touching me, kissing me, playing with me, and each time he did I felt the malignancy within me grow.

One morning I woke up exhausted. I laid in bed most of the morning, actually embarrassed to show my face, and hoping to give Meyersohn a chance to get up and get on with his day. But when I finally crept out of bed he was still sitting at the table wearing only that godforsaken terry cloth wraparound. The morning paper was spread out before him. He sipped coffee and fed from his bowl of oatmeal in petite quarter-spoonfuls.

"Morning, Neal! Feeling better?"

I said I was much better and very formally thanked him for asking. I got some coffee and sat down at the table with him. I didn't really want to, but I had to find out what was going on in his head. As soon as I sat down, he leaned over the table and kissed me. I brought the coffee to my mouth and singed my lips with it. But still I didn't leave the table. I really wanted to clear something up with him.

I noticed he had the paper open to the help-wanted section.

"Probably it's really tough to find a job these days," I said suddenly.

"I imagine."

"Probably you'll have to do some belt-tightening around here," I said, consciously, brazenly echoing Meyersohn's own words. "Get rid of unnecessary things," I added.

"Actually I made a phone call this morning to a man I know here in New York. He's going to throw a little freelance consulting work my way."

"That can't be enough," I said, frustrated, crestfallen, and amazed to hear myself voicing those feelings so bluntly.

"That's nothing you have to worry about, Neal." I started to feel a little nauseous. "But I'm glad you're finally up. There's something we should talk about."

I didn't say anything. I didn't move.

"It occurred to me that you and I haven't been doing enough together lately. Like when we wrote that proposal together."

Oh God.

I told him I didn't feel like doing anything today. "I'm so tired," I said.

"Yes, you should rest today. But I'm sure you'll feel fine by next Friday."

I looked him straight in the face. The obvious question was, "What's going to happen next Friday?" and Meyersohn, true to form, was waiting for me to ask it. Finally I looked away and mumbled, "What do you mean by that?"

Meyersohn reached across the table and grabbed my hands. His hands were hot and moist, his face was bright. "Neal," he said, "what would you say to us having a dinner party on Friday night? I used to have them all the time, years ago. I'd invite everyone I knew! And everyone always had such fun at them!" As he talked he stood up and rounded the table and knelt next to my chair, never once letting go of my hands. "I don't know why I ever stopped giving them. But this is the perfect opportunity to begin again!"

"What is?" I said uneasily.

"*This* is!" he said, and squeezed my hands tightly.

I got up, breaking away. He let me go without a struggle. I made a pretense of needing to wash my hands at the kitchen sink. The announcement seemed to bust something inside my head, inside my chest.

"And you can invite anyone you want to, Neal!" he said.

I couldn't get his sweat off my hands. "It's really your party, Ben," I said. "Besides, I don't know anybody."

"It's our party, Neal. You live here too. And as far as I'm concerned, my friends are your friends!"

And I thought, You don't have any more friends than I do. I felt right then that if I were a piece of paper, I'd ask Meyersohn, as a friend, to crumple me into as small a ball as possible and light me on fire.

From that moment on, I had no peace. In the days leading up to the dinner party, I started to view it as a point of no return for me, something that, if carried through, would doom any last chance I had of saving myself. And there was no talking him out of it. Meyersohn was possessed with the idea of the party and enthralled in the preparations. I knew Meyersohn's main objective was to use the party to show off "us." The thought made my insides retch. That anyone could think I was in love with Meyersohn! I even worked myself into a crying fit. But Meyersohn, convinced that I loved him and he loved me, only put his arm around me and said, "There, Neal. This will pass. Now what do you think? The napkins can match either the tablecloth or the china . . ."

He spent all week planning for it, running in and out, buying food and favors, consulting cookbooks. He compiled a list of the people he would invite and sprung it on me one morning while I was still in bed. Most of the names meant nothing to me, but I did recognize Van's name, and also that of Lynn, formerly Edward, who had exposed Meyersohn at his last party all those years ago. Why Meyersohn would invite him—or her—probably not even Meyersohn knew. He seemed to be following some inner dictate for self-destruction. I was convinced Van would refuse but when I came out of the shower, Meyersohn was just hanging up the phone: Van would be happy to come, he said.

"And he's going to call up Lynn for me and ask her to come as well."

"Oh."

"And he says hi."

I looked at Meyersohn. I had no desire to lie, not now.

"Oh, yeah. I met him once." After I said it I realized it was twice.

Nothing more was said of Van, but the incident made me realize that of course people would come to this party. There was no chance at all that they wouldn't. Nothing attracts a crowd like a spectacle, especially when it's been so long since the circus was last in town. And I was the main attraction, the new young boyfriend. Nothing brings them out like a new young boyfriend. The dread I felt was so heavy it was nearly impossible to move. I didn't fear that these people would think I was Meyersohn's lover—they already thought that—but that, simply by meeting me, they would discover what I really thought: that Meyersohn aroused in me a hatred and disgust the virulence of which I had never encountered before. It seethed hot in my chest, frightening, enraging, inciting. And while the reasons to hate Meyersohn flocked around him like gulls at a landfill, the reason I hated him fully now was because I was supposed to love him. He had given me sustenance, shelter, nurturing—even understanding, even love. All regardless of my giving nothing in return. And it was precisely this which made me the truly hideous one, the truly pathetic one. I felt weak and grabbed the table for stability. When I looked up again, I got my first indication of how far the illness had advanced.

Seated at the table with Meyersohn was a short, thin man, maybe a few years younger than Meyersohn. They were having coffee. The man had thick, very white hair that was real but was somehow arranged to look like a hairpiece. He also had a bushy, snow-white moustache that was very unbecoming on a man of his pallor.

"Neal," said Meyersohn. "This is an old friend of mine, William. I ran into him at the supermarket when I was buying food for the party. I've just been telling him all about you!"

That enraged me, of course. I didn't want William to know all about me. I started to move backward but William stood and extended his hand and I seemed to have no choice but to take it. It felt to me like grasping a small bundle of dried twigs.

"Hi, Neal," he said.

I hated him instantly. I was convinced there had to be something wrong with anyone who would willingly spend time with Meyersohn.

"Sit down, Neal!" Meyersohn said.

I didn't move.

"You know, Neal," he went on without missing a beat, "you and William have something in common."

William and I looked at each other, both of us waiting, perhaps dreading, to hear what Meyersohn had to say. But Meyersohn let his imminent comparison remain imminent, shamelessly savoring his grip on our attention.

As usual, he let it go on too long. William leaned toward me and said, with a calm, almost apologetic air, "He means we're both Irish."

"Faith and begorah!" Meyersohn broke out, adopting his brogue. "You've both got a bit of the old sod in ya, yes ya do! Ay!"

William just smiled pleasantly. I folded my arms against my chest. Meyersohn smiled stupidly and said, "We have fat-free pound cake. Why don't you have some with us, Neal?"

I shook my head no.

"Would you like some nice tea, then?"

I refused to respond at all.

Meyersohn went into the kitchen. William said to me, "Ben's done nothing but talk about you."

I didn't even move the muscles in my face.

"He says you're really smart."

Any movement and I would explode.

"One thing he didn't say, though, was how you two came to be together."

We met at the Fred Astaire School of Dancing, you fucking idiot.

Meyersohn returned with the cake and three plates—couldn't he take no for an answer? "William's coming to the party, Neal," he said. Then he turned to William and said, "I've invited everyone from the old crowd. Even Edward!"

"She's Lynn now, don't forget," William said. "She's had the operation."

"Oh, that's right! I forgot!"

What a liar.

The two of them yakked on about the "old crowd" for thirty minutes or so as they devoured the pound cake. I stood a short distance from the table with my arms folded, saying nothing. I would have just gone into the other room, but their conversation was so perversely fascinating and it was giving me a clearer idea of what the party would be like. "George and Eric broke up months ago," William said, "because that whore just couldn't keep it in her pants." To which Meyersohn replied, "She's always been that way." The only person they referred to in the masculine was the one who was no longer a man. Meyersohn was particularly nasty: "I suppose he thinks now that he's had his cock cut off he's special. He's about as special as a three-legged dog."

I was relieved when William announced it was time for him to leave. I might have wished him goodbye, as he did me, if I had been able to speak—or rather, if I had been able to speak without saying the one thing I would say to Meyersohn once we were alone.

Meyersohn walked William out to the elevator. Even from out there I could hear Meyersohn's lisping, which ratcheted up my disgust several notches. I couldn't understand what was being said, but I was sure it was about me. Then Meyersohn came back. He looked right at me.

"It's sad," he said, though his expression was not sad at all. "Poor

William has AIDS. I've known him for twenty-five years. He won't be long for this world."

This distracted me a little. "He told you that?" I said.

"No. He didn't say a word about it. But it's obvious just looking at him that he has it. He used to be so robust!" Meyersohn seemed to be trying to carry on in the same gossipy vein as he had with William. I wanted no part.

"You don't know if he's sick," I said firmly. "Why imagine the worst?"

"No, no. I can tell. She's been a bad girl." A smile curdled his lips. "And he likes you a lot, Neal. He told me so in the corridor."

Lying scumbag.

"Listen, Ben." I could feel myself trembling. More than anything I wanted to say, "I hate your guts," but instead I said, "I don't want you to have this party."

"I know you don't, Neal," he said, clearing away the dishes. "But that's just nerves. You'll see. Everything will be fine." I suddenly felt very tired.

I spent the next few days entirely in bed, listless and sad, my hatred dulled by a low but persistent fever. My body ached as if I had been beaten up. Meyersohn tended to me sensibly and comfortingly, but he also acted rather distracted and, at times, even disinterested. He seemed not to understand the gravity of the situation, or else he didn't believe it. Besides, he was preoccupied with getting ready for the party. We talked very little during those days, since I usually pretended to be asleep when he was in the room. The one conversation we had went like this:

"I saw a dog once, drowning in the Hudson River."

"Really?"

"Yes. It was in the middle of the river, fighting to keep its head above the water."

"Really?"

"Yes, really. What do you think, I'm lying?"

"I believe you, Neal. I'm sorry. I just meant 'really' in the sense that—"

"—in the sense that you don't believe what I'm saying."

"No. It was just to keep the conversation going. Like nodding your head." He nodded his head, stupidly demonstrating his point.

"It's the way you said it then. Accusingly. Like I was making it up."

"Oh no, Neal!" He leaned forward, toward me. I recoiled. He leaned back.

"So tell me more about the dog," he said.

"There's nothing more to tell," I said.

The morning of the day of the party, I awoke feeling much better. This wasn't due to any improvement in my physical condition. I still felt hot and weak, and when I sat up there was a dizziness in my head that wasn't there before. But I awakened with a clear idea of what I would do.

I emerged into the main room, showered and fully dressed.

"Neal! Aren't you looking healthy this morning!"

He was seated at the table, making place cards. He had already made several. They sat like tiny tents in a row in front of him. A name had been painstakingly inscribed on each one. They were cream-colored, like the napkins, and each one had glued to it a hank of frilly pink ribbon. I remembered Meyersohn saying at some point that the men would get pink and the few women attending would get blue. I could read only the first two. One said BEN MEYERSOHN—YOUR HOST. The one next to it read LYNN FRENETTE. Meyersohn's transsexual friend had been cruelly given a pink ribbon.

Meyersohn said it would be a good time to discuss what my role would be that evening. "You are also the host!" he said. He picked up one of the place cards and showed me. it read NEAL SPENCE —YOUR HOST. I shuddered inwardly.

"It's your party, Ben. I have no idea—"

"It's *our* party, Neal! We're doing this together! And the fact is a lot people are coming tonight, so there'll be plenty for both us to do."

As he outlined my duties, I was thinking that it had gone past the point of limits here. One of us would eat the other alive. There was no way to stop it. And I was thinking I couldn't even cry about it, because I had used up all my allotted tears for at least the next six years, a time when I doubted I'd be alive. Knowing my luck, though, I probably would be. Still, I listened carefully to everything he had to say, and found all my duties acceptable and agreeable because they were all meaningless to me.

Throughout the day I was very handy to Meyersohn. I wrapped the hors d'oeuvres in tinfoil and put them in the refrigerator. I hauled up from the basement of the building many extra chairs and a table extender, a piece of wood that fit into the middle of Meyersohn's table and doubled its length. I helped him move some of the furniture to make more space. Meyersohn talked all the time, which I really didn't mind, for a change. He said, "It's important to remember a dinner party is an occasion more for socializing than for eating." He said that the guests should feel relaxed at all times but that they could only feel that way if the hosts have made every preparation beforehand. The one time he ventured away from the topic of the party, he said, "I'm glad you're feeling better today." There was a mocking quality about that lilting voice.

"Who said I was feeling better?"

"Well, you're up and doing things."

"So. That doesn't necessarily mean I'm feeling better."

"Oh. I'm sorry, Neal. Are you still feeling bad?"

"What do you care?"

There was a minute of silence. Meyersohn went on folding the brand new napkins he had just laundered—so they wouldn't feel rough against the guests' lips, he had said—into small squares. I apologized for snapping, and said, "Yes. I'm feeling bad."

Still, I knew what I would do. I was waiting for five o'clock, an hour before the party was set to begin. Meyersohn was still cooking away in the kitchen. He had all four burners going. The food smelled over-spiced.

When five o'clock came, I casually announced that I was going for a walk—at least, I was trying for casualness while feeling a little anxious. Meyersohn seemed to pick up on the slight quiver in my voice because he looked over at me.

"Don't go far!" he said. "Remember, you're the greeter!"

"I just need some air"—what a lame-sounding excuse—"I mean, I need to clear my head"—that wasn't it either. I was hoping the right words would just come to me, but I was less confident than I planned to be. I should have thought it out better. I looked around like there was something I couldn't find. But I had everything I needed. I just wanted my leave-taking to look as casual, as unintended as possible.

When Meyersohn turned back to his cooking, I snatched from the elaborately laid-out table the place card with my name on it and crumpled it in the palm of my hand. I didn't want any trace of me here when the people showed up. Maybe they'd all think I never really existed. "Guests," Meyersohn would say, making a toast, "here's to my figment of the imagination, Neal Spence!"

"Neal?" I heard him say, of course when I was already in the corridor. He came to the door and opened it wide. He stood inside the threshold. "I just wanted to ask you: is this light bulb okay? I mean, I don't want it to be too dark, and yet I don't want the light so bright that we all can see how unattractive we are!—except for you, of course. What do you think?"

I couldn't say.

"Or am I just being silly?"

"I really wouldn't know. I'll see you later." I wondered if that sounded too abrupt.

On the street, I tossed the place card into a trash basket after tearing it up into the smallest pieces possible. I tried but couldn't tear the pink ribbon, nor could I really crumple it as it kept returning to its original shape. So I just tossed it. I was glad to be rid of it. That people would know who I was by that card . . . And then there was the placing of the card. At the right-hand side of Meyersohn's position, exactly the spot my mother used to sit relative to my father at Thanksgiving (the only time my family ever ate together). That way everyone would see that I was Meyersohn's! The woman behind the man! Perhaps I would gaze adoringly at him while he related one of his anecdotes. How about the one about the cunt at work? They'd sit mesmerized while I, Mrs. Meyersohn, cleared away the salad plates! And of course I'd interject supportive praises along the way, and he'd tell the guests that whatever I said or did was all due to the old sod in me, and he would undoubtedly adopt his Irish brogue when he said it and then, to prove him right, I'd stick my finger down my throat and bring up several mounds of moist reddish soil. And the crowd would spontaneously burst into applause and everyone would ask me to do it again. And because the good host always obliges his guests' requests, I'd try it again, but what comes up this time isn't reddish soil but bright red blood, which I inadvertently splash across the three guests to my right. *I'm so sorry!* Then William—why do gay men always insist on using their full given names?—gets up and tells the delightful story of how he first met me, how "charming" I was, how he really did like me after all. He says it was my smile that won him over. And then Van gets up and says what charmed him was the way the sperm trickled from my cock, like a gang of sleepy prisoners led from their cell at sunrise. He says, "We all know how rude it is to shoot—you could kill someone that way if it gets in your eye!" And the whole time I feel woozy but am still smiling, since it's only my guests' happiness that I'm concerned with. Then, just as I'm about to get up and make the grandest toast of the evening, my dear beloved Meyersohn leans over and asks if I'm alright. I'm looking a little peaked, he says. But I just pat his hand and say, "I'm fine—SWEETHEART!!!" The guests coo. But then, when I stand, hoisting my glass in tribute to the beautiful things that ultimately make life a tolerable, even a worthy thing, I suddenly collapse. But wait—am I only pretending to collapse? The crowd decides no and I'm rushed to the hospital by ambulance, with dear beloved Meyersohn at my side. Would the guests speak of the tragedy and the shame of it in someone so young? Is that Meyersohn speaking in lisps to the doctors outside my room: "Tell me, doctors, is it AIDS or is he just faking it?" It doesn't matter, AIDS or fakery, because either way it kills me. I rant fearfully at God for doing this to me. When people grow bored with me, I start feigning delusions. I think I hear my mother coming down the hall. (Even though I always said I would never tell her if I was dying, I tell her anyway.) Is that my family? My favorite ones, my sister Patrice, my brother Vincent? No. It's only Meyersohn, the only face I see in my final days. The medical bills will be a lot for him to have to pay. I die ignobly, since that's the way I lived and habits are so hard to break.

Out on the street, I tried to think of my ducking out as a great escape, a kind of adventure. I planned to be gone until well after the party was over, which I calculated to be a good six or eight hours. I was really good at killing huge amounts of time. I started missing those long train rides between cities.

"You can't be fucked up in the place where you live," I suddenly said out loud. I don't know why I said it out loud—in fact, I was embarrassed when a couple of people on the street turned around and looked my way. Always so concerned with what other people think.

I was trying to feel free and easy, but I was nagged, nagged the way Meyersohn nagged, even after you were on the other side of the godforsaken door. I had to go somewhere to get my mind off the party. Despite all I felt about Meyersohn, despite what an asshole he was, I did feel guilty about leaving him in the lurch this way. But I didn't turn back. There was just no way.

After wandering around a long time, I got tired and went to the only place it occurred to me to go: the bar.

Well before evening fell, the bars in New York were full. Of course, they were full with the same group of drunks that were there every day, but if you only went occasionally, as I had been doing since Meyersohn moved back from Washington, they were not so bad. This particular bar had dark walls and dim lighting except for the places on the walls where tiny spotlights showcased parts of the leather/western regalia—a pair of boots with spurs here, a studded vest there. It also had a jukebox, and it was playing a pretty good song for a change. The one bartender was tending about fifteen customers. I slid up to the bar and ordered a scotch rocks. I pulled some cash from the pocket of my coat—Meyersohn kept me supplied—and paid for it, leaving a generous tip. The bartender winked and thanked me. I surveyed the pickings at the bar, more out of habit than horniness, then turned and looked to the back, where a few small round tables were set up. A pay phone hung on the wall. I toyed with the idea of calling Meyersohn and actually explaining the truth, but I had gone too far down the road of deception to do that, and I knew it.

So I took a seat at a table, with my back to the pay phone. Slowly I sipped my drink. Suddenly the people all looked as sad as I felt, as fucked up. A man at the next table, who I only now noticed, looked extremely sad, even though he was trying to cover it up with sunglasses. I glanced at him then looked away because I couldn't tell if he was glancing back. Then I took another, longer look. The man had frizzy, afro-like hair (though he was white) and was very lanky. He was nursing a dark-colored drink and I couldn't tell if he was plastered or not.

It was J.J., the man I had tricked with just before fleeing to Meyersohn's. I sat up and turned to him in a rather obvious way, but still he made no sign of noticing me. My horniness began to act up at the sight of him, despite the strange time we'd had together. And though I had fantasized about parts of that night many times since then, J.J. probably didn't even remember it.

I got up and sat down frankly at his table. He looked up at me, then looked back down. I said to him, "Hey, J.J."

He sort of laughed through his nose in response. I smiled like an idiot.

"You probably don't remember me."

"I remember you," he said in a loud voice. "You went running out of my apartment like a girl in a panty raid." He snickered. "You remember that?"

"Vaguely," I said. I was embarrassed. It didn't seem to me that I actually ran out of the apartment. I just sort of left when things got too weird.

"How about giving me a second chance?" I was still really horny for the guy, for his big dick.

He shook his head. "Nah."

"Oh, come on. It was just that I had too much to drink last time."

"No."

"Oh, come on, buddy."

He lifted his drink and took a big gulp. He was dead set against the idea of me, but that made me want him all the more.

"Come on, J.J. Be my Daddy and do to me whatever you want."

He shook his head no. Then he leaned further into his drink and he seemed to be crying. He lifted his glasses and wiped his eyes with a napkin. He really *was* crying, although it was hard to tell with him, just like you couldn't tell if he was really drunk or not. Because with a man like J.J., he was always a little drunk and a little not drunk, a little crying and a little dry-eyed. He was truly in a state of limbo, suspended in his own despair. I realized for the first time that J.J. was in a great deal of pain.

"Take me home, J.J.," I said. "I want to suck your huge cock."

"You threw up all over it last time," he said, replacing his glasses and clearing his throat. "Remember that?"

"I told you. I had a little too much to drink that time. I've hardly had anything now. In fact, I don't even want this"—and I put my drink down, sort of far from me.

"Go away," J.J. said. He slumped further into his drink and gave out what seemed to be a light sob.

"Listen, sexy," I said.

He looked up at me and said, "You're a disgusting human being."

It hurt me when he said that, and it kind of embarrassed me again because I knew it was true. The exact thought had occurred to me in the last few minutes, when I persisted in trying to lay him even after I found out how unhappy he was. And he wasn't even forcing his unhappiness on me; it was me who was imposing on it. Time after time I was refused and even told flat-out to go away, yet there I was, still. I was like one of those ticks your mother found on your scalp. That little tick would hold on and hold on against all kinds of scraping and pulling and dousing with alcohol. And even with part of its body ripped away, it still held on with its pincers, sucking and sucking out of sheer instinct. And if the tick was really lucky, maybe the host would say, "It's more trouble to get rid of it than to just let it stay," and the host would even forget that the tick was poisoning him and would kill him eventually. Of course, he would never forget the tick was there, due to the soreness and the itching, the infection. But he could learn to live with that—who doesn't have problems? But if the tick was unlucky, the host would just scrape and pick until every last bit of vermin was gone. Those were the tough ones, like J.J. The ones who would never let you think of yourself as anything other than what you were.

I sat back in my chair, suddenly very sad. I put my hands to my eyes and squeezed them with my fingers. I pulled my drink toward me and downed almost half of it. The scotch scoured the inside of my mouth. Then I dropped both hands between my legs.

"So what's the matter, J.J.?" I said in the quiet voice of a person who regrets having gone too far.

J.J. stretched his elbows sideways on the table and leaned down into his clasped hands. His neck and shoulders bounced slightly as if he had springs for joints. I'd never seen anyone cry so hard so quietly.

"Tell me what's wrong, J.J. Please."

"Floyd is gone."

The one in the bedroom, sitting on the floor.

"Where'd he go?"

"I don't know. He just left. I thought he was just trying to get me mad."

"What do you mean?"

"He'd say, 'I'm getting tired, J.J.' Of sitting on the floor, he meant. 'You don't think I'd ever leave,' he said. He was right."

"The door wasn't locked," I said.

"But I thought he loved me."

J.J.'s crying became more audible. Other people were looking. Normally that would have made me scared, but I kept right on sitting there, holding my drink. My show of bravery, it turned out, had the same outward appearance as my show of cowardice.

The bartender called over to me to "take him outta here already."

The idea of assisting a drunken, crying person out of a bar, I admit, appalled me. But I took him by the arm and lifted him. He didn't resist me at all. When he stood up, I saw the outline of that enormous cock in his pants. That sent a new wave of sexual desire through me, which I ignored.

I walked him to the curb and tried to hail him a cab. They kept passing us by. J.J. kept breaking down and was now crying harder than ever.

"It's too late," he said, very loudly. "I hated him when I should have loved him! And look at me now!" It seemed as though everyone on the street was doing just that. But again, I made like I didn't care. All I could think was that my body below the waist had been ripped away, how much pain that caused, and how I was holding onto J.J., arms wrapped around his torso, on the pretense of holding him up. Finally a cab stopped. I put J.J. in it. He looked up at me, a face full of despair. I said, "Don't worry. He'll come back." Then I slammed the door and started walking briskly in the direction from which I came. J.J. stuck his head out the window and shouted to me, "Get out of the place where you are! And don't lie about it! Just say the truth and leave!" I didn't turn around.

My head was swimming, partly from J.J., partly from the alcohol, and partly from the fever that was beginning to surge again. I wasn't sure how long it had been since I left. Several hours, at least. Undoubtedly all the guests had arrived by now, perhaps some of them were even beginning to leave. By now everyone would be over the surprise of my not being there. By now everyone, privately or not, had offered his own suggestion as to why I didn't show up. I seemed to know exactly what everyone would be thinking, even the people I never met. But why did I care?

Meyersohn didn't care. Maybe that was the best way to be. Or at least it was better than pretending not to care but really caring, which is what I did. It was less phony. For all my scheming and deception and nastiness, I somehow held on to the appearance of caring—and that made me worse. In truth Meyersohn and me were exactly the same except he was honest about what he was and I tried to trick everybody into thinking I was alright. That is, everybody except myself.

I somehow felt that if I could tell Meyersohn all of this, if I could just let him know, then I could get out of there, like J.J. said. Just say the truth and leave. And I would gladly leave then, too, rightfully leave, after I told what I believed was the truth, after I made that crucial distinction between him and me.

I felt weak and was breathing heavily as I entered the lobby of Meyersohn's building. I wasn't conscious of time at all, but judging from where the bar was, it must have taken me another hour to get back. The night doorman was on duty. He usually made a point of not speaking to me, but tonight he said, "How are you?" like he could see something was wrong.

I rode up the elevator. I didn't have a clue as to how I would say what I needed to. I only knew I didn't want to lie anymore.

Even before I got off the elevator, I could hear the noise on the other side of Meyersohn's door. I walked up to the door and stood there for several minutes. I could hear the people talking, the music playing. It didn't sound at all like a Ben Meyersohn party.

Finally I slipped my key into the lock. Only it wouldn't turn. The door wasn't locked.

I pushed it open. An unexpected sensation of warmth rushed at me, then seemed to envelope me and take me in. Light classical music, ideal for conversation, was playing, but I didn't know where it was coming from. Everywhere there were people, sitting, standing, leaning, talking, in clusters of two and three, holding drinks and cigarettes and joints. I looked around at them and recognized nobody, nor did anyone acknowledge that I had come in. The meal had been eaten and the party was in the stage of fervent after-dinner socializing. Clinging to the ceiling was a layer of smoke from all the cigarettes. It seemed to muffle the music enough so that people could hear each other, and to absorb the light and reflect it back, casting everyone and everything in a subtle but flattering un-focused glow.

I saw no sign of Meyersohn. I guess I had expected him to come rushing up, all excited and happy to see me. When that didn't happen, I took a seat in a chair that had been left against the wall. Calmly I took in my surroundings. The apartment looked and felt so much bigger and so much more relaxed than it usually did. Everyone seemed to be truly having a good time. From what I could pick up in the rising and dying volumes, the discussions were passionate and smart and entertaining, about movies and books, about politics. Many of the voices lisped and lilted, but, unlike Meyer-sohn's, they sounded natural, musical even. I was pleased by the fact that people were ignoring me. If no one was trying to get to know me, I didn't have to deceive anyone. It was an unexpectedly pleasant respite, this party. Rather like being on a train.

Without my seeing her come up, a woman appeared kneeling at my side. The first thing she did was hug me. I hugged her back. I smelled the thick scent of her, so familiar. I felt the pleasing way her skirt and blouse hung on her body, even though she was very large for a woman. I thought it might have been Lynn, but when I pulled back I saw it was my mother. Her blouse was covered with cheap gaudy sequins and she was holding a highball. I stood up. It seemed improper for me to be sitting while she was standing.

"How are you, Neal?"

"I've been sick."

"Well, if that's really true, you should maybe see a doctor about that."

"How do I do that, Mum?"

"How does anyone do it?"

She adjusted her bra strap underneath the blouse.

"You working?" she said.

"No," I said. I didn't want to lie.

"Who's supporting you?"

"Guy named Ben Meyersohn." I looked around and didn't see him.

"A Jew. That's nice."

"You must have met him. He's the host of this party."

"I haven't met anyone here. They're all kooks and fags." She leaned into me. "There's a man dressed up as a woman, for chrissake. I thought you were the host of this party."

"Why would you think that?"

"I just assumed."

Mum sipped from her glass. The ice cubes gently knocked one another, a sound I could hear clearly despite the noise of the party. She made a face that said the drink was not to her liking.

"So you plan to just go on using this guy?" she said.

"No. Not for much longer. There isn't much time left."

"What's that supposed to mean?"

I didn't say anything.

"You dying, Neal? Or are you just being melodramatic?"

"I'm not sure. I feel so bad. It could be disease. It could be just me."

"Why don't you go to the doctor and find out?"

"Because I'm a coward."

"You always were."

"Just like Daddy."

She shot me a look. I'd gone too far. But as long as we were being honest, I felt I might as well say it.

"I don't ever want to hear you talk about your father like that again," she said sternly.

"Why? It was obvious he was afraid to die."

"So? Who isn't? That's not your problem, anyway. You're not afraid to die. You can't wait for it to happen. Your problem is what to do *before* you die. You don't have a clue as to how to get along."

"We only know what our parents teach us," I said huffily.

"Oh," she said. "You've got problems, so I'm the mother who doesn't love her children?"

"I never said anything about love."

She realized she overspoke. She sort of laughed to herself and said, "Well, as long as we were being honest." She sipped her drink. "You're a very hard person to love, Neal." Suddenly she leaned over and kissed me, right on the lips. Her lips felt like cold plastic against mine. Her scent became so heavy I nearly choked. I wasn't really kissing her back, which she sensed, and soon she stopped.

"So you *are* gay," she said.

"Sorry," I said.

"That doesn't answer the question, Neal."

"Oh. Yes, Mum. I'm gay."

"Oh well," she said. "You can't win them all. Anyway, it's time for me to leave. Say goodbye to ... your boyfriend ... what's his name again?"

"I will. Hey Mum, what did you think of the party?"

She downed the last of her drink and put the empty glass on the table. "All kooks and fags," she said. She left.

When I turned back to the party, several of the men were eyeing me disapprovingly.

Suddenly Van bounded up to me. He was wearing his customary smile. He looked like he was having a great time.

"Neal! I didn't see you before! How've you been?"

I told him I was just fine, and asked him how he was.

"Oh, just great! Listen, I've got a joke for you. What's the difference between a new boyfriend and a new job? After a year, the job still sucks! Ha! I'll talk to you more later, Neal. I've got to catch up with Lynn." And off he went to join this rather large person in a sun dress and a bouffant. Lynn did not look so much like a woman as she did a cartoon character, but what struck me most about her was how totally comfortable she was with herself.

Just then I noticed William coming toward me, holding a glass of wine. He appeared to be weaving a bit. He might have been smiling, but that bushy moustache of his kept the secret.

"Hi there, Neal," he said. "How ya doing?"

"Very fine, thank you. And you?"

He blinked his eyes once, and very slowly.

"Always so formal all the time, aren't we?" he said.

"Have you seen Ben?"

"Your boyfriend? Oh, he left shortly after dinner. Said he'd be back. But he was very upset, crying almost. I've never seen Ben like that. Usually he's so . . . unemotional."

"What was he upset about?"

"You, of course."

William staggered away from me and right into the table with a loud crash. Then he fell on the floor, face first. The people in the room looked at him, then at me, like they were expecting me to do something about it. So I went to William and tried to help him up. When I turned him over, I could see his arm was bleeding from where he fell on his wine glass. The crowd gasped and moved back. I lifted William into a chair. He no longer seemed aware of anything around him, but sat muttering with a pained, angry expression. I turned to the person next to me and said, "In the bathroom. Get a clean towel. Hurry."

The man hurried off and returned. He handed me the towel. I heard someone in the crowd say, "Who's that?"—referring to me, no doubt. I ripped the towel in half and tied it around William's arm. That checked the bleeding, which hadn't been all that bad. Then I helped William up and brought him into Meyersohn's bedroom. There were a lot of people in there, sitting on the bed, poking through Meyersohn's books. I had to kick them all out, saying William needed to lie down. Some of the people were put off. I heard them saying again, "Who the hell is that?" and "Make way for Florence Nightingale." William passed into unconsciousness the instant I laid him down.

I went to the bathroom to clean up. I had to kick out two men who were kissing and groping each other. When I came out, the party was going on as before.

The light classical music that seemed to come from everywhere suddenly became a fuzz of static in the air, which made everyone look up and around, like a great swarm was about to descend on them. Then someone tuned in a kind of polka music, only it was more raucous than polka. Shouts went up in the main room. I went to see what was happening.

I was startled to see that the dinner table had been pushed back and two people were dancing—a young blonde man about my age who I had never seen before and Lynn. They both had their shoes

off and were dancing wildly, arm in arm. They were almost galloping across the floor, tracing a triangular pattern. It looked like a lot
of fun. Their faces were so happy, so free of thought. Lynn was
leading, confidently, joyously. The young man was totally concen-
trated on keeping up, and doing a good job of it too, watching
Lynn's big feet with an unconscious smile. The crowd was cheering
them on, clapping, shouting. It was hard not to feel good watching them.

One polka song ended and another began. Lynn was ready to go
again, but the young blonde man declared himself exhausted.

"You, then," she said, coming up to me, taking my hand. At first
I resisted, and felt very embarrassed, but Lynn was so strong she literally pulled me onto the floor. And apparently I didn't need any
more coaxing because the next thing I did was kick off my sneakers.

Lynn led me in the galloping polka. She had very strong arms
and hands. She said, "Up! Pick your feet up!" though not loud
enough for anyone but me to hear. I picked up my feet. The music
was noisy and the station was not tuned in exactly but that made
more sense of my clumsy, lumbering steps, which nevertheless all
came down in time. Between the two of us, the floor was rumbling.
We completed one triangle and were starting on another when I
tripped over one of my kicked-off sneakers. I fell hard but never hit
the floor since Lynn, who never let go of my arms, used them to pull
me up again, all the while never missing a step herself. I fell right
back in with her. The crowd cheered our recovery. Their shouts ex-
hilarated me, made me want to go even faster. I began to match
Lynn's strength and confidence, then started to exceed her. "Easy,
young bull," she warned. We completed the second triangle and
started on the third. But when we turned, I stopped in my tracks.
Lynn tried to pull me along, and nearly pulled my arms out of their
sockets, but I didn't budge. I stood facing the open door, where
Meyersohn was standing, his hand still on the key that was still in
the lock.

The crowd stopped clapping and shouting. Lynn trotted to a
standstill. The polka music continued to play, though the static was
beginning to overtake it. In the next instant it became complete
static, which then phased back into light classical. Murmuring and

milling resurfaced among the guests. Several started to put on their coats.

Meyersohn and I had not stopped looking at each other. His eyes were angry and hurt. There seemed to be a rage in them that I had never seen before. Finally he turned away from my gaze and said, in a general way, "Well. What fun you're all having." He shut the door behind him and took off his jacket. Then he walked straight into his bedroom and did not come out again.

A cluster of guests was leaving. They all stopped by me and thanked me for my hospitality. "I'm glad you had a good time," I said warmly, sincerely even. William came running out of the bedroom wearing a frantic expression, apparently awakened by Meyersohn. He said, "My arm! It'll get infected!" and he ran past me and out the door, not even bothering to grab his coat.

It took over an hour for all the guests to leave. They streamed out casually, all of them thanking me and bidding me good night and I doing the same in turn. Meyersohn remained in the bedroom, with the door shut. None of the guests seemed to mind that, or even notice it. When the last of them was gone, I shut the door quietly. I saw my sneakers laying on the floor. I put them back on. Then I looked around. The place was a mess. Naturally I started picking up. I brought all the dishes and cups and glasses to the sink and washed them. I went around the place with trash bags and collected all the garbage, which I then hauled out to the trash chute. I emptied all the ashtrays and put them away. I even moved the furniture back into place and put all the extra chairs out in the corridor. The whole time, I was happy to be doing something, happy to be thinking only of what I was doing. When I finished, the apartment looked almost like there never was a party.

That was when Meyersohn chose to come out of the bedroom. He was wearing his blue terry cloth wraparound. His expression was once again very familiar. He came toward me with outstretched arms.

"Neal. I was so worried."

I deliberately sidestepped his hug. Then he came at me again. I pushed him away, pushing against his scarred chest. He fell back.

I said, "Goodbye." But I was leaving something out.

His face registered a look of real hurt. It killed me to see it. I said, "The truth is, we're both disgusting people. And we probably deserve each other. But the difference is, I can't go through with it. Which I hope makes me a little better. So, goodbye."

I ran out the door and into the stairwell. I didn't want to have to wait for the elevator. I ran like I would from a killer. And though it was likely that I had killed myself already, I ran as if there was still some hope of salvation.

I ran through the lobby and out the door and kept on running down the avenue. I was headed for the corner, where I would make a turn—because I was sure Meyersohn was still looking at me from the window in the study, the window I had used to spy on him.

I made the corner and halted. I needed to catch my breath. I sat down on the steps of a brownstone. I put my head in my hands and cried, right there on the street. I didn't care—which seemed like some kind of breakthrough. Anyone passing by would think I was just some sort of crazy homeless person—and they'd be right, now that I thought of it, except for the part about me being crazy. I was definitely not crazy, though I might have wished it.

I stayed there until an old lady in a hairnet called to me from a window in the brownstone, saying that the spot I occupied was not for sitting. People were covetous of every inch in New York.

"Anyway, I won't stay in New York much longer," I shouted back at her. She looked at me as if I'd used some obscenity and disappeared back into her window. I picked myself up and headed in the direction of the train station to look for someplace, anyplace I could rid myself of the infection of love.

Acknowledgments

The following stories have been previously published, some in slightly different form: "Bypass" in *Press*; "Cookout" in *Confrontation*; "Infection" in *StoryQuarterly*; "The Right of Way" in *Clockwatch Review*, "Fellow Feeling" in *Berkeley Fiction Review*, and "The Host" in *The Southern Anthology*. Thanks also to the MacDowell Colony, the Millay Colony for the Arts, and the Ludwig Vogelstein Foundation for their generous assistance. Special gratitude goes to the following: Jonathan Rabinowitz and Turtle Point Press; Elaine, who never failed to be there for me; Ken, who showed me more kindness than I often deserved; Hugo, who came and went and never left; and especially Dennis, who has been my partner, my guide, and my love.

Daniel Scott was born and raised on the
South Shore of Massachusetts. His stories
have appeared in many national magazines
and he has been awarded fellowships from the
MacDowell Colony and the Millay Colony
for the Arts. He lives in New York City.

www.ingramcontent.com/pod-product-compliance
Lightning Source LLC
Chambersburg PA
CBHW060632260626
47161CB00008B/2865

* 9 7 8 1 8 8 5 5 8 6 2 1 6 *